OUT ON A LIMB OF THE FAMILY TREE

Kathi Harper Hill

Copyright 2012 by Kathi Harper Hill

Out On a Limb of the Family Tree

Published by Yawn's Publishing

210 East Main Street

Canton, GA 30114

www.yawnsbooks.com

This book is a work of fiction. Names, characters, incidents, places, businesses, organizations, and events are either the product of the author's imagination or are used fictitiously. Any similarity to locales, incidents, or actual persons, living or dead, is entirely coincidental.

All rights reserved. No part of this book may be reproduced or transmitted in any form, electronic or mechanical, including photocopying, recording, or data storage systems without the express written permission of the publisher, except for brief quotations in reviews and articles.

Library of Congress Control Number: 2012949433

ISBN: 978-1-936815-62-3

Printed in the United States

Cover photography by Kathi Harper Hill
Special thanks to front cover model Anna Kate Hill

ACKNOWLEDGMENTS:

Many, many thanks to all the people who gifted me with their 'blonde' moments, fond memories, and interesting stories. As you will discover, lots of them made it to the written pages in this book, living right alongside stuff that came directly out of my deranged imagination.

Blonde moments gratitude: Janice Evans Burgess, Anna Kate Hill, David Hill, Myra Pierce, and Shannon Holloway Sumner.

Fond memories gratitude: John Bailey, who told me stories about my grandfather Harper's grocery store when we 'just happened' (Thank you, Lord!) to meet outside a restaurant one day. Janice Burgess for her grandfather's memories, and another fellow we remembered fondly on the way to Dalton. To my sister-in-law, Barbara Ann Dunn. To the first woman who ever babysat me, Jane Eller, gone home to be with The Lord many years ago. To Sue Hansard, for her brother's story. To my mother, Coleeta Sawyer Harper. To my paternal grandfather, John Henry Harper and my great-grandparents, Macy Victoria McGuire Harper and Jesse Harme Harper. To my father-in-law, JT Hill. To my great-grandfather, John Hill. To James M. Holt, my pastor off and on most my life. To Myra Pierce for the story of her grandmother. And to Mary Jane Reece Weeks, for permission to share a story her mother told me many years ago.

Please understand I have handled your stories with loving care. Even though I may have added a smidgen or a whole bucket full of fiction to wrap around them, I hope you recognize them and feel I've done them justice!

Also to Debra Gibson Adams and Betty Jo Holt who insisted their names be used in this book – here they are, hope you like your new, improved personas! I love it when I can personalize a book, and couldn't wait to abuse, er, use your names!

A special thanks to Marsha Benson, Bobbie Green, Anna Kate Hill, and Denise Davis Moser for taking on the brave job of trying to proof read a book such as this.

PREFACE:

I come from many generations born and raised in the Appalachian Mountains. This is where I call home. There is a language that is rapidly fading into faint memory that my people spoke. It's part Queen's English, Scots, Irish and Gaelic with some Cherokee mixed in. When I was a child, one was careful not to speak it away from home because of the fun that would be made of you for being a hillbilly, a redneck, an ignorant fool.

My great-grandparents spoke it because they knew nothing else. The mountains were secluded, and some people never left the county they were raised in.

If you come to my hometown, you will see at least one redhead everywhere you go. Before 'foreigners' moved here, one out of every three person's hair was some shade of red. Scots and Irish have powerful genetic influence here. So did their way of speaking.

My great-grandparents spoke Appalachian and my grandparents to a slightly lesser extent. My parents spoke it to a much lesser extent (although I've noticed as my mother has become elderly, she's reverted to it more). And me? Well, if I'm around someone who speaks it, which happens less and less as older people die out, I am fluent. If I'm around someone who speaks regular Southern, I speak that, at any degree of educated English. Giving a speech in front of a hundred people, I even clean up my Southern a lot. At home with my husband, we get very 'Appalachian'.

So, in "Out on a Limb of the Family Tree", you will find Missouri, who is an eighty-eight year old woman in 1997, and her sister, Kizzie who is eighty-seven years of age, speaking fluent Appalachian. If you ain't never heared of sech words, sound 'em out. You kin do hit!

And you will notice by the time the language filters down to even Wylene, who is in her forties, it's almost gone...

I've only used words and phrases that I grew up with, heard with my own ears and have even used. I'm sure there are more in other towns that I don't know, and some I've used that other towns don't know. I'm a local yokel, so please be kind.

And, if you cain't cipher it out, gimme a call. I do speak English, you know.

Dedicated to all the fine Appalachian women I have known and loved.
And to my God, may I always serve Him!

Rise in the presence of the aged, show respect for the elderly and revere your God. I AM the Lord.

Leviticus 19:32

What do you do
With the motley crew
Who's been given to you
As a family?

Table of Contents

Prologue. The Right Direction	1
Chapter One. The Family Tree	5
Chapter Two. Kizzie Mae McGuire Johnson Malone	16
Chapter Three. Things That Go Bump	22
Chapter Four. The Wedding Day Blues	34
Chapter Five. When the Honeymoon is Over	41
Chapter Six. Trick or Treat	48
Chapter Seven. We Gather Together to Ask the Lord's Blessings	57
Chapter Eight. Six Months and Counting	68
Chapter Nine. In the Meadow, We Can Build a Snowman	77
Chapter Ten. Happy Birthday to You, and Valentine's, too	87
Chapter Eleven. The Family Tree Sprouts Another Bud	98
Chapter Twelve. Busy as a Bee	113
Chapter Thirteen. Two's a Crowd	121
Chapter Fourteen. And Baby Makes Three	130
Chapter Fifteen. Come to Dinner!	138
Chapter Sixteen. In Your Easter Bonnet	144
Chapter Seventeen. Escape from the Hen House	154

Chapter Eighteen: Hemmin' and Hawin'	159
Chapter Nineteen: Family Reunion	165
Chapter Twenty: A Day in the Life	181
Chapter Twenty-One: Rain, Rain, Go Away	189
Chapter Twenty-Two: Happy Birthday Little One!	200
Chapter Twenty-Three: Well, I'll be Dogged!	204
Chapter Twenty-Four: True Tall Tales	213
Chapter Twenty-Five: Dot or Feather - Watch the Weather!	220
Chapter Twenty-Six: To Serve and Be Served	230
Chapter Twenty-Seven: As Time Goes By	236
Chapter Twenty-Eight: When the Mornin' Comes	240
Epilogue Part I: May 2002	244
Epilogue Part II: Spring 2063	248

Out on a Limb of the Family Tree

PROLOGUE:

The Right Direction

1997

Mint came flying into the house, ponytail bouncing behind her. She hurried over to the desk, tearing through drawers until she found her Duck N Hearts stationery and her grape scented pen. She flopped onto the couch, propping her feet up on its threadbare arm. She started to write, pausing for a moment for one last bubble, then stuck her gum onto a coaster where an old glass of tea lived.

Brow furrowed, she began to write furiously:
Dear Donna Jo,
    Sorry it's been so long since I wrote, but have I got something to tell you!
    Now I know it don't seem like the Lord would lead you in a direction that would cause a wreck. But that's exactly what happened to me. See, I always ask the Lord which way to go when I'm driving, if taking a left or a right will get me to the same place, no matter which way I go. I figure He knows better than I do what's up ahead.
    So, a few months ago, I did my usual and got the immediate answer, "RIGHT", so right I went. I hadn't gone a quarter of a mile when this red Buick bowed up and stopped slap dab in the middle of the street. And of course, I hit it, being as I was busy with the radio knob at the time. Thank goodness, I had on my seat belt and it did nothing but jar the fool out of me. My horn stuck when we hit, so when I got out to see about the other driver, I was

somewhat distracted by the unnerving sound of it. Just as I got to the driver's door, it was flung open and this really big man got out, looking like he was fixing to hit something – or somebody. Now, my eyes teared right up. I was already nervous and the look on his face just tore up my last nerve. He started in, saying, "Lady, lady, lady," and I began to think he couldn't say nothing else. I guess it shook him up too. I finally pulled myself together and blew my nose on the handkerchief he handed me. I could tell right off he was sensitive; he flinched when I blew my nose, even with the horn blowing all at the same time.

I started telling him how sorry I was, that I had no idea he was going to stop like that, and it just took me unawares. He explained he was trying to keep from hitting a dog, and thought I was far enough behind him to stop too. (I guess I was – if I'd been actually watching him). I looked around, and sure enough there was Billy Hill's old blood hound, standing next to the road, eyeing us like he knew exactly what we was saying.

"I guess we best call the police, don't you?" the man asked. I can tell you right now that started me bawling again. I figured my insurance would go sky high, and with my job, who can afford that? He started in again saying "Lady, lady," and that made me cry even harder.

He reached in his car and pulled out a phone (if you can believe that) and called Ron Taylor at the police department right then and there. Ron said he'd come on out in about fifteen minutes. While we was waiting on him, I introduced myself. I said, "As long as we got to wait, I might as well introduce myself. My name is Samintha Sanders. Everybody calls me Mint." I stuck out my hand, *friendly like, and he did the same. That's when I noticed he had the biggest blue eyes I ever seen. (Made me worry if my mascara had run when I was squalling.) His face lit up real nice when he smiled, and he told me his name was Ben Sanders! Well, we laughed at that coincidence, I can tell you that!*

After Ron wrote me a ticket and explained when the court date would be, Ben asked me out for a cup of coffee. I certainly couldn't refuse!

When we got to the restaurant, I excused myself for a few minutes and tried to spruce up a little. (After all, a girl's gotta look her best, even in the midst of bad times). As we were fixing to eat some pie and drink coffee, he explained that he had moved here to Sweetapple to work for the school as a coach, and didn't know a soul. I felt right sorry for him, and told him I'd be glad to show him around. (Just being polite, you know).

Well, the court date is next Wednesday. I wanted to let you know, because as soon as we're finished with the wreck business, the Justice of the Peace will be waiting. Yeah, you guessed it! We're tying the knot! I can't hardly believe it myself, but it's so. I hope ya'll can come. Sissy could hold my bouquet and carry the ring, if you'll let her. Her Easter dress will do just fine.

Ain't it funny how things turn out? I guess I'll just keep on trusting the Lord for directions, He didn't steer me wrong after all! And just think! I won't even have to change my last name.

Just my address.

Love and kisses,

Mint

    With a flourish, she used her special signature handwriting to sign off and folded it carefully, ready to mail. She started for the door, admired the way her new engagement ring caught the light, popped the gum back in her mouth, and was post office bound.

    Before she pulled out of the driveway, she paused, and as always, asked the Lord which way. "RIGHT" she heard and right she went.

CHAPTER ONE:

The Family Tree

Missouri Pickett came in from her kitchen garden where she had been admiring posies and vegetables alike. She stopped on the porch to use the old hand pump for washing off the dirt on the vegetables and herself. Although she had indoor plumbing installed years ago, she still preferred the icy cold feel on her skin from the water that came straight out of God's good earth. It was a better way of cooling off than any man made air conditioning she'd ever been introduced to.

She walked on into the kitchen and saw by the mantle clock that her great-grandchild would be arriving soon with a feller who was to become her husband in a few days. Missouri shook her head. That girl was something. She only hoped the intended had a little common sense to make up for what Missouri knew her great-grandchild lacked.

She turned on the gas oven, went into the pantry, and gathered up potatoes and onions. She filled the bottom of a black iron skillet with fat back grease, and set it aside as she began to peel the potatoes.

Missouri could hear the car approaching from a distance, and since she didn't recognize the sound of it, she figured it was the happy couple.

She took her stout frame to the front door, watching the dust swirl behind the sports car as it neared the house. When the car came to a stop, she opened the screen and walked out on the porch. "Come in, come in," she hollered as the young couple got out of the car. "It's hot as blazes out here."

Her great-granddaughter came flying up the steps, pony tail bouncing. She embraced Missouri in a bear hug. "I told Ben you was gonna teach me how to make cornbread, and he's as excited as I've ever seen him." She turned and grabbed the big man's hand. "Ben, I'd like you to meet my great-grandmother, Missouri Pickett. Missouri Pickett, Ben Sanders."

Ben ducked his head. "I'm pleased to meet you, Miz Pickett."

"Call me Missouri. That's what I allow everbody else to call me. You and Mint come on into the house." Missouri opened the screen and they all went in.

"Lord, it feels good to be out of that sun." Samintha turned to Ben. "This house has always been cool, no matter how hot it gets outside."

"Well now, Ben. I hear from Mint that yur a edgi-cated man." Missouri crossed her arms over her great bosom. "But what I want to know is, are you a Godly man?"

Before Ben could speak, Mint chimed in. "Of course he is, Missouri. Why, just yesterday I heard him praying out loud as we was going to town."

Missouri's eyes narrowed. "Who was drivin' at the time?"

Mint dimpled. "I was."

Missouri shook her head and looked at Ben. "I told her Mama they ort not to have had any young'uns, them bein' cousins and all."

Ben blushed. "I think it's sweet when she does that." He put his arm around Mint.

"Have you let her drive again?" Missouri asked.

"Lord no, ma'am. I ain't that big a fool." He answered sincerely.

"Well, I guess that's a step in the right direction," Missouri conceded. "Come on in the kitchen and let's us git this cookin' lesson started."

"Is Mama coming after while?" Mint asked.

"Said she was. We'll see. She said Herbert might have other plans."

"Oh, Daddy will be here." Mint giggled. "I think he's jealous of Ben."

"Most likely. Daddies are like that with thur little girls." Missouri turned to Ben. "You have a seat here at the table while I larn this girl suhum."

Missouri slid the skillet into the oven. "That's so's the grease and pan will be real hot when we're ready fer 'em." She turned to Mint. "All right, girl. I'll stand back and you do the work."

Mint looked at the big blue bowl as though she'd never seen one before. "What do I do first?"

Missouri silently handed her the corn meal sack. Mint poured some in. Then some more. Missouri handed her buttermilk, Mint poured till Missouri said stop. Next came an egg. Mint dropped shell and all into the bowl. "Hellzapoppin' child, ain't you got NO sense?" Missouri quickly dug the egg out of the bowl.

"Missouri, you ought not to talk that way. What would Preacher think?" Mint looked shocked.

"Preacher ain't thankin' nothin', least ways about what I'm a'sayin'. He's been six feet under fer ten years. And besides, he loved me like a husband ort to, faults and all." She glared at Ben. "You got plenty of faults to larn about onct you marry this 'un. Are you ready to put up with 'em?"

"Yes ma'am. I surely am not perfect either." Ben tried to look humble.

Missouri grunted. "Very well." She then returned to the task of making the bread. Then she turned to Mint and warned her, "Kissin' wears out, cookin' don't."

By dinner time, not only had Mint's Mama and Daddy arrived, but so had the other generation, Missouri's daughter (Mint's grandmother) and her husband. This left Ben thoroughly confused with all the generations of parents. But all that confusion was worth the meal he had consumed. The cornbread, which Missouri graciously gave Mint credit for, had been accompanied by fresh green beans from the garden, fried chicken, stewed potatoes and the sweetest onions he'd ever put in his mouth.

Conversation at the dinner table was lively, and sometimes Ben could hardly keep up with all the begats. Gradually the talk turned to weddings, and as long as they were talking about other people's weddings, Ben felt pretty safe.

"I remember gittin' married like it was yester-dey." Missouri said. "I know my mama and papa talked about thur courtin' and marriage often, too." She grinned, and Ben could tell she was warming up for a tale.

"Now my mama loved workin' in the yard and garden, she was a fair housekeeper, and she gradually larned to cook without burnin' the whole meal slap up. But I will say the house often smelled of smoke durin' the meal. My papa used to laugh and tell when he went to Mama's pa and ast fer her hand in marriage. He said Mama's pa leaned back in the chair on the porch and puffed on his pipe fer a few minutes as they watched Mama workin' out in the garden. Her back was to them, and she didn't know Papa was thar about to ast. Then he looked my Papa square in the eye and nodded. "Yur gittin' a fine gal. But she ain't much takin' to housework unless she has to, and she ain't a cook a'tall." He gazed out into the yard and garden and continued. "But she's the best little hoer in the county."

Ben choked on his chicken and the rest of the family laughed heartily. After Ben got banged on the back and his breathing returned to normal, he got the pun. He also got this family was going to be full of interesting times.

He'd drunk three glasses of iced tea, and was now sitting in the living room listening to Missouri and her daughter, Georgia. They were arguing about something out of Proverbs. He couldn't really listen well because he had to pee so badly. He hated to interrupt. He was half afraid of Missouri, and Mint had fallen asleep with her head on his shoulder, and he didn't want to disturb his sweet baby.

His silent misery was interrupted when Georgia asked him would he care to go in the guest room and get the good Bible that was on the night table. "Yes, ma'am I'll be glad to." He raised gingerly and laid Mint's head on the couch. He hurried out and found the bathroom first.

"Well, Mama, what do you think of him?" Mint's mother asked Georgia.

"He's big. That's all I can say for sure now. I just met the boy. What do you think Mama?" she asked Missouri.

"He's arse over teakettle in love with Mint, that's fer shore. And Lord love her, it'll take somebody spa-shull to have the patience to put up with some of her foolishness."

Herbert bristled. "Now Missouri, don't go talking about Mint that a'way. She's a smart girl."

Missouri snorted. "Maybe by yur measurin' stick, Herbert, but not by nobody else's."

Further discussion was ended as Ben re-entered the room with the Bible. He handed it to Mint's mother. "Here ya go, Miz Wylene."

Wylene looked at the Bible. "I certainly am not able to argue with those two about any Bible subject. Why, Mama taught Sunday School for years, and Missouri ain't missed a Sunday of church that I know of since my Mama was born." She handed the book to her mother. "Here, Mama, you and Missouri figger it out." She looked at Ben. "Why don't we go out on the porch and talk a little about the wedding plans?"

Ben felt himself go pale, but he managed a feeble smile and held the screen door open for his soon to be mother-in-law.

Wylene sat in the rocker, Ben took to the swing. She looked coyly at Ben. "Now Ben, I really want to talk to you about this idea of getting married at the courthouse in front of the Justice of the Peace. It's not the way people should get married."

"But Mint says that's what she wants." Ben squirmed in the heat—both kinds, the kind coming from the Georgia summer and the kind coming from Wylene. "She thinks it will be romantic, since us meeting over an accident will cause us to be at the courthouse anyway."

Wylene was silent for a moment. "That's pure foolishness. Mint is prone to foolishness and I think it's your place to make sure ya'll have a nice church wedding."

Ben tried to formulate an answer that wouldn't make Mint or her mother angry. As he was about to give it a try, Missouri stepped out. "Wylene, leave this boy alone. It ain't none of yur business if they git married over by the outhouse, much less the courthouse. It's clur to me Ben here is just near gone enough on Mint that he'd walk down the aisle on his hands if she ast him to. If yur wantin' to bicker do it with yur daughter."

Wylene stood up and stormed back into the house. Ben looked at Missouri, relief written clearly on his face. "Thank you, Missouri. I thought I was a goner for sure."

Missouri grunted. "I thank it ort to be a church weddin' too, but it ain't yur place to change Mint's mind. That's up to me, cause I can always do it, one way or the tuther. I want to know first, if a church weddin' is acceptable fer you."

"Oh, yes ma'am. It would make my mama happier too." His face went all dreamy. "I can just see Mint in one of those long white dresses."

Missouri shook her head. "Even with them rosie glasses you got on yur mind's eye, you know Mint ain't exactly a genius."

Ben sighed. "I know that. But she's got a good heart and I truly think we can be happy."

"As long as you know. Yur a smart man, college edjycated and all. If you both share feelins' fer each other, I thank you'll do all right."

She sat down in the swing next to him. "I was a scant sixteen when I met Preacher. He was as good lookin' as he was good natured. Now most boys that handsome – why – thur as handsome as the devil and act like him too. But not my Preacher. They was done callin' him by that name 'cause he'd knowed he'd been called to preach when he turned twelve." She looked up at Ben. "His real name was Benjamin. Is that yur true name too?"

"Yes, ma'am, it surely is."

Missouri nodded her head as if settling on something in her mind. "We got married when I was seventeen and he was twenty. I had two babies before Georgia. They both died when they was still infants. So I really loved on Georgia. She's the last baby I had. Now looky." Missouri stopped for a moment, gathering her thoughts. "I got Georgia and her Sam. I got Georgia's baby Wylene and her husband Herbert. And now Wylene's baby, Mint, is all growed up and we gonner have you too. That's enough blessins' fer a old woman like me. But I do hope that as soon as it's time, I'll git one more sweet baby to hold before I join Preacher." She patted Ben on the knee as she rose from the swing. "I'm prayin' that ain't too much to ask fer."

Ben stood up too. "Sounds like a reasonable request, Missouri. I promise to do my part." He grinned down at her.

She slapped at him and smiled. "Now, how about some blackbury cobbler? I made it early this mornin'."

"It's a good thing I'm a big man, the way ya'll expect a feller to eat."

"With four generations of women, plan on eatin' plenty. Consider yurself lucky too. From the looks of today's lesson, Mint will need all the help she can git keepin' you fed." They both laughed.

"She'll do fine. I can cook a little too."

As they started in the house, Missouri turned to him one more time. "Now Ben, even though Mint depends on the Lord fer direction when she's drivin', my advice is to stay behind the wheel as much as you can."

Ben shuddered as he remembered the terror Mint's skill level at driving had induced in him. "Don't worry, Missouri, I plan on beating her to the driver's seat every time."

Missouri patted him on the back as they went into the house. "Smart boy. And Ben – welcome to the fam'ly."

"Thanks." Mint joined them at the door, practically jumping into Ben's arms.

"Mint, I need to talk to you about dresses fer yur weddin'." Missouri started in. "The one I's married in seventy years ago comes to mind first, but it is way too fancy fer the courthouse, so we'll have to come up with another idey."

Mint's eyes got big. "You mean I could borrow your dress?" She looked thoughtfully at Ben. "Ben, maybe we could talk some more about the wedding plans."

"Sure, honey, whatever you want." He looked at Missouri and winked as they all walked into the kitchen.

It looked like a sure thing that another branch of the family tree was in the making, and as far as Missouri was concerned it would be a strong match. She smiled to herself, thinking of the fine dress she had in storage that Mint could wear with pride.

Before they began to eat, Missouri bade them bow their heads and ask the Lord to lead the family in the right direction, as He always had.

Laughter and talk filled the big kitchen as Missouri

dished out cobbler to each of her clan.

Unnoticed, she slipped out the door for one more look at her garden before dusk overcame day. As she walked along the rows of beans and corn, she smiled at her own smug satisfaction. Before turning back toward the house, she looked skyward and told Preacher goodnight. Then the lights of the house drew her back in to the heart of her home where her family was gathered and waiting.

Lying in bed that night, Missouri reminisced about dinner, and how easy it was now to feed all them people. She remembered when Georgia was just a little girl and the Great Depression had hit so hard. Her and Preacher had been blessed, all right. Space for a big garden, a pig to kill at first frost to see them with meat through the winter, laying hens, and even a cow to give milk. The only thing they'd done without of much was sometimes they'd run out of sugar, and tobacco for the occasional pipe Preacher smoked.

And Preacher had been generous, too. If he heard of anyone who was without, he made sure they had a part of what his family had. And God saw to it that in spite of that generosity, they had never gone hungry, not one time.

Georgia may not have always had new dresses or very many shoes, but she'd never suffered an empty belly. Neither had she nor Preacher, for that matter.

And when times had got especially hard, they had kept up Kizzie, Missouri's sister, and her bunch, too. Her husband, Homer, had been a saw miller and when he'd been laid off there hadn't been enough food in their garden to feed them and their three young'uns. They didn't have a hog to kill nor a cow to milk and very few hens to provide them eggs to eat. By the second year they'd done a bit better with a bigger garden and such. But they hadn't gone hungry because of Preacher's love and generosity.

How she had loved that man!

Still did.

CHAPTER TWO:

Kizzie Mae McGuire Johnson Malone

Kizzie was startled awake by the phone ringing right in her ear. She looked up at the TV and realized she had once again slept through most of her favorite soap opera. "Foot!" she muttered as she reached for the receiver.

It was her sister, Missouri. "Sounds like I woke you up. I thought this was when you was watchin' that sin program ever day."

"It is, and you don't have to be so judgmental. I fell asleep, as usual. Must not be too bad. I was always a believer that sin was more excitin' than this." Missouri laughed. Kizzie smiled herself. "What bad news are you callin' about today?" Kizzie wasn't much to mince words, and she figured her older sister – and only living sibling – would probably have some gloomy tale to tell. When you were in your eighties, usually one of your few remaining friends passed on a fairly frequent basis.

"No bad news. Just wantin' to know if yur plannin' on comin' to Mint's weddin'. You know it's in five days. She's wearin' my old weddin' dress." Missouri sounded pleased, and Kizzie just bet she was. She knew Mint had fully intended on a tacky courthouse weddin' to some feller she'd only just met when she'd whacked into him with her car. Lord, relatives!

"I reckon I'll come if my rheutmatize ain't too bad that day. I got that dress laid back I'm gonner be buried in, and I 'speck it'll do. Ain't much different, a funeral and a weddin', when you thank about it." Kizzie snickered.

"Well, you've had enough of both to know, I guess." Missouri snickered too, but Kizzie suddenly fell out of the mood.

"Just because I been married twice ain't no reason fer you to go and be snide. I'd of stayed married to Homer if he'd had the decency to live. And God forgive me fer marryin' that smooth talkin' preacher, the holier than thou Reverend Martin Malone. You know I couldn't've stayed married to that snake. I never seen a man with so many hands when a purty girl was around. I hope he's toasty warm where he is."

"Kizzie! Judge not lest ye be! You don't know. Maybe he got fergiveness in the end."

"Maybe he's sittin' on Hell's front porch, more likely." She changed the subject before Missouri could go on. "What time is the nuptials? Is this a rush job?"

"If you're askin' if she's expectin' sooner than nine months, the answer is most certainly not! You know she was raised better'n that!" Missouri's voice had a warning edge to it, but Kizzie could not resist.

"So was her mama, but you know it happened." Kizzie sighed. She was getting tired of the usual bickering she and her sister were so adept at.

Missouri was silent for a few moments, but apparently she was tiring of the game too. "The weddin's at four. Family needs to be seated by quarter of. If you want any of the men folk to pick you up, tell me, and I'll send one of them after you."

"Well, it's that or walk. Just don't send me Georgia's husband. He smells funny, always has."

"Lord, Kizzie, don't go sayin' that about people. He's

got that breathin' condition, it's the salve that smells, not him."

"Just send somebody else, all right?"

"All right. I'll call you d'reckly and let you know who it's to be. I'll hang up now and go feed before it gits dark."

"You need to git rid of them chickens. Yur gittin' too old to go out at dark. What if you fell?" Kizzie had fussed on Missouri about this before, but it didn't seem to do no good.

"Don't go takin' simple pleasures away from what's left of my life. God give me them chickens so's I wouldn't sit around watchin' soap operas."

"I'm hangin' up Missouri, it's useless talkin' to you." And she did.

Kizzie sat for a few minutes, thinking about her sister. There was a year between them, and they'd always been so close they could fight and hug at the same time. The biggest fear her heart could imagine would be for Missouri to pass and leave her on this earth alone. She'd lost a husband and even one of her children. The rest of her children were spread out and she saw them a few times a year – now grown strangers, more than anything. The grandchildren, in her opinion, hadn't turned out so grand, and she was relieved when they left after visits. But Missouri – she didn't know life without her.

Kizzie sighed and hefted herself off the couch. She turned off the television and hobbled into the kitchen to fix herself a bite to eat. She figured she'd need the strength when she went into the spare bedroom closet to search for her burying dress. She hoped it didn't smell like mothballs and she hoped even more it didn't have to be pressed. As far as Kizzie was concerned, permanent press clothes was the best miracle the Lord had ever performed, out shining every one of them in the Bible. She was forever tired of ironing, remembering the formidable chore it had been growing up. Plus, her ma had made them iron everything they owned, from bloomers to collars and back.

She stepped onto the back porch and got a ripe tomato out of the basket sitting by the door. She'd had a small kitchen garden this year, comparatively speaking, but the few tomato plants had been fruitful, and she'd been eating them three times a day. She picked up two pods of pepper and stepped back into her kitchen. She got two biscuits left over from breakfast, sliced them open, and spread a generous helping of Blue Plate on both sides. The tomato was rich and juicy as she cut into it. She rinsed the peppers and reached in the refrigerator for a Co-Cola. She refused to drink it unless it came in the glass bottles, like God intended. The rest tasted funny. She popped off the cap and joined her food at the table. She looked heavenward and said, "Thank you Lord fer this good food," and set in eating.

"Best call Missouri back when I git through eatin'," she said out loud. "I plumb fergot to warn her about Essie's gas problem. If they invite her, we'll all be embarrassed to death." She got up from the table, nibbled on a vanilla wafer for desert and stacked her dishes in the sink.

Walking down the hall to the spare bedroom, she reminisced about her own young wedding, and how beautiful she had looked, and how beautiful she thought her life was going to be. And it had been, she guessed, for the most part.

She opened the closet door and tried to feel way back in the back. There it was – still in that big heavy zipper bag they'd bought for her to put her 'good clothes' in. Her children didn't like moth ball smells either. She hung the dress on the closet door, unzipped the bag, and took out the dress. Well, she thought, it ain't so bad. She shook the skirt of it a little and decided it would do without ironing. She left it hanging out so it could air.

That chore done, she went back into the living room to call Missouri. She wondered how long they would talk this time without ya-yaing at each other. The thought made her smile. Missouri answered, and once again, the sisters commenced to talk.

Kizzie reckoned she and Missouri had fussed all thur lives. Between Missouri gettin' her in trouble, and then tryin' just as hard to get her out, thar was always suhum goin' on.

And it seemed no matter what one of them got, the other wanted it, instead of what they'd received themselves.

Kizzie reckoned sisters were just borned to be that way.

Yet, there were times when they shared effortlessly. Like one doll between them. They never fought one time over her.

And the times they'd had together! Being raised in the tiny rural town of Sweetapple, Georgia, other children weren't available for day to day play, and at school no more than twelve children were in the whole room, age six to sixteen. The only child that had been close to their age had been Homer Rudolph and he'd been meaner than a two headed snake. The other girls were either much younger or much older. So they had always depended on each other.

Kizzie secretly prayed the good Lord would take her first. After all, Missouri had family close by and she didn't. Missouri wouldn't suffer near as much as she would, so it seemed only fair to get to die first.

Kizzie sighed. That meant she'd probably die years after Missouri did.

CHAPTER THREE:

Things That Go Bump

Wylene rolled over, opened one eye, and saw that it was nearly time to get up. The clock would alarm in about five minutes, so she reached and turned it off. Her movement woke Herbert, and he scooted closer so they could spoon.

Wylene felt tears come to her eyes. "I can't believe our child is getting married."

Herbert grunted. "Be glad she seems to have latched on to a good one. He's respectable and will be able to provide for them, so I don't have to, like Jane and Larry are havin' to with theirs."

"Well, of course I'm grateful, but she's so young!"

"She's twenty. Same age you was. It didn't hurt you none." He scooted closer.

"I know, but Mint is so immature, you know that Herb." She sighed. "I guess I'm just feeling sad. I have a daughter getting married, what does that make me?"

"Free at last!" They both laughed. Wylene turned toward him, and they kissed. Then the phone rang. He moaned. "Just as things was heatin' up!"

Wylene shushed him and picked up the telephone. "Hello?" She paused, then back onto her pillow. "Yes, we were awake. Not up yet, though." She sat up again. "What? Is she all right?"

Herbert sat up too, feeling his pulse quicken. Wylene looked scared. "What's wrong?" He whispered to her. She waved him away as she listened.

"Okay, we'll be there as soon as we can." She hung up and turned to her husband. "Missouri has had some sort of spell. Kizzie called her about six this morning and said Missouri sounded confused. Mama went over there. She says they're on their way to the hospital with her. Missouri's talking nonsense."

"Reckon she's had a stroke? She's pushing ninety."

Wylene got out of bed and started grabbing clothes out of the closet. "I don't know. Lord I hope not! Mint lives and breathes for Missouri, she'll be killed if anything happens – especially now!"

Herbert pulled up his jeans. "We may not be having a wedding this weekend after all."

Wylene picked up the telephone and dialed Mint's number. It rang several times till Mint answered, sounding far away. Wylene hollered into the phone. "Mint! Turn the receiver around; you've picked it up wrong!"

"Geez, Mama, don't scream. You woke me up, and now you're yelling. What time is it?" Mint sounded more than half asleep.

"It's a bit after seven. Listen honey, Mother just called me. She's over at Missouri's. She thinks something's wrong, and she's taking Missouri to the hospital. Me and your daddy are going to meet them there. Do you want us to swing by and get you too?"

"What's wrong with her? Is she hurt?" The panic was clear in her voice.

"We don't know. Do you want us to pick you up?"

"Yes, I'll get dressed. Hurry Mama!" She hung up without waiting for a response.

They arrived at the Sweetapple General Hospital just

as the wheelchair was rolling Missouri through the emergency room doors. Georgia hurried over to her daughter. She hugged Wylene, then Mint, who was already tearful.

"I first thought she'd had a stroke. But then, I was helping her get dressed, and she had blood all over the back of her head! I think she's fell or something. She don't remember at all."

They all walked into the ER, and rushed to Missouri's side. The nurse was by her, asking her to get up on the examining table. "Would you like me to turn cartwheels while I climb up?" Missouri asked the nurse. "I'm dizzy as it is and I just cain't hop up thar. Plus I'm nearly a hundurd! Why would you ask a old woman to do suhum that foolish?"

The nurse looked irritated. "I'll be more than happy to help you. But we want you up there so I can take your blood pressure before the doctor comes in here."

Georgia bent over her mother. "I'll help you up, Mama. The nurse can get the other side." They did, Missouri grumbling the whole time.

Missouri looked up at Mint. "What are you doin' here child? Ain't it still early mornin'?"

"Well, I got scared when they said something was wrong with you. What happened, Missouri?" Mint asked.

"If I knowed, I'd a'done told somebody by now. All I remember is Kizzie hollerin' at me over the phone about some foolishness. My head hurts, though."

Mint leaned into her and Missouri patted her head, as she'd done for twenty years. "Oh, Missouri, please be okay. I thought you might be dead forever!"

Out on a Limb of the Family Tree

The doctor walked in. "Who's the patient?" He asked, as he looked at Mint clinging to Missouri.

"Well, ain't it obvious I am? I'm the only one in here with blood on her head." Missouri looked at the doctor threateningly. "And I don't want you causin' me no more pain. It already hurts."

Mint moved away as the doctor got closer. "I don't intend to hurt you, Mrs. Pickett. Just let me take a look." He helped her turn, and popped on gloves. He gently parted her hair to look at the injury. "You don't remember what happened?"

"No. If I did, I woulda told so everbody'd quit askin' me the same question over and over. What does it look like?"

"Like you've gashed your noggin." He straightened, pulled the gloves, ditched them, and turned to the nurse. "I think it'll take about four or five stitches. Clean her up and stitch her up." He turned to the family. "She's fine. I think there's a mild concussion; nothing serious. But head wounds bleed a lot, so she's lost a great deal of blood. Plus, a bump on the head at her age -"

Missouri glared at him. "I know I'm old, but I ain't deaf. I'm hearin' ever word yur sayin'. And I ain't foolish in the head yet, bump or no bump. So, talk to me, boy."

He grinned, then turned to face her. "Sorry. They just look so scared I thought I'd better reassure them. You don't seem to need reassuring. But you're fine, as you heard. I'd be interested in finding out if you ever remember what happened. Sometimes memory does come back. If it does, will you let me know?"

Her eyes glinted a little. "Don't know if I can

remember to or not. If I happen to recall, and then remember to call you, I might, if the mood strikes me to. Just make sure you write yur name real clur on the bill."

He laughed out loud. "I'll be sure and do that, Mrs. Pickett." He shook her hand.

"You call me Missouri. That's what I allow everbody else to call me."

"I'm honored. You can call me John." He turned, nodded to the family, and left the room. The nurse was ready to stitch. Mint whimpered and Wylene took her out so she wouldn't see.

"You can leave too, if you need to Georgia. I'll be fine. This nurse will take care of me." Missouri sounded a little more unsure than previously.

"Why, Mama, I ain't leaving you in here. The men folk always run out, and you know poor little Mint can't take nuthin' hardly. Wylene had to take her out, but I'm staying, don't you fret."

The nurse finished up and gave Missouri two tablets. "These are Tylenol II; take them as soon as you get home, so you can get some rest till the pain goes away."

Back home, they all fussed over Missouri, insisting she go to bed. "I ain't never took to my bed in the daylight unless I was bad sick. And Dr. John said I was fine." But to bed she went, and not twenty minutes after swallowing the pills, she was asleep.

The other three generations gathered round the kitchen table, coffee in hand. Mint still looked somewhat pale, as though it was she who had been stitched up. Her lip trembled as she spoke. "I can't stand the thought of something happening to Missouri. Mama, I don't know what I'll do."

Wylene looked at her and sighed. "Mint, you know Missouri is very old. She might be around another few years, she might not. The main thing is to enjoy each other like you always have. Why, she's so excited about your wedding, she ain't going nowhere!" They laughed.

"My Mother has a will of iron. Ya'll know that." Georgia said. "She passed it on to me, and I have passed it on to you, honey." She patted Wylene. "Looks like it run out before it got to you, Mint."

"I know I'm a crybaby. I just love her so much. She's always made me feel like I was special." She looked at Georgia. "You have too, Grandma, but Missouri has just always lifted me up, like I was going to be somebody."

"I know child. There's a special bond there that don't take away from mine or your mama's love. We're just glad you've got it." She stood up and put her cup in the sink. "I'm gonna go check on Mama."

She left Wylene and Mint, and walked down the hall to Missouri's bedroom. She pushed the door slightly open, trying to be as quiet as possible. She watched Missouri breathing deeply. She looked peaceful. Georgia stepped on into the room, gazing at her mother's face. She felt tears sting her eyes, knowing that someday – and not far away – her mother would no longer be with them. Georgia was an only child, and never talked about the dread that encompassed her when she contemplated the future without her mother, the last person that linked her to her childhood. Missouri had been the matriarch for years, and Georgia wasn't sure she was anywhere near ready to take her place.

Missouri stirred and looked up at Georgia. "You all

right?" She asked.

"Yes, Mama, I'm fine. Just checking to make sure you are."

Missouri smiled. "You got it backerds. I'm the one what's supposed to check on you. Yur my baby." She closed her eyes again, and seemed to sleep immediately.

"You're right." Georgia whispered. "I'm your baby." She stood another few moments, then quietly left the room, back to the kitchen to join the others.

Missouri was dreaming. She and Kizzie were out at the pond feeding the ducks. It was a day she remembered well from her childhood. Fall had just touched the air, colors blazing everywhere, but not cold enough mid-day yet for a coat. Kizzie was dressed in the frock and bonnet Mama had made especially for her. The tiny blue violets that made up the print of the fabric were the exact color of Kizzie's eyes. The bonnet was hanging down her back, and her white-blonde hair was coming loose from its binding, curling in ringlets around her face. Missouri could see herself, as one can in dreams, and she was standing beside Kizzie. Her dress was a print with yellow belles, which she hated. Everyone said it matched her bright red hair, which she also hated. Her Sunday boots were brown instead of black, and she had remembered pouting about that at the store till she'd nearly got a whipping for it.

She and Kizzie had gotten bored that afternoon after the huge Sunday dinner her parents had hosted for their Bible Study Class. All the grown ups were sitting on the porch, full as ticks. After contemplating a climb to the barn loft and deciding that was too dirty a trip, the girls snuck around once or twice, seeing if they could catch some gossip. But Tommy Bishop was hanging onto his mama for dear life. They figured nobody would say anything out of the way, unless they forgot about him, which grown ups sometimes did, especially if a child was still and quiet.

Kizzie and Missouri had tried to convince Tommy to feed the ducks with them earlier, but he was having none of it. In later years, the two sisters had wondered if Tommy had somehow sensed his mama would be in her grave not three months from that Sunday.

Lois Shoemaker and her husband were there too. They had three month old twins. Kizzie and Missouri had speculated over and over how in the world Mrs. Shoemaker fed them babies. Was it at the same time? If so, how did she hold them? If she nursed them one at a time, did the other baby put up a ruckus till it was his turn?

They made a special effort to be around when the babies woke up and tried to follow when Mrs. Shoemaker went inside. But their mama kept a sharp eye out and told them they needed to stay outside and play. They slowly made their way back out, snatching glimpses out of the corner of their eyes of the half closed door. Kizzie told Missouri that Mrs. Shoemaker was rocking and nursing, but she couldn't see if it was one or two she was feeding. Kizzie said all she could see through the crack in the door was the back of Mrs. Shoemakers head as she rocked back and forth.

They'd stood under the big poplar tree, just sort of hanging out, till the adults settled again. Then Missouri suggested Kizzie try to stand on the outside of the porch steps and hold onto the banister while stretching to see if she could see in the window. Mama had closed the shades *to the porch windows to give Mrs. Shoemaker privacy, but had left the shade up on the side window.*

Kizzie had about stretched her neck out of shape, but to no avail. Plus their mama had fussed on her for getting her frock dirty from the outside of the banister. That side was never swept, seeing as nobody was ever on the outside of the steps.

Missouri half smiled in her sleep. She nor Kizzie knew the answer to that mystery to date. Wondering around in sleep, Missouri tried to recall if either of the twins were still alive, and even if they were, would they remember being nursed at their mother's breast? Probably not. And right embarrassed if asked, she guessed.

Missouri slept on. She remembered that evening, as everyone left, Mama and Papa had stayed on the porch, listening to the frogs. The lightning bugs were gone, as were all the other insects, but the frogs still noised about. They talked low, so she and Kizzie had to squat close to the window sill to hear their conversation. It was mostly about nothing, the goings on of the day, what tomorrow would bring, things like that. Missouri remembered the comfort she felt, the security she knew in this marital ritual of common conversation.

Her mother had been a pretty woman, blonde and blue eyed. Her father handsome, even if his nose was too big, his jaw too square. He had a fine head of auburn hair and green cat like eyes. Both of them had a bountiful sense of humor and it seemed to Missouri they always stood out in a crowd. Some of it, she knew, was because they were both taller than most. But there was something else, too, something indefinable. She was always proud they were her parents.

She had wished she had Mama's blonde hair and good looks. But what she got was Papa's auburn hair turned fiery red and his strong jaw. Thank God she hadn't inherited his nose! She did get Mama's blue eyes. Kizzie had received all the beauty, though. Mama's flaxen hair, Papa's green eyes and the softer, more feminine features.

Missouri turned in the bed. And kept on dreaming/thinking. What did those looks matter now? They were both old, old women, hair color gone with the years, eyes sunk and behind spectacles. Their beauty all wrinkled and faded. But they were still who they were, and maybe more so.

Old age made her think of Papa. She remembered the last few years of his life. He'd been so lonely after Mama died. Five years of being widowed had never eased the grief from the day she left. He talked about "his beautiful Esther" every day. She and Kizzie tried to soften the blow by being good daughters, and she guessed it had, in some ways, helped.

The day Papa died he had smiled a lot and told them both he was going home and couldn't wait to see Esther. "I'll greet my Savior first, but I know Esther will be right thar with Him, waitin'!" She'd never seen anyone so happy to just die and go on.

Missouri missed Preacher. And she believed him and her babies would be waiting on her. But she still loved this life too, and wasn't ready to leave.

This roused her from her sleep, and for a minute she couldn't figure out why she was in bed in broad daylight. Then she remembered the fall. She gave serious thought to trying to get up, but she could tell the medicine had made her woozy, so she pulled the covers up around her neck and slept on.

****

Three days later, the day of the dress rehearsal, Georgia hauled Missouri to the doctor's office to have stitches removed. Missouri insisted on going on to the examining room alone, she was, as she said, "purty growed up to be so young."

Georgia had just settled into a nice magazine when Missouri stomped back into the waiting area. "Georgia! Come here, child! They's wantin' me to make water in this little plastic cup. Now how am I gonner squat over a toilet and do that, me near a hundurd?"

A man in the corner had a violent coughing fit, and Georgia felt herself turn crimson to the roots. "Lord, Mama, hush!" She threw down the magazine, picked up her purse, and raced across the waiting area. "Come on back here and I'll help you figure it out."

"Don't know what in tarnation they's thankin', makin' a old woman do such." Missouri muttered as they walked back down the hall. The bathroom door stood open, and although it was a small space, and Missouri and Georgia both fairly large women, they squeezed in and Georgia locked the door.

Ten minutes later they were out, triumphant. But Georgia sure did feel sorry for the doctor when he got in there with Missouri. Georgia settled back down, prayerfully, with a magazine, and read till Missouri came back out, this time looking only slightly miffed.

After making sure nothing was owed, they started for the car. "What did the doctor say, Mama?" Georgia asked.

"Fool said my blood pressure was up. Well, no wonder! I

told him what I'd been through in that two by four they call a bathroom and that man actually laughed at me! I contemplated right then and thar on givin' him a whippin'. But he got a right smart nicer when he saw I's gittin' madder'n an old wet hen. So, we both calmed down."

Georgia shook her head. "You know, Mama, he's just trying to help keep you healthy."

Missouri snorted. "You know, Georgia," she mimicked, "He's just tryin' to keep his pocketbook healthy."

Georgia threw her hands up in surrender momentarily and then quickly grabbed the steering wheel. "Did he have anything else to say about your health?"

"Took the stitches outta my head. Said it was healin' right nice. Wants me to come back after the weddin' and have my blood pressure checked again, when I ain't 'a little upset'." She snorted again. "I informed him I'd probably be a 'little upset' ever time I run into him."

"Did you agree to come back?"

"Yeah. I reckon he's a right smart doctor. Fer a young'un."

Georgia made a mental note to check her mama's blood pressure herself. She had a kit at home for when Sam needed his checked, as he was on medicine.

But she sure wasn't going to mention it at the moment.

CHAPTER FOUR:

The Wedding Day Blues

Mint looked at herself in the mirror. The sapphire earrings circled in diamonds were old, borrowed, and definitely blue. She tilted her head this way and then that way, making the light dance around in her hair. The earrings (or earbobs, as Missouri called them) made Mint's blue eyes even bluer especially with the snow white of her veil for background. She'd had her hair pulled up in a 'Gibson Girl' and tiny ringlets framed her face. Her cheeks were pink with excitement. "Twenty more minutes," she murmured as she glanced at the clock.

A light tapping at the door and her mother entered the room. "Hi, honey." Her mother teared up. "You look so beautiful."

"Thanks, Mama. I feel beautiful too." She giggled. "I hope this knocks Ben's socks off!"

They both laughed. Wylene hugged Mint gently, careful not to mash all the fabric surrounding her daughter. "Mama and Missouri will be here in a few minutes. They sent your granddaddy to get Kizzie."

Mint rolled her eyes. "I bet Kizzie will complain the whole way to the church." Mint walked over to the window and opened the blind a bit. "It's a beautiful day. Oh, Mama, I feel so blessed!" She twirled around and faced her mother. "How did you feel when you and Daddy got married?"

"Nervous, excited, giddy. I felt like I had waited my whole life for it to take place. I wore those same earrings."

She reached up and touched one of them. "I didn't wear the dress, though. I'd seen one in a wedding boutique, and I thought I just had to have it instead. I'm sure it hurt Missouri's feelings, but she never let on. Mother took it to the cleaners for me while we were on our honeymoon, and I never saw the gown again! They lost my dress! I thought my mama was going to kill somebody. All they could do was pay us for it – they never knew what happened either."

They both turned as the door opened. It was Georgia and Missouri. Missouri stopped and took Mint in. "Lord, ain't you a vision!" She walked over to Mint, touching the wedding dress she had worn nearly seventy years ago. "What memories this brangs back." She placed her hands on Mint's face. "Time respects no one. Before ye know it, it'll be you lookin' back."

Mint kissed Missouri. "I think you look beautiful today, too." She turned to her grandmother, Georgia. "You look great!" Mint beamed. "Look at all of us! Four generations of women." Tears threatened to smear her make up. "This is a perfect day."

Another knock at the door, this time Miss Barnes coming through with an authoritative look about her. "Now, Samintha, it's time for a last minute touch up. Don't show your face out that door lest Ben see you! Bad luck. It's almost time to seat these ladies, so out you go!" she shooed Missouri, Georgia, and Wylene out. She turned, and gave a critical eye to make-up and hair. Then she smiled. "You're a beautiful bride, Mint."

"Thanks." The door closed behind Miss Barnes. Mint shut her eyes, counted to twenty and opened the door a crack. She could see the back of Ben as he stood, waiting for his cue. "Sssssppt." He turned. His eyes widened as he saw part of Mint's face. "Come here." He hesitated for a second, then started forward. "Don't look!" Mint scolded. He dutifully ducked his head.

"You're going to get us in trouble, Mint!" Ben whispered. "That Miss Barnes is as rigid as they come."

Mint giggled. "That's why this is so excitin'! If no one cared, it wouldn't be fun." She stretched out one lacey arm and stroked his chest. "Mr. Sanders, I can't wait to get my hands on you."

Ben's eyes widened again and he looked at her. Blushing, he looked back down. "You're doing this on purpose, Samintha Sanders, and you ought to be ashamed!" He heard a noise and quickly shut the door, catching Mint's dress in it. One expletive later, he'd reopened the door, shut it, and strode hastily to where he should have been standing all along.

He could hear her giggling again behind the door. Ben just shook his head, said a prayer of thanks and grinned.

****

As weddings often are, Mint and Ben's seemed half dreamlike, half seriously earthbound. The thrill of seeing the church festooned in green and white, seeing her cousin Sissy solemnly strewing petals on the old oak floor, feeling the thrill as the congregation stood in honor when she began her holy march down the middle aisle. Then Ben's eyes. Oh, his eyes! He had turned toward her and she could feel herself becoming lost in his eyes. As she neared him, she could see the tears pooled there. He had touched her cheek with his hand before turning to the minister. Then, afterwards, as they were presented to the congregation as husband and wife, seeing Missouri, her grandmother, and mother, all tearful yet triumphant. The beautiful, bountiful reception, the laughter, the kisses, the photographs.

Then, it was over.

Missouri stood between Georgia and Wylene, watching the car drive away. Mint stuck her head out the window and yelled, "Great catch, Missouri!" as the crowd erupted into laughter. Missouri had caught the wedding bouquet and still held it clasped to her bosom. The car drove out of sight, and the crowd began to disperse. Ties loosening on the men, women with their high heels in hand, moseying to their own cars, reflected the lazy letdown.

Georgia patted Wylene's back. "Well, dear, she's flown the nest."

Wylene smiled. "Yes. I still can't believe it. My baby."

Missouri, with a glint in her eye, spoke to them both. "I suspect yur baby ain't gonner be a baby much longer. She'll be havin' babies herself afore you know it."

Wylene groaned. "Don't remind me, Missouri! I'm trying desperately not to think about that!"

Missouri snorted. "And I guess you and Herb tweren't thankin' nothin' of the sort as ya'll drove off."

Wylene laughed. "Well, we did stop and wash the car – you know how Herb loved that car."

"Now don't go telling family secrets, Wylene." Herb said as he walked up to the group. "They'll think I wasn't a normal boy."

"Done know that. But we love ye anyway!" Missouri looked up at the sky. "Well, I reckon we best be a'headin' back. Where'd Kizzie git herself to?"

"She had one of the Farley twins take her home right after she ate cake. Said her knees was bothering her." Herbert explained.

"Didn't have enough manners to tell me bye!" Missouri huffed. "Well, take me home, Herb, I need to call and check on her afore it's time to feed the chickens."

"Yes 'um."

Herbert walked around to get the car, and Missouri turned to her daughter. Wylene had wondered over to tell neighbors good bye. "Now, Georgia, I want you to pay special attention to Wylene this week. Yur her mama and she's gonner need you. It won't hit her till dark and she'll start thankin' about what Mint and Ben are up to and -"

"Mama, hush up! Somebody might overhear you." She glanced around nervously. "I promise I'll take care of Wylene. Like you said, I'm her mama. I've been through it; I'll help her do the same."

Herb had pulled the car around and was opening the passenger side for Missouri. "I'll be back to pick ya'll up as soon as I can," he told Wylene.

"Take your time. We've got the reception area to clean up." She turned, then impulsively walked to Herb and gave him a peck on his cheek. "Be careful."

He looked at her funny and grinned. "I will. Don't carry nothing heavy. I'll take care of that when I get back."

With Missouri safely tucked in and belted down, he waved to Wylene and drove off.

Missouri hung the wedding bouquet out the window and waved with it.

Georgia and Wylene looked at each other, laughed, shook their heads, and went in to clean the church.

Out on a Limb of the Family Tree

Missouri got home none too soon. Lord, her feet was hurtin'! She got them Sunday shoes off as soon as she could get in her bedroom to her house shoes. She shucked her good dress and hung it up, and reached for her old dress. Frowning, she muttered, "Well, this dress'll need arnin' now." She sighed, then a sly grin appeared. She had a good mind to call Kizzie just for meanness and ask her if she'd mind ironing her dress. That'd make her put up a good fuss!

She wandered on into the kitchen and got a glass of water, then settled on the back porch in her favorite rocker to rest. She looked out over the fields her Papa had worked so hard in. Most of it was fallow now, just her small garden spot. Near all the outbuildings were gone too. Her chicken house had been salvaged and redone from an old storage building, as the barn had been too dangerous for her to walk in for many years. She'd parked a car in it until she'd sold the Ford the day she turned eighty. She'd almost hit a child on the way back from town because her foot had hit the gas instead of the brake pedal. She'd hung the keys up that day and made Sam sell the car. The barn still stood, dark and looming. Missouri often wished it could be restored and used again, but she knew she was far too old to be the one to do it. She used the smokehouse for her garden tools and the lawn mower and hedge clippers and water hose and such as all that.

Then her mind turned to the wedding today. What a beautiful bride Mint had made! Missouri reckoned all brides were beautiful, least ways all she'd seen. She was pretty sure she'd been a beautiful bride, she remembered how beautiful she had felt!

Looking in the mirror, Missouri could see her red hair under the veil, but it was softer today, somehow. And how blue her eyes had looked, making the sapphire earbobs show up. Or was it the other way around? And the gown had fit her young body perfectly.

She remembered how Preacher's eyes had purely lit up when he saw her.

The house was full, the porches were both packed, and it was pouring the rain.

Kizzie was dressed in a new pale green silk, and stood by her after Papa had given her away. Her Mama had on a new dress too. It was of palest blue and almost hid the fact that she was pregnant. A change of life baby that had lived barely three days. They had named her Laura Christine. She was deformed, and as far as Missouri knew, she never opened her eyes.

Missouri sat up straighter and wondered aloud, "Now what was that boy's name? It started with a dubya…Walter! That was it!"

Relieved that she'd thought of Preacher's best man at the wedding, she got up from her chair to call Kizzie and ask her to 'arn' for her.

CHAPTER FIVE:

When the Honeymoon is Over

The phone had already rung six times before Missouri could get to it. She'd been stringing beans on the front porch, and what with putting the pan and knife down, heaving herself out of the chair, and unsticking the screen door, it took time. As soon as she answered, she heard giggling on the other end, and knew it was Mint. That child never did know how to use a phone properly.

"Good mornin' to you, too. I see yur back from the honeymoon."

More giggling. "Morning Missouri. We got back yesterday but with unpacking and all, I'm just now getting around to calling you." She paused and Missouri heard some rustling in the background. More giggling again. Missouri rolled her eyes heavenward. "Would you happen to know where Mama and Daddy have got off to?"

"They was goin' over to Georgia's early this mornin' to finish pickin' the beans so we can git them all canned tomorrow. Are you and Ben comin' to help?"

"I will. Ben has to go back to work tomorrow."

"You can wash the cannin' jars. Don't fergit to brang them you got at yur house."

"Can't I help -"

She didn't get finished before Missouri interrupted. "No, you cain't help strangin' the beans. You always mess up, and thar ain't nuthin' I hate worsern tryin' to strang the beans while I eat 'em."

"Aw, Missouri, I'll do it right this time. I'm a grown

woman now." There was a very un-grownup whine to her voice.

Missouri snorted. "You may be growed up, but you still cain't strang. I'll tell you what. When you git so growed up you have yur own garden, you can strang yur beans, I'll wash the jars."

Mint sighed "Okay, okay, you win. What time do I need to get there?"

"We'll start about eight. I'll have breakfast cooked, and soon as we clean that up, we'll commence on the beans."

"I'll be there. I love you Missouri. I missed you while I was gone."

"Uh-huh. I just bet you did. Now git off this phone and tend to yur husband afore he has to git to work tomorrow."

This brought on a fresh gale of giggles as Mint hung up the phone. Missouri had to act quick and stifle her own giggle.

She barely made it.

****

The next morning was another clear, hot day, and Missouri had got up extra early to make biscuits. She'd fried tenderloin and made milk gravy, scrambled eggs and put three kinds of jelly on the table. The coffee was strong, the milk sweet and the butter creamed. All had arrived on time, save Mint, and they were sitting around the table, with second cups of coffee in their hands. They heard the car come up the drive, about three dozen empty canning jars chattering in the backseat like ladies at a tea party. The door slammed, and Mint's footsteps were heard as they came across the porch. All eyes were turned to the door as she opened it, but what they saw was certainly not what they were expecting from the new bride. Her face was tear streaked, her hair a mess, and her clothes were wrinkled. She went straight to her mama, sat in her lap, and began to wail.

Missouri shook her head, stood up and started clearing the table. "Honeymoon over?" she asked. Mint wailed louder.

"Now, now, Mint, honey, what's wrong?" Her mother asked, patting her back.

Mint sat up, sniffing loudly. "Ben fussed on me before he left for work. I got up special early to iron his shirt, but I forgot when I went to the bathroom and left the iron on it, and it burned a big old hole in the back. I didn't mean to!" She burst into tears again.

Missouri put her hands on her hips. "Well, it sounds like you did ruin it. Did you tell him it was a accident?"

"Y-yes. I explained to him I'd never ironed before, and I didn't realize it would get so hot so quick. He just shook his head, threw down the shirt, and went back to the closet to get another one. He said he'd wear that one wrinkled, thank you, and walked out the door. He didn't even k-kiss me 'bye!" The last sentence was wrung out of her and she flung her head back on her mother's shoulder. The women looked at each other and grinned.

"Well, Wylene, it looks like you need to go and make room fer yur child to come home. She done give up that apartment she was rentin' afore she married."

Mint raised her head. "What are you talking about? This was just a fuss, not a reason to divorce!"

"Exactly." Missouri said. "So git up from thar and quit actin' like it's the end of the world. We got beans to can."

The telephone rang. Missouri answered it and smiled. "It's fer you, Mint. It's Ben."

Mint grabbed the phone and pulled it as far into the next room as the cord would allow. "Mama, it looks like you need to get one of them cordless phones." Georgia said.

"I guess I know what I'm gittin' fer Christmas, in that case, 'cause I shore ain't spendin' money on a phone I don't need."

Mint came back in, a dreamy look on her face. Missouri put a clean plate on the table. "Git suhum to eat while we finish up the dishes, so we can git started."

Mint began to fill her plate, then suddenly went pale. She ran out of the room. The women looked at one another. "I'll go see about her." Wylene walked into the bathroom. Mint was washing her face with a cold cloth. "What's wrong, Mint?"

"I don't know, Mama. The smell of that food just suddenly made me sick. I did this yesterday, too. I must have a bug of some kind."

Wylene looked at her closely. "Turn around."

Mint did so. "Why?"

"I want to see your back side. Oh, Lord."

"What is it?" Mint craned her neck trying to see her own bottom.

"When a woman gets pregnant her butt is usually the first thing that changes."

"I'm not pregnant! I just got married!"

"Not married two months and – Mint, did you and Ben

have relations before you got married?"

"Mama!" Mint looked shocked. "I have you know I'm a grown woman, and I don't have to discuss this." She glanced at her mother and the wind went out of her sails. "No, we didn't."

"Have you used precautions since you got married?"

"Of course we did – except the second day when we – uh – sort of got in a hurry." She blushed scarlet. "But we thought that was okay, because Ben – uh – you know – stopped before it was over."

"One thing for sure, you need to have a test and find out. You call your doctor right now and make an appointment."

Mint again began to cry, this time silently with tears rolling down her face. "Please don't mention this to Ben unless we know for sure. We planned on waiting two years, not two months!"

They walked back into the kitchen where Missouri and Georgia stood gazing at them. "Well?" Missouri asked.

"I've told her to call the doctor and have a pregnancy test done."

"Turn around, Mint, and let me see yur backside." Mint rolled her eyes, but did as Missouri asked. "Praise the Lord!" Missouri clapped her hands together. "She's carryin' fer shore!"

Mint once again picked up the phone, dragging it to the floor. After a few moments of conversation, she turned to the women. "They can see me tomorrow at ten."

"Give me that phone." Missouri grabbed the receiver away. "Now listen here. I'm nearly a hundurd years old, and I may not have tomorrow. This would be my first great-great grandchild and I'm tellin' you to see her right away." Silence. Then, "Fine. She'll be thar in forty-five minutes."

Three hours later, Mint returned to Missouri's house. The look on her face told the tale, and all the women gathered around her. "Missouri, can I ask Ben to come out here to tell him? I'm afraid he's going to be so disappointed in me."

"Samintha Sanders, you hush! Ben is as much a part of this as you are. Thar ain't mistakes when babies is made, so you thank the good Lord fer this. Why, I can almost guarantee that Ben will be tickled pink, soon as he gits used to the idey. Call him, and we'll have him and all the rest of the fam'ly here fer supper."

As Mint went once again to the phone, Missouri gathered her straw hat and basket. "I'm goin' to the garden to git some tomaters and onions fer supper."

As she got between the rows, she pulled some green onions, and then walked further into the garden. She looked skyward. "Well, Preacher, my prayers is answered! We're gonner have another baby fer me to hold. I'm so grateful; I don't even want to mention that I'm a' hopin' it's a girl. And you know Ben will make a fine daddy. He's so much like you was. I wish you was here to share this." Then her voice changed, and she bowed her head. "Now, Lord, I know the Bible don't say nuthin' about talkin' to dead husbands, and I thank You know it's just suhum I do fer comfort. I don't mean nuthin' sacrilegious. And I do thank Ye, Lord, fer this child. I know it'll be a blessin'."

She picked a few ripe tomatoes, and some cucumbers for good measure. She looked up at the house as she heard laughter. It made her smile. She knew soon that the house would fill up with the men folk, and the table would be crammed with family. Well, that was just fine with her. The more the merrier.

That night Missouri tried to keep her mind from worrying overmuch about the baby like a dog worrying a bone. Just because she'd had so many miscarriages didn't mean Mint would. But the pain of the death of all her babies lived within her always.

She looked up toward the ceiling and prayed. "I know the old devil is eatin' at me, Lord. I know You have plans fer us afore we are even knit in the womb. And if this baby is meant to come outta the womb whole to live on this earth, it will. And if You see fit fer it to come back home to You afore it has to suffer this old world, well, then, that's exactly what's gonner happen. You already know. Give me peace, Lord. That peace that defies all understandin'."

And He did. Missouri slept, and instead of dreaming about the grief and sorrow of losing babies, she dreamed of Georgia as a baby, and giving her the joy she'd longed for.

The next morning she called it blessed assurance.

CHAPTER SIX:
Trick or Treat!

The last week of October started off with a cold wind and snow flurries. Missouri stood at the kitchen sink, eyeing the left over gravy and eggs she'd warmed and mixed with some dry cat food. She could see the cats sitting at the edge of the wood, waiting on her. She sure wished one of 'em would tame up, but they were too wild to change. She wanted a housecat, but was fearful it would trip her, and falling at her age was certain death, most times. Besides, she figured no cat could ever top Saddle.

Papa had surprised them that evening with a tiny kitten hidden under his coat. He was the prettiest thing she'd ever seen! Long, silky hair, snow white except for the black u-shape fur across the middle of his back. They had named him Saddle because that's exactly what the patch resembled. He grew very fast. His feet were huge, his ears were huge, and he looked more like a bobcat than anything, except for the plumed white tail he was so proud of. Sadie Dillion had took one look at him and asked to breed him to her white Persian, Eleanor. They had nine kittens, all but one snow white, the other with the patch just like Saddle's. Sadie and her Papa had made a lot of money on that litter, folks just could not turn them away. But Saddle became more likely to roam, although when he was with Missouri, he was like a guard dog. Papa decided to have him cut so he'd stop roaming. Even took him to the animal doctor to make sure it was done right. Saddle came home groggy and Papa pale as the cat. The doc had given the cat something

Out on a Limb of the Family Tree

to sedate him, and Papa thought he'd killed him. And then the doc cut the cat and the cat yowled, even though he was 'out like a light'. Papa slid down the wall. If the doc's wife hadn't been close by he'd probably knocked his noggin. And all this coming from a man who regularly cut bulls, killed hogs, and the like. He was sheepish about telling it, but honest. Said he could not have stood it if that cat had died. A few days later, no worse for wear, Saddle was back to himself, except he was done with wandering. He then went wherever Missouri went, and grew to twenty-one pounds. He lived to be twenty-two years old, and the grief they suffered when he died was as if a family member had passed. From age five to twenty-seven that cat had been her closest companion. He comforted her as nothing else could when her babies were born still and lifeless. Preacher teased her Saddle came before him, and even Georgia sometimes. And, truly, sometimes he did.

"Stop wool gatherin' and git out thar. Ain't gonner warm up anytime soon," Missouri muttered, and picking up the bowl, exited the kitchen. The cats scattered as she approached, but she could see them out of the corner of her eye, waiting for her to get far enough away so's they could eat. She backed off and here they come! Four of 'em, lookin' near starved. She fed them some every morning and afternoon, but it was never enough.

As she came back in, the phone was ringing. "Hello!" she hollered.

"Missouri, are you okay?" It was Mint and she sounded alarmed.

"Fit as a fiddle. Why ye askin'?"

"Because this phone has rung twenty times, that's

why." Missouri heard her sigh heavily over the phone. "Were you outside?"

"I was. Feedin' them cats. Pitifulist bunch I ever saw. What are you up to this mornin'?"

"Ben and I want to come over when he gets outta school this afternoon. We have a surprise!"

"I'll be here unless I git a better offer. You gonner give me a hint?"

Mint giggled. "Nope. Except it's gonna to be fun!"

"Well, I could use some of that. How's the baby?"

"It's fine. Kicking me this morning, so I guess it's awake. My bump is turning into a basketball."

Missouri smiled. "That's good news, girl. I guess I'll see ya'll about four thirty or so?"

"There abouts! I love you, Missouri."

"I love you too, child."

Hanging up, Missouri groaned at the kitchen dishes, but set to. Wadn't no use puttin' it off.

****

Ben and Mint rolled in that afternoon and Missouri had to smile as she gazed upon the growing belly of her great-granddaughter. Ben made them both go in the living room and wait till he unloaded the car with the 'surprise'.

In a few moments, Ben hollered from the back door, asking Missouri if she had some big knives. Raising her eyebrows, Missouri hollered back, "I've some thar in the pantry in that Piggly Wiggly poke in the floor." She turned to Mint. "What's he doin' anyway?"

"You'll see in a minute. How you been today?"

"I plumb give out afore I could finish washin' them

dishes this mornin'. I thank it's cause I'm gittin' so old." She grinned. "Or maybe so lazy."

"Ha. That's one thing you are not."

Ben stepped into the room. "What are you not?"

"Lazy. I do believe the laziest person I ever knowed was Ider Mae Chumley."

Mint interrupted. "It's Ida Mae, not Ider. I never knew her real name till I saw it on her tombstone because of the way you and Kizzie mispronounce it."

Missouri gave her that look and said, "Well, somebody orta told her before she died six years ago." Then she went on to say, "Anyway, we didn't call her Id-duh or Ider. We called her Idle. She was so lazy in school the teacher give up. Her mama probably dusted her when she was cleanin' house. But she snagged her a feller, and after they was married a spell, she got all panicked and come bustin' in on us one day while we was havin' a quiltin' bee. She was tearful, and said she couldn't cook, and Osborn – that was the poor man she married - was gittin' tared of scrambled aiggs at ever meal. And she couldn't even make biscuits to go with 'em! She was a'beggin' us to help her. Said her Mama was gonner show her how to make biscuits and cornbread, but 'man could not live by bread alone'. Well now, everbody was just starin' at her. Then Izzie Prater spoke up and sez, 'Anybody can larn how to make stone soup.'"

Mint interrupted again. "Barney used to read that story on TV when I was babysittin' kids as a teenager!"

Missouri nodded, "That's the one. So she looked all hopeful and ast Izzie how to go about makin' stone soup. So Izzie tells her to git a big pot of clean water and boil it, and then find the smoothest stone she can, and wash it real clean and put it in the boilin' water. I imagine Izzie thought she was settin' up poor old Osborn as well as Ider Mae fer a evenin' no one would ever fergit. But the rest of us wadn't as mean as Izzie. Clara Blanton spoke up and said she always put a little left over ham or roast beef in hers to make the soup have a thick broth. And she had a little left over roast she'd be glad to give Ider if she'd wait till quiltin' was over. Ider was ever so grateful and said she would, and she'd help with the quiltin' while she waited, if we wanted her to. Some thar liked to dropped thur thimble in shock. So I spoke up and told her I always cut up some taters to go in mine, cause Preacher and me liked taters. Ider said they did too. Then Kizzie said she put carrots in hers, and Ider Mae allowed she had some carrots…and so forth. Turned out she had the best beef stew a feller could ask fer, and her Mama had sent home the cornbread she'd larned Ider Mae how to cook. The point is, Ider Mae changed after that. Her house still looked like a tornado had struck, and her childern always had food on thur face 'cept fer Sunday. But they was fed. And she started minglin' with the other women, and helped with other quiltin's and thangs."

Mint and Ben were silent for a moment. "Kindness really does pay, doesn't it?" Ben asked.

"Shore does." Missouri slapped her knees with her hands. "Now, what's that surprise I'm a'hankerin' to know about?"

Ben grinned. "Come this way, ladies." He led them through the kitchen to the back porch, where five fat pumpkins sat lined up. Ben had newspaper spread all over the floor, and Missouri's big butcher knife ready. "Do you have a pan so I can scoop the guts out?"

"What are you gonner do with five pumpkins?" Missouri asked.

"I'm making jack o'lanterns. One for you, one for Kizzie, Georgia and Sam, Wylene and Herb, and one for us."

"That's right nice of you, I reckon." She looked at him, trying to figure out why in thunder he'd do all that.

"Now, Missouri, what do you want carved on yours?"

Missouri blinked. "You mean I can tell you a picture and you'll carve it?"

"Ben can do just about any picture you please, Missouri. He's a right good artist."

"That so? Well, will wonders never cease." She thought a moment. "I want me a big old hissin', arched back cat. Can ye do that?"

"Sure can." And as the evening proceeded, Ben created a haunted house, a scary moon with clouds, a scary face, and a regular smiling jack. All works of art the likes of which Missouri had never seen.

"My Papa cut us a jack o'lantern ever year. But it was just a face with snaggle teeth. Claimed he copied from old man Winder Gravitt's face." Missouri shook her head. "I ain't never seen such, Ben."

As he finished, he stretched his back and interrupted Mint, who had been babbling ninety miles an hour. "What do you think?"

"They is absolutely fine." Missouri turned to Mint, who looked blank and then frustrated.

"You interrupted me, Ben. And now I don't know what

I was saying."

Missouri turned to Ben. "Don't never interrupt Mint in mid-stream, Ben. She's a'liable to drown."

Ben laughed and apologized to his wife. She came around quickly so she could brag on her husband's art work.

"I'm plumb tuckered out just watchin' you do all that. Now ya'll come on in and I'll fix us some supper."

"No thanks, Missouri. We've got to deliver all these and then get home. You want me to throw this pumpkin gunk out to the chickens?"

"No. I'd just step in it and break my neck. Throw it out yonder way in the woods. Maybe suhum'll eat it."

Missouri got up out of her rocker, and she and Mint started into the house. Missouri wobbled and hit her shoulder on the doorframe. "I'm a-warpin' into thangs. Let me stand here and git my balance."

Ben put down the pan and got her by the arm. "Let me help you in. Do we need to call Georgia or Wylene?"

Missouri gave him a look that would kill weeds on the side of the road. "I do not. Just let me git set down at the table." Ben and Mint exchanged looks over Missouri's head as he guided her to the table.

"Well, I'll just go throw this out." He started to the back porch, slowly.

"I see what he's doin'. Tryin' to walk like a turtle so ya'll stay longer. I'm fine. I just got up too fast."

"It won't hurt us to stay two more minutes. You gonna feel like helping me hem up that maternity dress in the next few days?"

"I reckon I will. I cain't work that new fangled

machine you got. Either you'll have to do it or it'll be done by hand."

"Okay. You need anything from the store when I start over here?"

"No, I got plenty laid by." Ben walked back in. "You git shed of the innards?"

"Yes ma'am. I rinsed the pan out and left it on the porch to drain."

"That'll do."

They said their good-byes and Missouri had no doubt she'd get phone calls from ever durn family member she had, checking on her.

It started with Kizzie. Took less than an hour. "What are you a'doin', Sister?" she asked.

"Eatin' a moon pie. And you?"

"I'm just a mite hungry. Feelin' a bit peckish this evenin'."

"Sorry to hear it. Take you a Alka Seltzer."

"Thankin' about it. Ben said you near fell."

"Ain't so!" Missouri felt herself get riled up. "I just knocked into the door frame."

"You ain't feedin' chickens tonight!"

"Yes I am. In fact, I'm a'hangin' up and doin' it right now!" She slammed the phone down, slammed her hat on her head, and got nearly to the pen when she realized she'd forgot the feed.

The phone was ringing when she got back in.

It was Wylene.

And so the evening went. Missouri thought as she fell into bed, *'I'm as tard as a rented mule with all this foolishness goin' on!'* But she slept right good.

CHAPTER SEVEN:

We Gather Together to Ask the Lord's Blessings

Missouri got up before daylight on Thanksgiving morning. She knew this was the only time she'd have today to be alone, as Georgia and Sam had spent the night to help with getting things ready for dinner today. She grabbed her old Bible and sat for a few minutes, hand resting on the front of it. She bowed her head and asked the Lord to truly bless this day with her family, and to give her wisdom as she read His Word.

Afterwards, she went out the back door, scooped some feed out of the box, and went toward the chicken house. "Well, I declare!" She exclaimed as she counted the eggs this morning. "You gals done a fine job today. I count eight fresh aiggs right here'n my basket. Good job, ladies!" She walked around where she'd scattered feed and looked at her hens. They were scratching and clucking, busy, and not knowing empty nests awaited. Making sure she fastened the gate-latch firmly, she walked on back to the house. She was surprised to see Georgia up and making coffee.

"What got you up so early?" Missouri asked as she came through the back door.

Georgia shrugged. "I guess I'm excited about today. Plus, the smell of turkey was driving me wild." She laughed.

"Couldn't stand it, could you? I bet you opened that oven door."

"Yes'um, I sure did. It looks fine. We'll have some good dressing after while."

Missouri smiled. "Cornbread dressin' has always been one of yur favorites, honey. I always try to make extrie so's you and Sam has some to sneak home. But I don't know about this year. Ben may be a big eater."

"Oh, he is, Mama. Worse than I thought. And Mint! Lord, she's eatin' everything in sight!"

Missouri frowned. "I hope Wylene don't make the mashed potaters too runny. When you mash arsh taters they is 'posed to be firm."

"I already warned her. She informed me she was grown with a grandbaby on the way, and she knew how to mash potatoes."

Missouri grunted. "We'll see." Looking at her list she muttered. "The rest of her brangins' is last year's canned green beans and that Silver Queen white creamed corn I like so good." She smacked her lips and grinned. "Now, that's good eatin'." Looking at the list again, she sighed. "And Mint is a'brangin' green onions, cucumbers, radishes and deviled aiggs." She looked up again. "Is Ben devilin' them aiggs?"

"Yes. He said he'd been doing that for his mama since he was a kid."

"And he knows how to make a blackbury cobbler, he claims. I give him the burries to do it with. So we'll see, I reckon."

Turned out, everyone did their job as planned. Even Mint, who had cut the radishes in cute little flowered shapes that 'took Missouri's time'.

The table was set with Missouri's Mama's old dishes, the ones she used on special occasions only. They had been her mama's Sunday dishes. The table had the extension in, so everyone sat comfortably around it. Sam had blessed the food, and bowls began to pass from person to person.

"Well, now that we're all settled into eatin'," Samintha began, "I have some excitin' news to share!" She looked at Ben and beamed. For once he didn't squirm or look uncomfortable, but just grinned at her. "Last night we heard an awful racket outside, and Ben went to see if a dog was in our garbage can. Guess what it was!"

"A coon?" Herb asked.

Mint looked aggravated at her daddy. "No, Daddy. And I didn't mean to really guess. Ya'll would mess up the story if you did." She looked around the table and smiled sweetly. Missouri shook her head. "Well, anyway, it was a big old mountain lion!"

"Shaw!" Missouri exclaimed. "I ain't seen one of them in years."

"It's true, Missouri," Ben interjected. "I think she's got kittens 'cause she looked like she was nursing. I guess she was just hungry enough to be brave. She had her head down in the can and when I opened the door, she looked up at me and growled. I liked to a'had a heart attack!" He put his hand to chest dramatically. "I just eased back in the house and started to get my gun, but then I reckoned she had babies that needed her." He looked a little sheepish. "And besides, I can't hardly stand for anything to go hungry."

"So he threw out a bunch of scraps that was in our refrigerator." Mint said. "She ate them all too, except for that stew I tried to cook." Mint looked dejected. "It's a sad time when even a hungry cat won't eat my cooking."

Missouri snorted. "Well, like Ben said, her babies

needed her."

Mint shot a near glare (as near as she dared, anyway) Missouri's way, then continued. "Anyway, it made me so proud of Ben! Why, he's just like Sigmund and Freud!"

The table got quiet for a moment, as folks tried to figure that out.

"Honey," Ben asked, perplexed. "You mean like the psychiatrist?"

Mint rolled her eyes. "Of course not. Why would I compare you to a psychic? I mean those guys that tame the big cats. You know, one of them got hurt real bad."

Sam guffawed. "Siegfried and Roy, you talking about, girl." Georgia nudged him under the table and he silenced. But it was too late.

"That was an easy mistake, Mint." Wylene said. "I remember years ago when Herb went into a bank to get his first paycheck cashed. It was exactly a hundred dollars, and he was so proud! The bank clerk had a fistful of cash to give him and asked him what denomination? And this fool here said, 'Baptist', pretty as you please! Told me later he wondered what religion had to do with cashing his paycheck."

Ben laughed till tears ran down his cheeks.

"Well, don't get so uppity, little Miss Wylene," her mother warned with a twinkle in her eye. "It was last week that we went into that chicken place and you ordered *Pomeranian* sauce instead of *Polynesian* sauce to go on your sandwich. I thought the poor waitress was gonna have a stroke trying not to laugh." Georgia leaned over her plate. "Wasn't three minutes until we heard the whole kitchen crack up."

"Well, now, Mama, that was a perfectly honest mistake. The neighbors just got that dog and I was thinking of it."

"It's a wonder you didn't order a durn hotdog." Missouri said.

Everyone laughed, then a truce was called before the food gave them indigestion from laughing at each other so much.

And Missouri had to admit, Ben's blackberry cobbler was some of the best she'd ever eaten.

****

Sitting on the back porch in the chilly evening after everyone left, Missouri thought about how cold Thanksgiving Day always was when she was a child. In fact, it was usually the day Papa deemed hog killing day…

Up early that morning, Missouri and Kizzie had to help in the kitchen as much as possible. The cooking was left up to Mama and old Aunt Dulcy Gardner. She had married Lum when she was thirteen years old and they'd had seventeen children. She was ninety-three and had outlived Lum and all of her children, the last one passing just a year before, right before Thanksgiving. So, of course, Mama and Papa had insisted she join them for Thanksgiving dinner. Mama told Dulcy she needed help in the kitchen as the younger family members would be helping with the hog killing.

Missouri remembered how surprised she was that Dulcy was actually helpful. She was a spry little thing, hardly taller than Missouri. She had about four teeth left in her head, so Mama always made sure she got served first in order to let her cornbread dressing soak in gravy to soften it by the time everyone was served. Dulcy explained that the rest of her teeth had been pulled out by the tooth-dentist, who said if they didn't come out they would pie-zen her haid.

Their Thanksgiving Dinners were usually mid-afternoon, after the men got the hog slaughtered and cleaned and the meat salted down. Papa always brought tenderloin in, and Mama would take it to the cellar to keep it cold till morning, when it would be served with hot biscuits and gravy, and some of Mama's homemade jelly, sweet butter, and eggs.

For dinner on Thanksgiving they usually had a baked hen or two, cornbread dressing, and whatever vegetables were available. And almost always potatoes. Dulcy was still able to bake some and she had brought a cake with her. Missouri tried to remember what kind that particular year, but it wouldn't come to the surface of her memory.

And Missouri and Kizzie loved the stories Dulcy would tell. She was fifty years old when the Civil War ended, but said she never saw anything about that war other than hearing terrible things about that 'darksome' time, because they lived so far back in the mountains nobody bothered them. Nobody helped them either, she added.

She told about her little brother, John Henry, deciding he wanted to catch him a wild bird, so he built a box, and propped it up with a stick, put feed under it, and set it out in the field. They could see this field from their house. They had a window of sorts where the eating table sat. Dulcy said the bigger brothers teased John Henry mercilessly about his "foolish old box". But one morning in the middle of breakfast (late because it was Sunday), they saw a flock of small birds light around the box. And sure enough, several birds wandered around under it and then Whap! The stick collapsed and the box closed shut. Every one of the brothers jumped up from the table and took off running, with John Henry in the lead, despite their Ma hollering 'Here! Here! Come back here!' Pa said, 'Aw, leave 'em alone, Dance, they'll be right back.'

Just as her little brother got to the box, a wondrous thing happened. The box slowly lifted off the ground and flew off! So many of them birds had gathered under there, they had strength enough to fly and carry the box with them.

Missouri had been fascinated with this story, and every time Dulcy visited she got her to re-tell it. And Missouri always asked the same question: "Was yur mama really named Dance?" *And Dulcy would assure her she was indeed.*

Kizzie was more interested in the story Dulcy told about another brother, J T, who, when he was just three years old, managed to climb up on the mantle, get the clock down, and take it completely apart. Their Ma had been horrified, as they didn't have much good stuff. But he had sat in the floor and put it back together. Only one piece had been left over, but the clock ran anyway. Good as new, maybe better. Dulcy said that baby still got a hick'ry lashing fer it.

Kizzie would always get mad about J T getting a whipping and tried to change the story every time it was told.

Dulcy would just laugh and say, "The truth's the truth,

child." She said her pa was a hard man, didn't even like her Ma to grow flowers because 'them purties take up space whur good food ort to be planted'.

A hard man, indeed.

And Mama, well she liked the story about the woman at the church house during revival.

Dulcy said, "The preachin' had been purty dry and folks was gittin' restless. Then suddenly Miss Loduska Jane Mulky let out a scream.

The preachers got all excited and said 'Amen!' and 'Yes, Sister!' and, to the speaking preacher, 'Preach on, Brother!'

"But Miss Loduska Jane waved her hands and said, 'No, no, I wadn't shoutin' fer the Lord! A mouse done run over my feet!'"

Dulcy would always get to laughing then. "Well, sir, the women of that church got up and commenced to head fer the door, all at once like, and nearly trampled the poor old deacons what was standin' at the back!"

Missouri had to admit that was a good story.

A few times when Dulcy would feel 'poorly' Missouri and Kizzie would be taken to her house to spend the night. Dulcy's house was not much bigger than their smoke house, and it was magical to the girls because of this. The front porch had a plank nailed between the two posts and laid flat, so Dulcy could put her pots of flowers on it in the summer; bright spots among the little unpainted shack. The house had two rooms: the front room was her sitting room and bedroom. There was a large rock fireplace that dominated this room, (in fact, the fireplace still stood to this day) and her bed sat catty-cornered across from it.

*Dulcy had hung a quilt on each wall to frame the little iron bed; and she told the children this helped warm the walls in winter so she wouldn't freeze. There was a night table, two straight chairs for company, and an ancient rocker that had come from 'across the pond'. The other room was the kitchen, and it held a large wood cook stove. The table was five feet long made of large oak planks, and this was what was 'made-up' for a bed for the girls when they spent the night. Much giggling occurred about them sleeping on the kitchen table. And there was always at least one cat to curl up at their feet to sleep. So winter nights were always toasty. Summer nights were torture, and they usually drug the table out on the porch to sleep there, trying to catch a breeze, for Dulcy was old and cold all the time. No one could stand being in her house for more than a few minutes **but** Dulcy when the weather turned warm.*

Missouri sighed, knowing it was too chilly for her to be sitting outside any longer. Which made her wonder why it had always been cold by Thanksgiving when she was a child, and now you never knew if you were getting snow or short sleeve temperatures.

The phone rang and she heaved herself out of the chair to the kitchen. It was Kizzie.

"Fed them chickens yet?"

"Long time ago. It was comin' up a cloud so I thought I'd better git it over with. How was yur dinner with yur childern?"

Kizzie grunted. "Glad to see 'em come, glad to see 'em go."

"I been thankin' about Aint Dulcy."

"Lord, that woman. She shore entertained us when we

was little, didn't she?" Kizzie's voice warmed.

"Sure did. I was thankin' about all them stories she told. Remember how we laughed when she told about old man Pine, who was the town drunk at that time? When Dulcy's husband died, old man Pine come a'wobblin' up her steps, looked in the door at all the food folks had brung to the house fer after the funeral, and started cryin'. He walked on in, put his brown sack with his liquor in it on the table, tipped his hat at her, and wobbled back out. Said she laughed till she cried. She never seemed to run out of her stories." Missouri chuckled.

"Even at her own funeral. Remember old Ezra Parks standin' up and a'tellin' how Aint Dulcy had been at a church meetin' when a strange man had come up to her and said he had a vision to share with her, if'n she was Dulcy Gardner?"

"I remember like it was yester-dey. Give me goose bumps then, gives me goose bumps now." Missouri shivered.

"Said that feller told her about seein' a man standin' behind a old woman in a rockin' chair in a flare garden, and the man in his vision said they was waitin' on Dulcy to come on."

"And Aint Dulcy swore the description fit Uncle Lum and his old ma to a tee. Did anyone ever know who the man was that told her his vision?"

"Not that I know of," Kizzie said. "Although you'd thank someone knowed at the time."

Missouri lowered her voice. "And we both remember Mama seein' them angels right afore she went home to glory."

Kizzie was silent for a moment, then sniffed. "I was scared to death at first, till I saw the look on Mama's face. She said the sangin' was beautiful. And they was handsome. And then she said she saw Papa."

"Praise be." Missouri's voice was barely above a whisper. She cleared her throat. "Well, we're gittin' on up thar, Kizzie. Won't be long fer either one of us. I wonder what it will be like to pass over."

"Now you hush, Missouri. I don't want you goin' first. I ain't got nobody else, you hear?"

Missouri laughed. "Like I git to choose, Sister. Maybe we'll be comin' out of the church house Sunday and git struck by lightnin' and go together."

"Talk like that and you'll git struck right now. I swan, Mama raised you better."

"But Papa made up fer it. He was always funnin'."

"Yes, he was. Sweet old Papa. It will be good to see them, won't it?"

"Indeed." Missouri eyed the stove. "But right now I'm hangin' up and gittin' me that one leftover piece of dressin' and some tea and call that supper. I'm turnin' in early tonight. I'm plumb tuckered out."

"So'm I. I reckon I'll talk to you tomorrow if the lightnin' don't git you first."

"Good-night, Kizzie."

"Night, Missouri."

Thanksgiving Day was officially over.

CHAPTER EIGHT:

Six Months and Counting

Missouri was in the back bedroom wrapping Christmas presents when she heard the car come up the driveway. She peeked out the window and saw Ben getting out and going round to the passenger's side to help Mint out. Missouri grinned as she watched the struggle. She saw Mint's hand reach out and Ben tug at it, then Mint slap at him and Ben moving out of the way. Finally Mint turned sideways and scooted to the edge of the seat. She then grabbed Ben's shirt and hauled her pregnant self up. Missouri shook her head. For Mint to be just barely six months along, she sure was boasting a big belly. Mint straightened and arched her back and Ben closed the car door behind her. Missouri dropped the curtain and hurried to the door to let them in. Just as Ben knocked on the screen, Missouri opened the wood door.

"Come in, come in. Mint honey, yur gonner have to git yurself a bigger coat to cover up that belly. It's cold now, and the weatherman says maybe some snow tonight."

"I know. I just thought Ben's would do for now." Mint looked down at her belly. "But things seem to be moving a bit quicker than I thought." She looked up at Missouri. "How can I grow three more months? Won't I explode before then?"

Missouri grinned. "I don't thank that's happened to anybody yet. He may just be a husky little feller." She turned to Ben as Mint waddled toward the bathroom. "Did the doctor give ye any news?"

Mint looked back and shot Ben a warning look. "Do NOT say a word till I get back, Ben Sanders!"

"Yes 'um." Ben turned to Missouri. "She'll skin me alive if I do."

"So I see. Come on in and set. Do ye want some coffee?"

"If you got some made." He pulled out a kitchen chair and sat down. "I see you got your tree up." Ben looked over in the corner of the living room. A small spruce stood in a watering stand. "It looks good. Did Herbert do it?"

"He come yester-dey with it. I wadn't gonnner put one up, but he insisted. I mean, it ain't like I don't want to celebrate Christmas, but I guess I'm just gittin' so old I'm lazy."

"You want me and Mint to help you decorate it while we're here? I've got the rest of the day off and we ain't got no plans I know of."

Mint entered the room. "Oh, please, Missouri! I love decoratin' a Christmas tree and we done ours over the weekend. Mama and Daddy did theirs too. Can we help?"

She sat the cup of coffee down in front of Ben. "Of course you can. After Ben drinks his coffee he can git the decorations out of the attic and ya'll can set to. I'll watch. I was wrappin' presents in the back room when you drove up, so I'll have two or three to put under the tree when it's finished."

Mint poured herself a glass of milk and sat next to Ben. "Come sit with us a minute Missouri. I'll tell you what the doctor said."

Missouri sat. Ben and Mint exchanged glances, and Missouri squinted at them. Something was up.

"Well," Mint started, "He said I was doing just fine. Still can't tell if it's a boy or girl cause it won't cooperate. Every time they try to do the ultrasound, it turns around and hides its privates! I reckon it's gonna be shy, like its daddy."

"Mint! Lord!" Ben turned beet red and Missouri hooted. "I swear she can be the most brazen girl!"

"I'm afraid that may be partially my fault, Ben. We've always been kind of bawdy with ar humor from time to time. Tell him yur sorry, Mint."

"I will not. Cause I ain't." She looked smug. "Anyway, we've picked out some names and wanted your blessing." She cut another look at Ben.

"Now wait a minute," Missouri said, looking at them suspiciously again. "I hope you ain't gonner tack on Missouri to some pitiful infant. I will not give a blessin' fer that!"

Mint squirmed, as if she hadn't considered the idea. "Well, no, Missouri, I guess I didn't figure on naming a girl that. I mean, there's only one of you, nobody else should have your name."

"Good. At least yur showin' some sense. So what do you have picked out?"

"Well, if it's a boy, we thought Adam Benjamin. Cause if it is a boy, it will be the first boy in several generations on our side, and Adam was the first man. And Benjamin because of Preacher and Ben too." Mint looked at Missouri expectantly.

"That sounds wonderful. I like it. I like it a lot. Will you call him Adam?"

"Yes 'um," Ben said. "I don't like it when there's too

many folks with the same name. You don't know who's being talked to. And we both liked the way Adam sounds."

"And fer a girl?" Missouri asked.

Once again, the look passed between Ben and Mint. Missouri tilted her head. For a second, it looked like Mint was not going to be able to say it, but she took a deep breath and began.

"Okay, you remember your mama was Esther?"

Missouri nodded. "I reckon I still remember my own mother's name." She said dryly.

"And Ben's great-grandmother was Polly."

Silence.

Missouri arched her eyebrows. "Well?"

"So, if it's a girl, we're going to name her after them. Esther and Polly, I mean."

Missouri glared at them. "Yur gonner name her Esther Polly?"

Ben grinned. "Nope. Polly Esther."

Missouri shot up from the table like she'd been stuck with a pin. "I'll not be havin' that!"

Ben and Mint looked at each other and burst into laughter. "Oh, Missouri, we got you so good!" Mint giggled till tears ran down her face. "We have been plottin' this for days!"

Missouri continued to stand there glaring at them. "I'm a good mind to decorate that tree by myself. Seems to be the only comp'ny here that's worth keepin'."

Ben stood up and hugged her. "Come on Missouri. You know it's funny. Sit back down. I promise we won't do that to our child." She reluctantly sat back down, not knowing for sure if she liked being had.

"So, if you thank you can, tell me what you are gonner name it, if it's a girl." She was glaring again, and this time she meant business.

"Well, the Esther part is real. And both of us like Sarah, and that was Ben's other great-grandmother's name. So, Sarah Esther and call her Sarah. How's that?"

"That sounds acceptable. Sarah or Adam. That sounds fine. But I want to know why you'd mess with a poor old woman who's nearly a hundurd like you did?" A slight grin escaped Missouri as she looked up at them.

"Ha ha, Missouri. You know good and well you was about to have a conniption fit and whip us both." Mint crossed her arms over her belly. "I have no worries that we could make a very big mistake, cause you wouldn't have let us."

"Well, somebody in this family has to have sense. It's pretty clur it ain't you two." She laid both her hands on the table. "So, the due date is still around March twenty-eighth?"

"Yeah, there bouts. Although the doctor said the baby is going to be so big, it may make an early March arrival. He figures if it keeps growing, I'll have an eight or nine pounder."

"I was nearly ten pounds." Ben put in. They both stared at him, and he blushed. "I guess I haven't mentioned that before." He turned to Mint. "I was afraid you'd be mad at me."

Mint continued to stare at him. "Why on earth would I be mad at you because you weighed ten pounds when you were born?"

"Well, that would make it my fault this baby is so big,

wouldn't it? And if that makes it harder on you, that will be my fault too, won't it?" He looked a little angry. "Actually, this is all my fault and if something happens to you, that'll be my fault." He finished with a dejected look on his face.

"Whoa, son, yur havin' a 'I done and pert near killed my wife' spell. You ain't supposed to do that till she goes in labor and curses the day she ever laid eyes on you." Missouri's face softened. "I remember how Preacher grieved over my birth pains and even swore to me he'd never touch me agin to keep me from goin' through it." She grinned at them both. "Course that idey passed in a short time." She patted Ben's hand. "Point is, that's the way babies git here, and we cain't do nothin' about it. Plus, I hear that bigger babies are easier to have, cause they's strong and help the mama by workin' thur way out, where littler fellers are weaker."

Ben looked at her hopefully. "Really, Missouri?"

"Really, Ben." She stood up. "Now, go pull the attic stairs down, and git them boxes marked 'tree decorations', and let's git busy."

When he left the room, Mint whispered, "Are you making that up to make him feel better?"

"Nope. I read it just the other day. Makes sense, I reckon. All my babies was little, so I cain't speak from personal experience. But it looks like you'll be able to." She patted Mint's belly. "Come in the back room and help me carry presents so we can put them round the tree when it's finished."

As they walked around the pull down steps in the hall, they heard a thump and a muffled phrase that made them both grin. "I thank Ben found the rafter." Mint giggled and agreed with her.

They gathered the gifts that Missouri had wrapped, and stacked them up on the kitchen table. Ben brought down the boxes and sat down in the floor to unravel lights. Mint and Missouri separated garland and found the star for the treetop. Half way through Missouri said she'd 'bout give out' and let them finish, although Mint suspected Missouri just didn't want to do it. She promised them supper, but they declined, Mint saying she was feeling tired and just wanted to go on home and lay down.

As Missouri watched them drive off, she felt a little lonely, which was unusual for her. Generally speaking, she enjoyed being alone, being used to it for so many years. She turned and looked at the little Christmas tree, lit up and proud in the corner. She still had a few presents to wrap, but thought she'd wait till tomorrow to finish, as it was getting suppertime and she still had to feed the chickens before dark.

As if the mere thought of her feeding the chickens made Kizzie mad, the phone rang and they bickered with one another for a few minutes. While they talked, Missouri had fantasies about the cornbread on the stove, and how that'd taste with a can of Luck's navy beans heated up and poured over it. With an onion too. And who knew? Maybe a fried potato if Kizzie finished her gripin' in record time.

Which she doubted.

****

Missouri remembered pulling on wool long johns under her flannel gown and rushing down the stairs, racing with Kizzie. They would have been in big trouble if it hadn't been Christmas morning. The fire was already crackling in the fireplace, and the tree smelled so good!

She sighed as she gazed up at it, brief as the gaze was. They had worked so hard on popcorn balls and stringing cranberries! Papa had made a few wooden ornaments – a Santa shape, a crescent moon, a bell and an angel. Holly, with its red berries shining, peeked out between the pine limbs. Missouri thought it was surely the prettiest any tree could look. She scooted on into the dining room where she knew her woolen stocking would be hung over her chair. It would be full of presents.

Papa had stopped her for a hug and pretended he wanted to talk, a merry glint in his eye. Squeals from both the girls had him laughing, and he turned them loose, just in time for Mama to come from the kitchen asking what the noise was about. Both of the girls knew she really came to see them get their stocking.

That year Missouri had eyed it carefully before taking it down off the back of the chair. The toe was round, an orange, she was sure. Ah, peppermint sticks peeking out of the top. Carefully placing them on the table, she found a new hair bow, a wooden whistle ("It sounds just like a train!") some walnuts (which she knew she'd give to Mama to help with the cake for New Years Day), and sure enough, a big juicy orange in the bottom.

Kizzie shared her own presents, very similar to Missouri's. They thanked Mama and Papa. Then Papa had said, 'shouldn't you look under the tree'? Puzzled, the girls had glanced at one another. Why would they do that?

Cautiously, they stooped and looked under the tree as instructed. And gasped. The most beautiful doll (and maybe the only doll, except for rag dolls) Missouri had ever seen. The doll had a porcelain face, a dainty lace cap, a soft rabbit fur coat over a lacey gown, and tiny knit shoes. Beside her was a red and green plaid dress, made from the same material Missouri's and Kizzie's Christmas dresses were made from. They immediately begged for the doll to go to church too! Dressed like them. Mama smiled and said maybe.

She very seriously talked to them as she stooped down before them. She explained that the doll's name was Deloris, and she belonged to both Kizzie and Missouri and they must never fight over her, or Mama would take her away for a whole week!

Papa said if they were very good and shared Deloris, he would build a cradle for her by the time their birthdays rolled around. That was February! Kizzie's was the fifth and Missouri's the seventh!

The girls had joined hands and danced around the living room until Papa made them stop so they wouldn't jiggle their insides too much.

Missouri smiled to herself. Memories got more precious to her every year. What ever would she do without Kizzie?

CHAPTER NINE:

In the Meadow We Can Build a Snowman

"Hot dog!" Missouri exclaimed as she looked out the window the second week of January. Her whole world was covered in white, and it was coming down hard. The snowflakes were large, lazy, and many. She grabbed the phone and called Mint. "Have ya'll looked out?" She asked when Ben answered the phone.

Ben laughed. "Oh, yeah. Mint is hurrying breakfast so we can come to your house. I hear you have a great sled."

"That's fact. My Papa made that sled when me and Kizzie wuz young'uns and it has served many generations well. However; I ain't too sure about Mint gittin' on a sled in her condition."

"I won't let her go down hills or anything like that, Missouri. I'm just gonna pull her around in the field. It'll be fun."

"You'll break yur fool back, but go ahead. Sled's stored in the barn, which is fallin' down, so you'll have to be real careful when you step in. It's in the first stall, wrapped in a old quilt. I'm a-callin' Kizzie and see if she wants ya'll to pick her up. I got a streak o'lean to cook to season my soup beans with. I put the beans to soakin' last night afore I went to bed. If you young'uns will stay, I'll make a cake or pie fer dessert."

"Sounds great. Tell Kizzie to call me if she wants me to pick her up. It will be about two hours."

Missouri hung up and called Kizzie. "Mornin', Sister. Want to come to my house and help me build a snowman?"

"Well, they say they ain't nothin' worse'n a old fool. I guess you just proved it." She snorted. "What's this I hear about soup beans? And are they white or pintos?"

"They's mixed. I didn't have enough of either, so I decided to do both. And I'll bake a big pone of cornbread. I'll stew some taters too, and we'll eat like kangs."

"You know I ain't gonner turn that down. All I eat fer breakfast was a cup of coffee and snow cream."

"You foolin' me?"

"Nope. I looked out and saw that stuff, and I dashed out, and got me a clean bowl full of snow, and eat the whole thang."

"Lord, Sister. I wish I'd thought of that afore I eat my aiggs!"

They both laughed, excited about the day.

As soon as Missouri hung up, Wylene called, insisting on baking a pound cake, if Missouri would fix enough beans and bread. "Well, we ain't gonner do this unless you invite Georgia and Sam. Thur feelin's would be hurt if you don't."

"I'll call and see if they want us to pick them up. We can build a snowman!" Wylene hung up, excited.

"I don't reckon nobody grows up no more." Missouri groused to herself, but she was grinning.

The family crowded in, beans simmered, Herb got out the playing cards, and promised Missouri nobody would stay out in the snow long, it was just too cold.

She watched out the window, Kizzie and Herb sitting with her, as Wylene, Georgia, Mint, and Ben built a snowman, threw snowballs at each other, and even played on the sled a little.

Ben was the only one to ride down the hill, (with Kizzie hollering through an open crack in the door "Blow the soot outta that thang!") until he apparently coaxed Wylene to get on with him – zip! Down they went. You could hear Wylene screaming and laughing through the window. Sam slept through the whole thing in the recliner in the living room.

Shedding boots on the porch, the crew came in, shivering and wet. They all talked at once, laughing, and bringing the cold in with them. Mint allowed as the snow was so deep they might have seen an abdominal snowman at the edge of the woods. Shaking her head, Missouri reminded Ben to wipe down the sled real good after dinner so the runners wouldn't rust, and he promised he would.

Waking Sam up, they told him tall tales of their adventures while they dished out beans to pour on cornbread with stewed potatoes on the side. Kizzie had brought a big jug of fresh made sweet tea and every drop was drunk. Moaning, everyone swore they couldn't have but a tiny piece of pound cake, but one bite did them in, and they all went back for seconds.

"This reminds me of the way I'd feel after dinner on the ground ever fifth Sunday." Kizzie said. "Ever woman in the county tried to outdo the other with the best food you ever put in yur mouth."

"That's truth, Sister. Easter Mulky could make the best fried chicken I ever tasted before or since."

"Her name was Easter?" Mint asked. She had become extremely interested in names since her pregnancy.

"T'was. Born Easter mornin'; just as the sun was comin' up in the east. Reckon her Mama thought that was a

Out on a Limb of the Family Tree

sign."

"And do you remember her firstborn was born on Easter too?" Kizzie asked.

"Did they name it Easter too?" Mint asked, giggling.

"No. Fer it was a boy. They named him after his Pa, but all I can recall is Hoss. He was the biggest thang, and to his dyin' day, that's what he was called."

Georgia rose and began stacking dishes in the sink. "Mama, your cats are looking for supper." She gazed at the feral cats, sitting at the edge of the wood, watching.

"Don't you know they's cold. I put a cardboard box with some towels in it on the porch, but if they use it, it's after all's quiet. Ben, will you throw them some cat food? Thur's a pan or two out thar. They'll run, but if yur real still, and don't skeer them none, they'll come right back and eat."

"Should I take water, too? I'm sure everything's frozen."

"Reach up under the cabinet thar and git that old saucepan. I don't use it no more no how."

So Ben trekked out with a box of cat food under his arm and a pan of lukewarm water in both hands. He tread carefully so he would not fall and bust his rear end, and slowly, so as not to alarm the feline population.

Georgia glancing back out the window said softly, "Well, will you look at that?"

Everyone got up to peer out windows and doors. Ben had squatted down to feed and water the cats, and one of the cats had come to him, and was rubbing up against his knee cap as he stroked its fur. They could see he was talking to it, and cautiously the other three cats approached and began eating. When the cat got its fill of petting, it too began eating. Ben slowly stood up, turned around, and walked back to the house.

When he opened the door, everyone stared at him. He blushed. "I've always had a way with animals, especially cats. Mint and I hope to get a kitten soon."

"Well, I ain't never seen nuthin' like it." Missouri declared. "Them cats are traitors! I been feedin' them fer nigh on a year, and not onct has any one of them let me even come close." She puffed up all mad like and glared at Ben. "You ort not to steal folk's pets."

Ben looked alarmed until he saw the twinkle in Missouri's eye. "Sorry Missouri. I guess I'm just a smooth operator. Want me to teach you a thing or two?"

"That'll be the day, boy. That'll be the day." Herb told him.

"I'm thankin' on gittin' me a pet, myself." Kizzie announced.

Missouri looked at her in surprise. "A pet? Now, just what kinda pet are you thankin' on?"

"A bird. I seen one at Elsie Simmon's house that talked up a storm. Now wouldn't that be a fine thang to have?"

Missouri shook her head. "They's a lot of trouble. Messy and all. We had one years ago. Do you remember it, Georgia?"

"I do. And we got it because of the one you saw Mrs. Weeks owned."

"That's truth." Missouri nodded, warming to the story. "Miz Weeks, well she was a fine lady. Always looked like she'd just stepped out of a hat box. Her house looked like that too. Ever time I went home after visitin' with her, I'd thank I needed to lick my calf over at my house cleanin'. But she loved animals, and she had this little old bird that talked. She'd larned him to say 'The Lord is my Shepherd' and when her husband got home, it'd say 'Ralph's home, here he comes!' and 'Is that you, honey?' and 'I'm a Georgia cracker.' Now, Miz Weeks, she talked real slow like. I know all us folks do here abouts, but hers was more deliberate than most. And this here bird sounded just like her. I swannie, I never heared nothin' like it in all my days. Anyhow, that bird got all mixed up one day. He puffed his little chest out and announced, 'The Lord is a Georgia cracker.'" Everyone laughed. "Well, sir, I made Preacher go out the next day and buy me one."

Georgia clapped her hands. "I remember that like it was yesterday. And as I recall, our bird never said a blasted word."

"That's truth. We got us a mute, I reckon."

"You mean thar ain't no garun-tee on them a'talkin'?" Kizzie asked indignantly.

"Well, 'course not, Kizzie. Why on earth would you thank that?"

Kizzie looked mad. "Cain't trust nuthin' nowadays. I may just git me a goldfish instead."

****

When Missouri went to bed that night, she felt pleasantly at peace with the world. Today had been a beautiful surprise from the moment she'd opened her eyes until she closed them.

Blessin's from God, that's what it was. "Lord, thank Ye so much! My family comin' and us sharin' dinner and conversation and such. And them cats! My, my! What a gift. Ben won't never fergit that. I know I won't. And Lord, last of all I thank Ye fer the snow. I know it's an aggravation fer some, but I've always loved it. Ever time I felt like You was doin' it just fer me. Amen."

She rolled over and slept the best she'd slept in years.

And Missouri dreamed:

Missouri and Kizzie were eight and seven, respectively. Lila Dover was spending the night with them, and they had experienced an exciting night. Lila was six, missing both front teeth and as feisty as they came. She bounced when she sat in a chair; she hopped when she was standing 'still'. She was never quiet, unless it was in church, and that was only under threat of a switching. She was tiny, freckled, and impulsive, with blazing red hair that put Missouri's own fiery copper color to shame. In a word, Missouri and Kizzie adored her. They had whispered and laughed far into the night, until, after Mama had come in twice, Papa had appeared. It had been hard to keep a straight face as he admonished them, because his hair was standing straight up and he was in his nightshirt. But worse than that, both of them could feel Lila's body shaking from barely controlled hilarity throughout the whole speech. Missouri had truly thought she was going to wet the bed.

When they had finally fallen asleep, exhausted from all the antics their guest had provided, it seemed only moments before Mama was making them wake up. She talked in a stern voice and made them get out of bed and go to the window. As soon as they staggered and looked outside, Lila started squealing, jumping up and down, and clapping her hands. Missouri and Kizzie looked outside and then at Lila, both with wonder.

There was more snow on the ground than any of them had ever seen, and Mama said that was true for her and Papa too.

They dressed hurriedly and got downstairs in record time for breakfast. All they could talk about was getting outside.

Papa came in as they sat down to eat, and after the blessing, looked at each girl. Then he said in his most serious tone. "Now girls, I know you cain't wait to git outside, and I don't blame you."(Lila bounced in her seat and made little high pitched noises, which Papa was trying to ignore). "BUT, you may not go out the back. The snow is at least three feet deep and it's too dangerous behind the house. The barbed wire fence (which he pronounced 'bobware) is under snow, as well as a stump with a axe nearby. You may play out in the front yard, where it is farly flat. Yur mama will watch you and you will come in the minute she tells you to. It's very cold and you cain't stay out long."

"Three feet!" Lila exclaimed. "I'm barely taller than that! Let's git goin', girls!"

Mama put her hand on Lila's tiny shoulder. "You must wait until we've finished eating, Lila. Then I will see that you are all dressed warmly."

After much squirming from all three children, Mama looked for things to wrap them up in so they wouldn't freeze. She found a few things from years past she was able to dress Lila in, and went from there.

Finally they were able to go out on the front porch. The snow was up level with their porch floor, which was at *least three feet off the ground, if not more. This amazed Missouri and Kizzie. The steps and yard had just disappeared. The porch floor was also covered with snow, so it looked like the snow came right up to the walls of the house.*

"Oh, this is fantastic!" Lila cried. "This is wonderful!" she jumped up and down, twirled around and; poof! Suddenly was gone.

Missouri, Kizzie, and their mama simply stared open mouthed for a moment. After all, it's not often you see someone vanish in front of your eyes.

Then Mama gasped and ran to where Lila had been twirling around. She barely got herself stopped at the edge of the porch, or she would have taken a dive too. "Lila! Are you all right?" she cried.

Mama was answered by a faint giggle, then slowly Lila stood, her hat and hair, face and shoulders, covered in snow. When she was upright, she was neck deep in the snow. "That was fun! I've never done anything like this before!"

As soon as they realized she was fine, Missouri and Kizzie immediately began to beg to do the same. At first Mama was adamant, but then, with a twinkle in her eye, said yes!

And off the porch they went! Missouri would never forget the shock to her system of landing and sinking into the snow, the exhilaration of the cold, nor the additional shock of seeing Mama leap into the air and landing in the snow, just like them! Mama warned them not to tell Papa, but at the supper table that night, seeing his bone tired body and weary face, she looked each girl in the eye,

shrugged and told him the tale from beginning to end.
 Papa laughed till he cried.

The next morning Missouri recalled the memory to Kizzie and they both enjoyed it thoroughly. Missouri pondered on whatever became of Lila. Kizzie replied, "Last time I saw her was about seventy years ago. I'd rode to town with Papa when he was pickin' up supplies. She was with her Mama and Papa, about to head back to home. They'd just bought lots of new material to make Lila a weddin' dress and a travelin' dress, fer she was gittin' married to some gent from Alabama way. I watched the wagon leave out, with Lila turned back lookin' at me. She was hoppin' up n down on the wagon seat, wavin' to beat the band, and grinnin' from ear to ear." Kizzie laughed. "I hope that Alabama feller had lots of energy to spare, fer he was in fer a tiresome life if he didn't."

CHAPTER TEN:

Happy Birthday to You, Valentine's too

February, 1998

Missouri awoke earlier than usual and lay there for a few moments trying to figure out why she felt so excited inside. It came to her gradually and she chuckled a little. It was Kizzie's eighty-eighth birthday. Today and tomorrow she and Kizzie would share the same age. On the seventh, Missouri would turn eighty-nine.

"Eighty-nine! Can you believe it, Preacher! Yur wife is a very old woman. Ain't lived but in two houses my whole life. Let me ponder on that fer a minute."

She and Preacher had built a tiny house when they had married, out about a half mile from Mama's and Papa's house. They'd lived there until Missouri's Mama had died, and then they'd moved back in the old home place where Missouri still resided. She got the house for taking care of Papa, but Kizzie had a much bigger house anyway. Husband number two had built her a pretty fine house and paid cash for it. At least, Missouri thought, he was good for something. She had always loved this house. It had been built to last, and last it had.

"Well, I reckon I like that just fine. I wonder what the young'uns have up thur sleeves fer me and Kizzie's birthdays."

Every year there was always some kind of big to do. When they were younger, Georgia and Wylene threw them a collective party on the sixth, usually taking them out to eat with a homemade cake waiting on them when they got back. Kizzie's children usually called and wished her a happy birthday. She got a few cards in the mail from grandchildren, but that was about it.

The last four or five years Georgia and Wylene had celebrated their birthdays separately. Missouri figured it was because they was so old her girls was afraid to wait a day after, for fear Kizzie might die in between! That made Missouri laugh again. But it was probably true.

At least they got two cakes out of the deal nowadays.

Mint had asked Missouri what she wanted for her birthday. Missouri had never really expected to need anything new this late in life, but she discovered she did. "I need some new drawers. Mine's gittin' too raggedy to wear to church."

Mint was horrified. "I can't buy you underwear for your birthday, Missouri! I want to get you something you really want."

Missouri raised both eyebrows. "And just what do you thank I'd be wantin' at nearly a hundurd?"

"You ain't a hundred. You are turning eighty-nine. And I'm sure you've seen something in one of those catalogues you get in the mail every day. I see you looking at them."

Missouri fidgeted a little. Well, there was one thing…She'd gone to the bedroom and come back, showing Mint a very frilly pair of gardening gloves. The page had been earmarked.

"I'm near ashamed to show you. You know I wouldn't want to use 'em after I got 'em. They's too purty."

Mint snatched the catalogue away before Missouri

could change her mind. "This is great!" She looked at Missouri slyly. "You might just get what you want and what you need!"

Missouri smiled at the memory. She knew it would please Mint more to give her the gloves than it would her getting them. They had been a passing fancy for her, but Mint would always remember it. Missouri found herself planning, more and more everyday, for her family's future without her in it, so memories were important.

She'd said good-bye to all her older family by now, of course, but she had lots of memories to sustain her until she was with them again…

They'd been turning seven and eight that year. Missouri remembered it so clearly! There was a mysterious gift up under one of Mama's old quilts in the corner of the living room. It had been there since they got up. Last night they'd had Kizzie's favorite supper in honor of her birthday, and tomorrow they would have Missouri's favorite. Today was what Papa called 'in the middle day', the day between their birthdays. This was the day they got a present each and a cake with dinner! Pa and Ma, Papa's parents, had come yesterday and would stay until tomorrow afternoon. Pa always teased them and said he could see them any old day, but it was fine eatin' around birthday time!

That dinner had been fine eating. Fried chicken (in the middle of the week!), potatoes and gravy, biscuits, green beans, kraut, and a big pone of cornbread. Missouri was so full she didn't think she could eat cake. Until she saw it! It was three layered with dark chocolate icing. She knew her eyes had to be as big as Kizzie's!

Out on a Limb of the Family Tree

They'd all had a piece. Everyone groaned about how full they was, they'd never eat another bite!

Then Mama joked and said, "Well, then, thar ain't no use in puttin' the tablecloth over all this fine food to save fer supper."

Papa reasoned they might be a little hungry by then. Everyone had hurried into the living room and Mama joined them as soon as she got the food covered on the table. Papa had teased, and wondered why in the world that old quilt was in the living room. Mama must be slackin' off on her housekeepin'. Reckon either one of the birthday girls would want to see if there was something under it?

They'd rushed to it and with Papa's 'careful now!' admonishment; they had slowly removed the quilt. Underneath it was the most beautiful dollhouse! It looked just like their own house! And there was a Mama and a Papa and two little girl figures. Each one of them was dressed and had faces and hair to match the family's real hair painted on the wood.

Both girls had squealed, then hugged their Papa and Mama, who had obviously worked hard to create such a fine gift for them. Ma walked over and inspected it all while Pa stepped outside to puff on his pipe a little.

In moments they heard Pa cry out and Ma laughing. They all rushed to the kitchen. When Pa had stepped back in, their old tom cat, Silas, had come in with him and promptly jumped on the dinner table and stuck his head underneath the cloth to help himself to dinner. Pa had picked up the big cat and 'flung him agin the door', hoping to throw him out. But instead Silas had pushed off the door and bounced back, and landed right on Pa's head! He was hollering to Ma, 'Vic, Vic, come help me turn this cat loose!'

But Ma was laughing so hard, Papa had to do it.

While Mama doctored Pa's wounds and Pa threatened to get the shotgun after Silas, Missouri and Kizzie slipped away and commenced to play with their birthday gift.

They were pretty sure Pa wouldn't really shoot Silas. He was the one who had nursed the cat with a bottle when he was a kitten when the mama cat had been killed by wild dogs. He loved that old cat.

And besides, he ought to have known better than to try and keep Silas away from fried chicken.

****

There'd been fine eatin' at Kizzie's dinner, and leftovers yesterday. Today was her turn to celebrate. She was eighty-nine years old!

She heard the horn honking and Ben's footsteps on her porch before she could even get to the door.

He peered into the living room as she rounded the corner. "You 'bout ready to go, Missouri?"

"I reckon. Ya'll picked up Kizzie yet?"

"Yes'um. She's in the car." He jiggled the lock to make sure her door was secure, then followed her down the porch steps. "Got any presents today?"

"Nary a one. Ain't talked to nobody neither, I mean outside the fam'ly." She grunted. "You'd thank the preacher woulda at least called me."

Getting into the car, she didn't see the big grin plastered on Ben's face.

"Howdy, Kizzie. You look mighty spiffy."

"Thank ye kindly, Sister. You don't look so bad yurself, fer a old woman."

"Hey, Missouri." Mint smiled from the front seat.

"Hey, lamb. How you doin'?"

"Fine. Gettin' bigger'n a house, though."

"Enjoy it, honey," Kizzie said. "It's the only time in a woman's life she's allowed to eat all she wants when she wants. Baby needs it anyway."

"That's what I been telling her." Ben said as he backed out of the driveway. "She can worry about getting her figure back after the baby gets here."

"Law, it's hotter'n all git out in here." Missouri said, fanning herself with a magazine she'd found lying in the back seat.

Ben turned the heat down, making Kizzie hug her sweater closer to her body.

"Ain't that where Harkness and Enoch Abercrombie got kilt when thur wagon turned over that time in that turrible storm?" Kizzie asked, pointing to a large field.

"I thank it was over yonder ways," Missouri said, craning her neck as they zoomed by. "That was pure awful. They left all them sweet babies orphans. Who raised 'em, do you recall, Kizzie?"

"I shore don't. All I remember is they was took far off. Don't even know how many they was. We was little too, and I reckon the memory just didn't stick good."

"Here we are." Ben interrupted as they swung into the restaurant parking lot.

"My, my, they shore is a lot of folks eatin' out tonight." Missouri commented. "I remember when we didn't even hardly know what that meant to a body."

"Yonder comes Georgia and Sam."

"Whar's Wylene and Herb?" Missouri turned to Samintha as she struggled out of the car.

"I don't know, Missouri. Maybe they're running late." She glanced up at Ben and winked.

All the women straightened up their clothing, Missouri and Kizzie secured their pocket books and they headed for the front of the restaurant.

Missouri frowned as Kizzie and Mint sort of pushed their way ahead of her, and it went through her mind it was rude, especially on her birthday. Ben held the door for all three of them, though, and she smiled kindly at him.

She thought the restaurant was awful dark, and started to grumble about how they was too cheap to turn up the lights, when the lights came on bright, and the whole restaurant hollered: "Surprise!" and started singing "Happy Birthday!"

Missouri stood there, mouth agape, and a few tears escaped to roll down her cheeks. "Well, don't this beat a hen a'rootin'." She said when they'd finished. That certainly explained why nobody had called her today! They was plannin' a surprise!

****

Bright and early Valentine's Day, Mint's car pulled up in front of Missouri's house. Mint pushed and shoved and heaved herself out of the car, reached back in for a box of heart-shaped candy and waddled around to the back door. Missouri was opening the door by the time she made it up the two steps.

"Howdy, child. What brangs you here so early?"

One look at Mint's tear stained face told Missouri she was going to have a long morning.

Mint stuck out the candy. "Happy Valentine's Day, Missouri." Her lower lip trembled.

"Uh-huh. Same to you." Missouri sighed heavily. "Come on in. I got hot biscuits." She turned toward the kitchen and Mint followed. "I slept kinda late this mornin', so you are lucky. I just eat breakfast and it's all still warm. You want a scrambled aigg?"

Mint sat down heavily. "No. But a biscuit with butter and jelly sure does sound good."

The butter and jelly were still on the table and Missouri put two biscuits from the pan onto a plate and handed it to Mint. "Sweet milk?"

"Yes, please."

After pouring Mint milk, she poured herself another half cup of coffee and sat across from her great-granddaughter. "All right. You obviously ain't here to brang me candy before noon. What's the matter?"

"Ben's all mad at me and I'm mad back! He was plumb rude to me this morning and we didn't speak when he left for work. And it's Valentine's Day!" She wailed.

"What in tarnation ya'll goin' on about at each other this mornin'?"

"Well, you know we're setting up the nursery. And I got to thinking last night while Ben was out exercising, that our bedroom needed rearranging, too. So I did a little redecorating in there. Now, I can't exactly move the heavy stuff, but I put the rocking chair closer to the door, so if I needed to rock the baby in the middle of the night, it'd be handy. Just a few things like that. When Ben came home he thought everything looked good. He said so, Missouri!" Having finished off the biscuits and glass of milk, she crossed her arms as best she could across her belly. "It's not my fault he forgot all about it when he got up this morning to get ready for work and run into the rocker and maybe broke his toe. I admit I laughed a little bit, but I couldn't help it! You know how I am. Anyway, I offered to help him any way I could, but he just glared at me. And when I tried to give him his Valentine's present, he wouldn't even speak to me! I told him not to cut off his nose to spoil his face and then he made fun of me for saying it."

Missouri took a quick swig of coffee to keep from laughing, herself. But Mint saw it. "Are you laughing at me too?" She accused.

"No, child. I was just thankin' back on Pa. You know, Papa's daddy? Ma was awful bad to rearrange furniture all the time, and one evenin' she put the sewin' machine at the foot of the bed. In the middle of the night the chickens commenced puttin' up a ruckus like they was a fox in the henhouse or suhum. So, Pa got in a hurry to go see about it. Somehow he got turned around and wound up straddlin' that sewin' machine. He calmly told Ma, 'Vic, if you'll help me git off this here sewin' machine, I'll go see what's got in the chicken house.'" Missouri chuckled. "I guess men folk just don't take to stuff bein' moved around."

Mint nodded miserably. "I guess you're right, Missouri. And I am sorry he hurt himself. But what am I supposed to do now? It ain't my fault, I shouldn't have to be the one to apologize!"

"Do you suppose he stayed mad on account you moved furniture or on account you laughed at him a little bit?"

Mint bit her lower lip. "Well…that maybe made him even madder."

"Looks to me like you ort to apologize about that. That'll give the boy a chance to apologize right back. Then ya'll will have made up afore it's too late to go celebratin' Valentine's."

Mint stood up from the table. "You're right as usual." She reached over and hugged Missouri. "I don't know what I'd do without you. I think you're about the smartest person I've ever met."

Missouri grunted. "Sounds like you need to meet more folks."

Mint laughed, grabbed up her keys, and out the door she went.

"Thank ye fer the candy!" Missouri hollered as Mint waddled down the porch steps.

Mint gave her a backward wave before wedging herself in the car and driving off.

"She orta peed first." Missouri muttered as she closed the back door better. "I swan that child gits in more uproars than anybody I ever seed."

The phone rang and it was Georgia wishing Missouri Happy Valentine's Day. She and Sam wanted to take Missouri out to eat to celebrate.

"That ain't very romantic." Missouri said.

"Mama, we are both nearly seventy. How much romance do you think we need?"

"Well, some, surely, just to make sure yur both still breathin'."

"With Sam's snoring, trust me, I'd know if he stopped breathing."

"I still believe I'll not go this time. But I thank ye just the same."

Hanging up, that gave Missouri an idea. All this Valentine talk had give her a hankering for chocolate. She banged around the kitchen till she found all the ingredients she'd need for her old timey fudge candy.

And that's the way Missouri spent Valentine's Day – eating chocolate, watching TV, and talking to Kizzie intermittently on the phone.

CHAPTER ELEVEN:

The Family Sprouts Another Bud

Way, way down a dark warm tunnel. Sitting in warm water... then, faintly a whistle, louder, louder, train coming! Get out of tunnel! Quick!

Ben sat up with a jolt. "What the heck is that noise?"

Mint opened one eye. "That's Mama's tea kettle. The water's boiling."

"Why does it sound like a freakin' train?" He was hissing, his heart beating fast.

"Cause the whistle – whistles," for now there were two whistles sounding, one high pitched the other a lower keen, "are made to sound like a train. That way, Mama says, you can hear it all over the house and you're not likely to forget and burn the house down."

They had spent the night at Mint's parents. Friends and family had thrown them a baby shower, and after packing up stuff and cleaning up, Mint was too tired to go home and wheedled Ben into sleeping over.

Mint stretched a little, then looked puzzled. "How come the bed's wet?"

Ben moved slightly and made a face. "So that's why I was dreaming about sittin' in warm water. Did you wet the bed?" He looked at Mint suspiciously. "I mean you have to pee ever five minutes, maybe you slept through one."

Mint looked indignant. "I have you know I do not wet the bed, Ben Sanders, and furthermore -" A surprised look crossed over Mint's face. "Oh! Oh!"

Ben looked down at her. "What's wrong with you?"

She was struggling to sit up, not very successfully. "I had a pain. A big pain. Ben! Maybe my water broke!"

Ben levitated off the bed, landing a safe distance from it. He pulled his boxers away from his rear, and looked at the damp condition they were in. "Oh, Lord. I'm gonna get your mama right now, don't move!" He started out of the room.

"Don't take another step!" Mint said. He turned and looked at her. "Put on your jeans. You can see clean through them wet drawers. No need to give Mama a heart attack." She giggled, then went all surprised again, "Oh, oh!"

He grabbed his jeans and hopped toward the door, trying to pull them on and run at the same time. "Wylene!" He sprinted down the hall. She turned from the stove and looked at him, a half smile on her face till she saw the expression on his.

"Ben, what in the world is wrong with you?"

"It's Mint. The bed is wet and she's having a pain and maybe it's time. Do you think it's time?" He said all this in one breath and thought forever went by before he saw understanding light Wylene's face.

"Well, let's us just go see, shall we?" She followed Ben at a more sedate pace, as he careened down the hall, skidded past the bedroom door, jerked back into the bedroom, and tapped his foot three times before Wylene made it in. She walked over to Mint and put her hand on Mint's forehead. "How are you feelin', honey?"

"I'm fine, Mama. Are you okay this morning?" She looked at her mother sweetly.

Wylene smiled back. "Yes. A little tired from last

night, but it was fun wasn't it? I just love what Joann got the baby -"

"Stop!" Ben yelled. They both looked at him, surprised. He sighed. "This could be a medical emergency we're looking at here, and ya'll are talking like it's a spring day in the park. I have to know – I *need* to know – if Mint is in labor. Tell me. Now." He crossed his arms over his chest, a fierce, frightened look on his face.

Wylene pulled back the covers. "Let's get you out of this soggy bed and get you cleaned up. I think we need to call the doctor." She looked up at Ben. "Why don't you help Mint to the bathroom and she can sponge off and get on some dry clothes. I think you'll both be needing to get ready for a little trip to the hospital." She smiled, looking as calm as a Buddha statue.

Ben helped Mint to a sitting position, and she told him what to get for her to put on. They waddled down the hall toward the bathroom as Wylene pulled the sheets off the bed. As soon as she heard the bathroom door shut, she did some sprinting of her own, to her bedroom. She jumped into the middle of their bed, waking Herb up with a start. "What in blazes are you doing?" He jerked the covers over his head.

Wylene jerked them back. "Get up, Gramps. I think our grandchild has decided to make an entrance."

"What? What?" Herb sat up. "It ain't time yet, is it?"

Wylene rolled her eyes. "She's not a bus. He's not a train. It's a baby. They don't come on schedule. The first day of spring is as good as any, don't you think?"

"I reckon. Have you called the doctor yet?" He stood up and stretched.

"Ben will as soon as he gets Mint cleaned up. They're in the bathroom. Her water broke in the bed and they were both wet."

Herb winced. "I could have gone the rest of my life without hearin' them details. Ain't you better be callin' Missouri and your Mama?"

"I'll wait and see what Mint wants to do. Do you want a quick bite to eat before we go?"

"Yeah. Any sweet stuff left from last night's do?"

"Cake. Help yourself." She heard the bathroom door open and she walked out into the hall. "How is everything?" she asked.

"Mama, I think I had another contraction. But it doesn't hurt as bad as I thought it would."

"Well, you're just getting started good. Trust me, honey, it'll get worse. Ben, why don't you call the hospital and let them know Mint's water broke and she's had a few contractions. They will tell you when to come on."

"Okay." He walked toward the den to the phone.

Wylene turned to Mint. "Do you want to call Mama and Missouri, or do you want me to?"

"Well you call Grandmama, and I'll call Missouri. She'd have a fit if I didn't call her."

Ben walked back in. "They said since her water broke we needed to come on. Not to run no red lights, cause it would probably be a long day." He turned to Mint. "Do you care if I shave and shower? Or do you want us to just go?"

"You go ahead. I'm gonna call Missouri, and Mama is gonna call Grandmamma. Mama, can I have some tea?"

"Sure, honey. I'll fix you a cup and some dry toast while you call Missouri." Ben helped get Mint seated before heading back to the bathroom. Wylene handed her the phone and left to make breakfast.

Mint sat there a minute, feeling her heart race. She was scared and excited. She sent up a prayer that all would go well, and she wouldn't be too much of a sissy during all this. As if a test, she felt another contraction come on her, then leave. Not so bad. She could do this. She looked at the phone, smiled in anticipation, and punched in Missouri's number.

****

Missouri was coming in the back door from feeding the cats when she heard the phone ringing. "Hold yur horses, I'm a'comin'." She grabbed the receiver and answered louder than she meant to.

"Dang Missouri, you don't have to yell."

"Is the baby comin'?" Missouri yelled again.

"How'd you know that?" Mint sounded incredulous.

"Because yur lazy tail is never outta bed at this ar, unless suhum has happened. So, I's right. Well, whur are you?"

"We're still at Mama's. My water broke and we're getting ready to go to the hospital. Mama's fixin' me some tea and toast, and Ben's getting cleaned up."

Missouri's voice softened. "Are ye hurtin' much, child?"

"Nah. I've had a few pains, but it's not so bad. Mama said it would get worse in a little while."

"That they will. But yur young and healthy, you'll do fine. The Lord will see you through it. I'll come on after while. Georgia and Sam can pick me up on their way. You behave now."

"I will. Just think Missouri, you're gonna be a great-great-grandmother!"

"Yes ma'am and that information shore makes me feel spry." Mint laughed and so did Missouri. "I'll see you soon, honey. I love you, Mint."

Mint felt her eyes tear up. "Oh, Missouri, I love you so much. I'm so glad you're gonna be there."

"Me too." Missouri heard Mint take a quick breath. "Is that another pain?"

"Yes 'um. Not too bad, though."

"Well, hang up afore you have that young'un in yur mama's livin' room and ruin the good sofa."

Mint laughed. "Ok. See you in a little while. Bye, Missouri."

Missouri hung up and slid to her knees. "Well, Lord, the time has come. Now, You know Mint ain't the swiftest of yur childern, but she's a good'un, and she'll be a good mama. I ast that You keep her safe through this, and let the baby be fine. Keep us all calm, Lord. Don't let Mint kill Ben, neither. She has a mouth on her anyway, and when she really starts a'hurtin' thar ain't no tellin' what she might say to that poor boy, so still her tongue some if Ye will. And I just want to thank Ye Lord, fer lettin' me be alive to see another child into this here fam'ly. What a blessin' You give me! Help me to be worthy this day. In Jesus sweet name, Amen." She knelt there another minute, then smiled. She looked toward the ceiling. "Well, Preacher, we've got a great-great on its way. I figger you already know what it is, and I bet yur as proud as punch, sittin' up thar in Abraham's bosom." She was quiet a minute. "Well, I've been down here so long, Lord, it may take two of them angels to help me up." She grunted, and finally managed to stand upright. Just as she did, the phone rang.

It was Georgia, and plans were made for Missouri to be picked up in an hour.

She hung up and called Kizzie, who got all excited and wanted to come too. Which made Missouri have to call Georgia back. This baby was going to have quite a welcoming committee.

****

The waiting room on the maternity ward floor looked more like a family reunion or a church picnic than a hospital setting within an hour of Mint arriving. Several of the ladies from the church had arrived, all bringing a 'little something' for the family to munch on. Ben and Mint's deacon, Missouri's deacon, Kizzie's deacon, Georgia and Sam's deacon, as well as Wylene and Herb's deacon, and their wives were all present. Kizzie's deacon and his wife had two of their grandchildren in tow because they were babysitting. The preacher and his wife showed up shortly afterwards, and then Mint's best friend and her boyfriend, plus Ben's buddy showed up. At one point a nurse came in to ask them to quiet down, but when she saw all the fried chicken and potato salad she had a change of heart, and helped herself before going back out on the floor.

Occasionally, Wylene would pop in to say how things were going – she was staying in the room most of the time with Ben and Mint – and then Herb, Sam, Georgia, or Missouri would take a quick turn to visit the couple.

After three hours everyone had gone home but family and the preacher.

After five hours everyone had gone home but family.

And after hour six, Kizzie gave up and had Sam take her home.

During hour seven they were sitting around, the men asleep, the women talking occasionally. They all perked up when a nurse came in and said 'it was about time'.

Georgia stepped into the hall and knocked. She asked for Wylene, who came to the door but didn't come out of the room. Georgia could hear Mint whimpering and felt goose bumps rise on her arms.

"I just don't know. She is so tired. The epidural didn't work, and she's in so much pain." Wylene choked up. "I can't let her see me be upset, but she's my baby, and I can't stand it!"

Georgia patted her hand. "Honey, I remember what it was like with me seeing you when you were giving birth to Mint. I would have traded places with you in a heartbeat. Do you want me to spell you?"

"No. It'd just be worse if I couldn't be with her. They say she's fine. Ben is doing a good job."

Georgia went back to the waiting room all teary eyed and got everyone nervous. Missouri left the room and went to a bathroom stall to pray in private.

****

Ben wiped Mint's forehead and patted her shoulder. He felt as helpless as he could possibly feel. He was worried because she was so tired, and he didn't know how much longer she could stand it. The nurses assured him things were right on schedule and both baby and mother were doing fine, but it didn't look that way to him. He spoon-fed her an ice chip and she closed her eyes to savor it.

Another pain started just as the doctor came in to check. "Well, it looks like it's time to start pushing. It's almost over."

"I can't. I'm too tired." She sounded small and far away.

"Mint, honey, you've got to push. This baby has to come out."

"You SHUT UP Ben Sanders. Why don't you push?"

"That's the spirit. Come on Mint, if you can get fired up at him, you can push." She looked at the doctor with murder in her eyes, but she pushed. And she pushed again. And one more time. The doctor grinned. "Congratulations, Mama and Daddy, it is now a done deal!"

They looked at one another and burst into tears.

Wylene started crying too, saying, "Praise the Lord, praise the Lord!" and making little jumps into the air.

As they cleaned the baby up, Mint looked at her mother. "Mama, will you please get Missouri in here? She needs to see her new great-great-grandchild."

"I will honey. I'll bring Mama too – I don't want to hurt her feelings. And what about your daddy?"

The doctor laughed. "Let's do it one at a time, okay? The oldest first. Tell 'em all I said so."

Wylene smiled her thanks and headed for the waiting room.

****

"What do you mean you don't know where she went?" Wylene was a little strung out, and when no one knew where Missouri was, she was incensed.

"She was here a minute ago. We just all sorta got upset when Georgia told us about poor Mint, and well -"

"And, well, *poor Mint* is asking for Missouri." Wylene threw up her hands in disgust and turned around, almost knocking Missouri down. "Where have you been!?"

Missouri narrowed her eyes. "I thank you should check yur tone of voice, Wylene."

"I'm sorry, Missouri, I just came to get you because Mint was asking for you, and you weren't here and –"

"Well, why didn't ye say so? Come on!" They both went off hurriedly.

By the time they got back in the room, Mint was sitting up and holding the baby. Ben was standing as close to the bed as he could possibly get, and tears were still streaming down his face.

Missouri walked over and touched the top of the baby's head. "Land's sakes, look at that."

Mint smiled up at her. "Ain't you proud, Missouri? Your first great-great-grandchild. You want to hold her?"

"Hand me the lit'un." Missouri took the baby into her arms. "Why, hello thar, Sarah. And how are you today?"

The baby grunted a bit and squinched up her face. Her little fists waved in the air, then she settled back down.

"How much did she weigh?" Missouri asked.

"Nine pounds and three ounces." Ben stated. "And twenty-one and a half inches long."

"Well, well, a husky lit'lun, but not a feller." The baby started to fuss and then cry. "Oh, she's gonner start a ruckus. I reckon that's what her mama's fer." Missouri smiled and gave the baby back to Mint. "How does it feel, lamb?"

"Pretty wonderful, Missouri."

"Well, I'm gonner let yur daddy in here before he has a hissy fit. And Georgia is knockin' down the door too. But I'll be back tomorrow." She leaned over and kissed Mint on the cheek and then gave Ben a good strong hug. "You done good Ben. Yur still alive!"

They laughed and Mint blushed. "I wasn't that bad, Missouri."

"I suppose not. Be good, childern. I'll see you tomorrow." She walked out the door and noticed Herb was already choking up as he made ready to see his first grandchild. She patted him on the shoulder. "Buck up, son. She's a beaut. Love on her and then take me home. I'm plumb tuckered out."

He nodded agreement and stepped through the door.

****

Ben and Mint said the last good-bye to her parents. The baby was asleep in the crib next to Mint's bed, and Mint looked spent. Ben smiled down at her. "Do you want me to stay tonight or leave you be?"

"I don't know. I'm scared for you to leave, and I don't want the baby took off to the nursery, but I'm so tired." Her lower lip trembled. "I think I need you to stay. They said they could get you a cot."

"That's fine. I don't want to leave ya'll, but I wanted to do what you felt was right." He sighed. "Ain't she pretty? I can't believe she's ours. How'd we do something so grand?"

Mint smiled. "Beats me. I guess the good Lord knows what He's doing, as Missouri would say."

Ben sat on the edge of the bed for a moment and simply held his wife in his arms.

****

Missouri watched as Herb and Wylene's car tail lights disappeared into the darkness. Herb had gone out and thrown some feed toward the chicken house, saying they wouldn't eat it anyway, as they had gone to roost some time ago. But Missouri just didn't feel right without it done. She clicked off the porch light, double checked the lock on the door and more or less shuffled into her bedroom. She found herself humming 'Amazing Grace' as she got her nightclothes together and felt again the powerful grace she was singing about. The bed had never looked so good, she thought. She pulled the covers up to her chin, snuggling the worn quilt. Home felt so sweet.

"Well, Lord, I thank Ye immensely. I don't reckon I been this happy since Mint was borned, least ways I don't remember it. I know miracles happen all the time, but the birth of a child just seems to top most of 'em." She cleared her throat. "I know I don't have a whole lot longer on this earth, I'm old and time is growin' short fer me. I'm all right with that, and I imagine when the time comes I'll be grateful fer it. But fer now, Lord, I sure am enjoyin' my stay. Especially days like this one. Yes, especially days like this one." She snuggled deeper into the covers. "I'm mighty tired, but I wanted You to know how deep I love the family You've blessed me with. May I do them proud the rest of my days." She felt herself drifting. "Amen, Lord. Good night Preacher." And just as she fell into sleep fully, she could have sworn she heard Preacher telling her the same.

Awakening with a start just an hour later, Missouri lay in bed, exhausted from her day at the hospital. Relieved Mint was safe and the baby here, she had thought maybe she could actually get a good nights sleep. At least for her, which meant she'd be up by five. But as she turned on her side, she began to remember the babies she had lost, and the sadness that she and Preacher had felt for so long after each death. And then, finally, Georgia was born. Missouri allowed her mind to go where she never allowed it to go.

The last pregnancy had gone well. She was in her eighth month. She and Preacher had traveled a few counties over when the revival there had sounded like a sight to be seen. They were planning on staying over night because of Missouri's pregnancy and had reserved a room at the inn there, a real luxury for them.

That night had been the worst night of her life, and the best. Missouri had gone into labor after the revival. A local doctor had been contacted and they had met him at the clinic behind his house.

Another woman, a girl, really, was there, and she too was in labor. The girl was terrified and clung to Missouri, who was not as far along in labor as she. A slip of a girl, she was obviously poor and alone.

Telling Missouri she had no one and nothing, she begged Preacher to tell her how to get to heaven. A very startled but determined Preacher explained salvation to her, even as the doctor was impatient for him to get out of the way. The girl had accepted Christ Jesus as her Lord and Savior and calmed some.

The doctor had instructed Preacher that he had to help, there was no way the doctor could deliver two babies from two women at the same time. The doctor was widowed and lived alone. He had been unable to find anyone in the middle of the night to help. Preacher was embarrassed, but was not about to leave a wife who had lost babies before.

They learned later, after the girl delivered a healthy child, that she was orphaned herself, and unmarried. Missouri had heard of women bearing children without a husband, she'd just never met one in her life.

As she lay dying, 'bled out', as the doctor had said, the girl gripped Missouri's hand, and begged her to take her child and raise it. Crying, she said she had no one, the child's father had been someone she did not know who had 'taken advantage of her' and left.

Missouri lay there numb, her stillborn child in her arms. He had been such a beautiful boy. Nothing wrong that they could see. They'd named him William.

As the girl had requested, they'd named their daughter Georgia.

The doctor had arranged the burial for the girl and their son. As sad as it had made Missouri, she had put her sweet boy in the young girl's arms and buried them together.

Missouri and Preacher thought it was the least they could do. And they both knew the girl and William would be there when they passed over. Missouri prayed the girl would take care of William in Heaven, and felt sure her Heavenly Father would allow it.

Preacher sent word by telegraph to home as to why

they couldn't come back the next day. He told the family all was well and the three of them would be home in a few days.

When she was able to travel back home, friends and family were thrilled that she and Preacher had a healthy baby.

They never told a living soul. The doctor died a short time after the births, and when Preacher heard about the death, he contacted a nephew of the doctor's and asked to say a prayer at the funeral. He explained how he knew the doctor and wanted to pay respects. Truth was, Missouri knew, Preacher wanted to snoop and make sure no one knew about the babies. As far as Preacher could tell, the doctor had told no one.

As best as she could recall, it was the only secret she'd ever kept from Kizzie.

Their secret was safe. By the time Georgia was a year old, she and Preacher stopped mentioning it, afraid Georgia might somehow pick up on their conversation. To Preacher's last day on Earth, it was never spoken of again.

Missouri dreamed for years about that young mother. She believed God had divinely placed all of them together at those moments. She had no doubt Georgia was meant to be her daughter. But she wasn't so sure God had approved of the lie.

Nevertheless, Missouri planned on taking that lie, that secret, to her grave.

Wiping the tears from her eyes with her gown sleeve, she asked for forgiveness again, and rolled over to attempt sleep, knowing it was she, not God, who needed to forgive her.

She loved Georgia with all her heart.

Wasn't that all that mattered?

CHAPTER TWELVE:

Busy as a Bee

Early the next morning Missouri set out on a mission. She wanted to get this done before Georgia and Sam picked her up to go to the hospital to visit Mint and baby Sarah. "I got a bee in my bonnet." She muttered as she looked for the piece of wire she kept in the closet. Finding it, she used it to hook the high latch on the door that led to the steps to the attic.

The door creaked open and Missouri sneezed at the dust that wafted toward her. She shook her head thinking back to how often the attic had been used in the past. Now it was plain old dusty and filled with its share of cobwebs.

"Well, I reckon I got enough steam in me to git up them steps. I just hope nobody finds out I done it."

The steps were narrow and steep, and the family had forbidden her to climb them two years ago after she'd slipped and sprain her ankle. Missouri set her jaw determinedly. This was her house, and by gumption, she was old, not senile, nor was she age three.

With great caution, she began the ascent. Huffing and puffing, she reached the top and stood, looking around.

Big shafts of light beamed through four windows, even though they were as dusty as the steps. The floors were solid pine and the ceiling high. She and Preacher had planned to make two bedrooms up here, one for all the boys they were planning on having, and one for all the girls. She shook her head. There had been plenty of room downstairs for Georgia, and the rooms, like the children, had never been.

Over the years lots of stuff had accumulated up here. Lamps, rugs, tables, a bed stead, and even an old pedestal sink was propped up in the corner.

Missouri headed to the far corner where the older things were stacked. She figured they'd started in the back and worked their way up.

She was right. Underneath an old claw footed parlor table sat the little bee stool. Missouri sat down next to it in a rickety dining room chair that threatened to dump her out. She hardly noticed. Her old gnarled fingers gently caressed the little stool. She traced the carved bee with her finger, touching the clover ring around the top of the stool that her father had so lovingly worked on.

She sat the tiny, three legged stool in her lap and could almost see the new baby becoming a toddler and using this stool for all manner of things.

A fat tear plopped down and hit the stool. She still missed Papa sometimes.

She'd been the apple of Papa's eye all her life, even after Kizzie was born. Of course, Kizzie had been Mama's little angel, so it worked out fine.

She had received the Bee Stool for her third birthday. Papa had presented it to her and explained she could sit on it instead of the hard floor and it would be warmer in the winter. He told her she could stand on it to look out the window when she was watching for him, and she could use it to be taller when she was helping her mama in the kitchen. He told her how he had carved the honey bee and then decided it needed clover all around it, because that made such good honey for them to eat with their biscuits.

Missouri had agreed, honey was one of her favorites! He told her that when Kizzie was three, he'd make a stool for her, too.

But somehow, he never did. Missouri reckoned that was the only thing she'd had that had been totally hers and not shared with Kizzie. Over the years, Kizzie would ask to borrow it, and Missouri never refused. But they both knew it was Missouri it belonged to.

Interesting, Missouri thought, why she'd never brought the stool out for Wylene or even Mint, that she could recall. Georgia had played with it some, long ago. She guess she'd just packed it up when Georgia outgrew it, and twenty some odd years later when Wylene was born, she'd simply forgotten about it.

She pulled herself out of the old chair and carefully toted the stool down the stairs, closing the door behind her. She felt a little like a child who had done something naughty and gotten away with it, even if she did feel a little swimmy headed.

****

Wylene was in the bathroom looking at the back of her hair and trying to decide what shoes to wear with the outfit she had on, when Herb stuck his head in the door. "Let's go."

His tone annoyed her. "As soon as I get my shoes, I'll be ready." She laid down the hair pick and frowned at him. "What's got you in such an all fired hurry, anyway? We aren't late."

"Your mama just called. Missouri fell again. They'd gone to pick her up and found her in the living room floor.

Out on a Limb of the Family Tree

The ambulance is on the way."

Wylene jerked the curling iron's plug out from the wall, put on her old loafers she'd worn to water the flowers and make breakfast in, and grabbed her purse as they ran out the door.

"I hope Mint doesn't hear about this before I can go up to the maternity ward and tell her." She fastened her seat belt as Herb backed out of the drive way. "Was Missouri confused again?"

"I don't think so. Something about her feeling faint and trying to get to the couch."

They hit the ER doors wide open and saw the backs of Georgia and Sam as they turned a corner. "Mama!" Wylene hollered and Georgia stopped.

"Hey, honey. They've just took Mama back to an examining room. You know she won't want to be by herself."

"I know, but is she all right, you think? I mean...do you think she's had a stroke?" Wylene put her hand to her mouth, trying to get her lip to stop trembling.

Georgia shook her head. "No symptoms that I could see. She was just a little weak. I think she hurt her knee. She said she felt faint and was trying to get to the couch to lay down, but didn't quite make it. She slid down the wall, so that broke her fall some."

"It's a wonder she didn't break a hip!" Wylene walked her mother to the exam door. "Do you think I ought to go tell Mint?"

"Lord, I forgot she was still here! I guess you better. You know as well as I do, some well meaning friend will try and beat us to the punch."

Wylene rolled her eyes, looked for Herb, and headed for the maternity ward.

****

"Well, well, Missouri, so we meet again. Do you remember what happened this time?" Dr. John stopped at the examining table and smiled down at Missouri.

"Yep. I remember feelin' a mite dizzy headed and thankin' I ort to lay down a minute. I's closer to the couch, so I tried to git to it and couldn't make it. So I put myself up agin the wall and slid down, easy like. I'm prob'ly gonner be stove up anyhow, and still hurt my knee." She grimaced as she tried to bend it.

"Easy now. Let me take a look at that knee in a minute before you start doing deep bends." He picked up the chart the nurse had left on the table. "Well, your blood pressure is high. Didn't we talk to you about that the last time I saw you?"

"Maybe. I've had so much goin' on, I guess I fergot."

"I don't doubt you have a lot going on, but this is important. Have you had any more dizzy spells besides this one?"

"Oh, one or two. But they wadn't as bad as this un was."

Georgia spoke up. "Part of this is my fault. I meant to take her blood pressure reading and forgot. My granddaughter had a baby yesterday and it's got us all distracted. She's here in this hospital, in fact."

Dr. John turned to Missouri. "What does that make you? A great-grandmother?"

"No, a great-great-grandmother, as a matter of fact."

"Congratulations. Now we need to get this blood pressure under control so you can watch that little one grow." His voice grew stern. "I'm serious, Missouri. I don't want you in here in a month with a stroke, unable to move and drooling all over everything. You are too healthy otherwise to let this kind of thing happen." He scribbled on a prescription pad. "This needs to be filled before the day's out, and I want you to start it the next minute. Okay?"

"I will." Missouri was meek. "I reckon I just didn't want to thank about it."

"Most of us are that way. But it is not a good way to be. Now, let's take a look at that knee."

He was ordering an x-ray when a loud commotion was heard outside the door. Mint came hobbling in.

"Oh, Missouri! Not again! I was trying to nurse, and thought it was gonna kill me, and then Mama came in and said you was down here hurt!" She burst into tears. "I can't take all this."

"Looky here, Mint!" Missouri scolded. "I ain't dead. I hurt my knee a little. Got dizzy, that's all. Don't you go gittin' all foolish on me and spoil that baby's milk! Shape up right now!"

Mint blinked. "I'm sorry. All my emotions seem to be wide open. Actually, I was crying before Mama walked in." She walked closer to Missouri. "Are you really all right?"

"Yes, child. I'm startin' on medicine today fer my high blood and pressure so I won't be dizzy. And Dr. John is havin' my knee x-uh-rayed." She patted Mint's hand. "Now you go back to little Sarah and keep her from starvin'. As soon as they's through with me, I'll come by to see the baby afore I leave. Now scoot!"

Mint hobbled back out of the room and Missouri caught a glimpse of Wylene outside the door, grinning.

"You see why I cain't remember squat? You see why my blood pressure is high?" Missouri fumed at Dr. John.

He laughed out loud. "I love it. You guys crack me up." He shook his head and left the room.

After having her sprained knee bandaged and taking a blood pressure pill, Missouri was wheeled to the elevator and did indeed visit Sarah and Mint. Ben was in the corner eating a doughnut and drinking coffee, watching Sarah sleep in the little crib, a moonstruck look on his face.

They locked the wheels on the chair and put Sarah in Missouri's lap. "Ain't she the sweetest thang?" Missouri cooed. Sarah opened her eyes and studied Missouri. "This here is yur great-great-granny, little lamb. You'll be callin' me Missouri afore we know it."

Missouri looked up. "Georgia, do you remember the little bee stool that was mine? You played with it some when you was little."

"Why, I'd forgot all about it. If I remember correctly it was really beautiful. Whatever happened to it?"

"It got stuck back in the far corner of the attic. I plumb fergot about it too. Don't reckon Wylene or Mint ever had a chance to play with it. But I commenced thankin' on it last night and hunted it up. It's as sturdy as the day Papa made it."

Georgia's eyes narrowed. "Mama, are you telling me you climbed those attic stairs this morning, alone?"

"Uh, well, I weren't tellin' you on purpose." Missouri decided maybe she *had* had a stroke when she fell. What in tarnation did she go and tell that fer?

"What if you had fallen up or down those narrow things? You'd had a broken neck instead of a sprained knee!"

Missouri knew winding up when she saw it. "Calm down, Georgia. You'll git the baby all upset. And none of that happened. The stool's safe in the kitchen, I'm safe right here, and I ain't gonner do it agin."

"That's what you said the last time."

"Well, that was before my high blood and pressure. I won't no more."

Georgia sighed and shook her head. "I hope not, Mama."

Mint, deciding the war was over, asked Missouri about the bee stool, and the rest of the visit was pleasant.

****

Georgia called Kizzie and asked was she willing to stay at Missouri's tomorrow, and insisted that Missouri spend the night with them.

"Dr. John said you could put weight on your knee day after tomorrow, so you are just going to have to be inconvenienced for a few days. That means my house for the next two nights and company of some sort for a few days."

Missouri had harrumphed around, but she knew it to be true.

So much for sneaking around and getting away with anything.

CHAPTER THIRTEEN:

Two's a Crowd

Missouri got home early the next morning. Everyone was excited because Mint and the baby were coming home today. Wylene was staying at Ben and Mint's house for a few days to help out, so Georgia had wanted to cook dinner for everyone, and Missouri hadn't wanted to stay for all that hoopla. They'd picked Kizzie up on the way, and after what seemed like an hour, got them both situated in the house.

Putting a cushion under Missouri's knee, as she was propped up on the couch, Georgia asked, "How's your knee after getting you settled? Do you need a pill?"

"Well, it's a'painin' me some, but I don't reckon I want nuthin' just yet."

"I've got the pills right here with fresh water, all you have to do is reach and get them. Kizzie, all *you* have to do is make sure Mama uses the walker anytime she gets up, like to go to the bathroom. If you don't care to, bring her dinner in here and put it on the little fold out table."

She turned back to Missouri. "And Mama, I mean it. Don't get up unless you have to go to the bathroom. The preacher's wife is coming over around two to visit, and somebody will be back before dark to get Kizzie home and you back to my house for the night."

Missouri felt acutely embarrassed and began to get riled. "This here is all a lot of foolishness. Ain't no reason not to let me stay right here. I have a phone. I can call somebody if I need 'em."

Out on a Limb of the Family Tree

Georgia rolled her eyes. "You know that doesn't even make sense. We'll see how the doctor thinks you're healing up tomorrow afternoon and go from there." She bent down and kissed Missouri on the cheek and whispered in her ear. "Don't fight too much with Kizzie. I'd hate to find her walking home on the side of the road."

Missouri grinned in spite of herself, patted her daughter on the arm, and bade her good-bye.

"Bossy little thang, ain't she?" Kizzie asked, as Georgia walked down the porch steps to her car.

"Yep. I hate like everthang this happened now. She's got so much on her, and she ain't a sprang chicken no more."

"That's so. Georgia's what – seventy?"

"Turns sixty-nine next month." Missouri snickered. "She'd knock the taste outta yur mouth if she heared you say she was seventy."

"I reckon so." Kizzie sat down in the rocker. "Want to watch some TV?"

"Not partic'ly. But the clicker's yonder on the side table." Missouri sighed. It was going to be a long day.

After sitting through two soap operas and Kizzie hooting at 'them women in them big old tall staccato heels, wobblin' around like they ain't got no sense', and Missouri asking, 'Don't you mean stiletto heels?' and Kizzie answering, 'No, Sister, that's a kind of a knife.', Missouri tried to keep her mouth shut.

But finally, an hour and fifteen minutes later, she sarcastically asked Kizzie for pain medication. "I don't mean to be troublin' you none, but my knee is killin' me, and I need some dadburn medication." Was the way she put it. "Not to mention I'm gonner be hungry in the near future, and as far as I can see, ain't no dinner been cooked."

Kizzie replied, "Well, seein' as how that's what I'm here fer, Yur Highny, let me git the almighty pill and start yur almighty dinner."

By the time the 'almighty dinner' had been served and they were on their second helping of coconut cake, sent over by a neighbor just minutes before, feathers had become unruffled.

Kizzie kept humming a little snatch of a tune and finally gave up. "I just cain't recollect how that song goes." She hummed a little more.

"Why, that's *'Smilin' Through'*!" Missouri said. "I ain't thought of that song since I's a girl. You remember when Mathias Gates sang that one Sunday afternoon at Mama's and Papa's? I thank him and Mercy Berry was datin' heavy and they'd heared it playin' when they got to see some silent film. Nineteen-twenty-two, that was. And ole Mercy picked it right out of the pianer when he sang it, too." Missouri turned to Kizzie. "They ever marry?"

"Yep. Just not to each other. Mathias married Tibby Berry, Mercy's first cousin. Like to killed Mercy. But a year or two later Mercy married Chib Drennon. Remember? They had a lit'lun nine months to the day they's married. Ever old biddy in the county was countin' down the minutes. On thur fangers and toes too, I reckon."

"That's right." Missouri nodded her head in memory. "Named that baby Sampson because he was a eleven pounder with the fullest head of hair on a new baby I ever seen. Called him Samp all his life, I guess people still do. Some of them old biddies you speak of swore he was a ten month baby 'cause he weighed so much." They both got a little chuckle out of that. Then Missouri turned serious. "Reckon why it is, Kizzie, that folks always want what's the worst in people? Me and you is just as guilty. We hear suhum bad on a body and we cain't wait to call each other up and chew on it fer a ar."

"You always say yur gonner pray fer 'em." Kizzie snickered.

"Well, and I do. But shame on me and you if we even git a little bit of pleasure from thur wrong doin'." She cocked her head. "I thank I hear a car." Glancing at the clock, she frowned. "It ain't but two. Shorely Georgia ain't back from all she had to do."

Kizzie got up and hobbled to the window. "It's the preacher's wife. I guess we'll straighten up and fly right now."

"Oh, I fergot she was a-comin'. Clur these dishes right quick, and don't fergit to offer her some of that cake."

"Yes'um. I'm a'liable to fergit." She snorted and took their dirty dishes to the kitchen. Brushing crumbs from her dress, she got the door just as the preacher's wife began knocking.

****

Missouri had no sooner gotten settled on the couch in the den at Georgia's after supper when Sam came in and handed her the phone. "It's Kizzie."

Missouri rolled her eyes, took the phone and said, "Did you fergit suhum?"

Ignoring the sarcasm, Kizzie started right in. "I just saw the local paper! Ransom and Reader are both dead!"

Missouri sat up, wincing at the pain in her knee. "What in the world happened that they'd both up and die?"

"Sezs here thur boy, Styles, remember him?" she went on without waiting on an answer. "Styles said his daddy – that was Reader – had been workin' in the garden and musta had him a heart attack. Ransom walked across the road to visit a spell, and found him. He got so upset he tried to run to the house fer the phone and had a heart attack hisself! They's both dead by the time the amb'lance got thar."

"Well, Lord have mercy. Them boys always did everthang together. I reckon they stormed Heaven together too."

They were both silent a moment. It was a lot to take in. Reader and Ransom had always been known as the 'Reynolds twins'. They were a year older than Missouri and had moved into town when Missouri and Kizzie were sixteen and fifteen. Missouri already had her eye on Preacher, but the Reynolds twins, well, they were a vision to behold. Hair black as soot, eyes blue as the sky, skin dark as the Cherokee blood that flowed in them from their mama's side. Those eyes danced with merriment of the Irishman their papa was, and they were full of mischievousness! They had a complete set of dimples between them, Ransom in the right cheek and Reader in his left. What Missouri and Kizzie's Mama called sugar bowl dimples, they were so deep. Standing just a bit over six feet tall, with shoulders wide and strong, hips narrow and attached to long, lean legs, they were, simply put, beautiful specimen.

"And they was two of them," Kizzie practically

swooned over the phone.

"They was, that. And as dangerous as they was handsome."

"Ain't that the truth, Sister? They liked to got me whipped by my own Papa fer the first time in my life, and me fifteen years old."

"And?" Missouri asked.

"And it was worth it." Kizzie answered.

Because Missouri and Kizzie were good girls, and the boys had been very polite and hadn't missed a church service, Papa had agreed they could go to a social one Saturday that their friend, Autrie Dobson, was giving. Papa had sort of frowned on Autrie and her family because they weren't regular church goers, and rumor had it that Mr. Dobson had a whiskey still deep in the woods. But that rumor wasn't confirmed as fact, and Mama had gently persuaded Papa to let them go to the social. He'd reluctantly agreed, sternly telling them they must be home long before the sun started leaving the sky.

Well, the social would have met with Papa's approval. Boring beyond belief, plus the weather had took a turn, and it was hotter'n all git out.

Missouri and Reader had gone into the house with some of the others where they hoped it would be a bit cooler. Kizzie and Ransom had stayed on the porch.

Except when Missouri excused herself for a quick trip to the outhouse, Kizzie and Ransom were no where to be found upon her return. To top that, Reader had disappeared too. Missouri enquired to everyone there where had they gone, but the boys just grinned and the girls didn't seem to really know – or care.

Finally, Missouri had no recourse but to ask for a ride home from some folks who would be passing by their house on their way home. Mr. and Mrs. Dobson were terribly upset, and Mr. Dobson had gone to find Reader and Ransom's papa and asked some of the boys to comb the woods.

Missouri had no more than got home, about to tearfully tell the tale, when the twins pulled up in their buggy with Kizzie between them. They looked sheepish and Kizzie, well, Kizzie looked drunk.

And she was.

The final story had been unclear, but Missouri pieced it out over the days as Kizzie squealed on herself.

When Missouri went to the outhouse, Reader came back out to the porch. He and Ransom started talking about this 'purty little place in the woods just beyond the house that had beauteous flowers'. Knowing that Kizzie was a fool for flowers, they kept it up, finally convincing her to 'step just right over here'. Right over here got further than she meant to go.

They come upon a contraption in the woods, the likes of which Kizzie had never seen. They boys told her it made country medicine, and their papa helped out Mr. Dobson with the still. For that is what it was. She asked about the contraption, and what was this stuff that looked somewhat like creamed corn?

Why, that was corn mash, they replied.

Kizzie asked: Is it sort of like the corn mush Mama makes? Looking over Kizzie's head, the twins held a complete conversation with their eyes.

Oh, yes, very much so. Would you like to taste it?

Out on a Limb of the Family Tree

She did. And for some reason, she ate quite a lot.

When the twins saw her go from giggly to almost unconscious in a matter of moments they got scared enough to bring her home, whether their hide was ruined or not.

"You got to hand that much to 'em," Kizzie said. "At least they didn't leave me in the woods, nor take me to the Dobson's house or suhum."

"I ain't never seen Papa in such a shape in all my borned days. If you hadn't been so drunk and needin' help, I do believe he woulda whipped both them boys with his bare hands, right thar in the yard."

"And he was even mad at poor Mama, fer talkin' him into lettin' us go in the first place. Only time I ever saw him mad at her, too."

"But, my, they was handsome boys, never seen any handsomer myself."

"Me neither, Sister. But that was the end of courtin' the Reynolds twins."

"I reckon they turned out to be right nice fellers. One of 'em married Lucy Davis and one of 'em married Joanna Anderson. Is either of 'em still livin'?"

"Let me looky here." Missouri heard the newspaper rustle. "Lucy is. She's Style's mama. Joanna is already deceased. They have two girls still living, Rhonda and Susan. I reckon they is all sad today."

They talked a moment longer, then hung up, each pensive, thinking back to that particular time.

Missouri found herself dozing on the couch, thinking of those two handsome boys. She went to sleep with a smile on her face, remembering Kizzie staggering out of the buggy, a look alike on each side of her trying to keep her from slithering to the ground.

Kizzie had told her she was nigh afraid to even take Communion and drink the wine, the way Papa looked at her every time the cup was passed.

Yes sir, that had been the end of the courtship with Reader and Ransom Reynolds!

CHAPTER FOURTEEN:

And Baby Makes Three

Missouri hobbled around the kitchen, greatly relieved she was at home, alone. Lord knew she loved her family, but they was nearly drivin' her crazy! Sam had brung her home just past day break, at her insistence, since she'd got around pretty good yesterday. At the doctor visit, the doctor said she could try walking with her knee bandaged and no walker, and she'd done so as soon as she'd got back to Georgia's. It didn't hurt near as much as she'd feared it would, and if she moved around easy-like, she was fine.

Mint and Ben were bringing the baby for her to see today! Of course, she'd seen her in the hospital, but had missed seeing her the following two days due to doctor appointments and such. She couldn't wait to hold that baby.

Missouri glanced at the clock and figured she had just enough time to finish her coffee and get ready for them to come. She peaked in the refrigerator and looked at the left over coconut cake from day before yesterday. It was still good, so if they wanted refreshments, she had it ready.

A bit later, she heard car doors and stood at the window to watch. Ben came around and opened the door for Mint, who still was careful how she moved about. He reached in the back seat and scooped up Sarah from the car seat, placing a light blanket over her as they headed toward the house.

A sudden sureness and sorrow filled Missouri. She would never see this child grow up, probably wouldn't see her enter first grade. Of course, she already knew this logically, but the knowledge hit her heart for the first time. "Thy will be done, Lord." She whispered, just before she opened the door.

"Come in, come in!" she hollered, opening the screen door wide. "I cain't hardly wait to hold that lit'lun in my lap."

Ben grinned at her and kissed her cheek. "Glad you're so happy to see us, Missouri."

Missouri grunted. "Who said I's glad to see the likes of you? I just want my hands on that baby."

"Well," Mint said as she walked through the door, "I hope I still have at least a little room in your heart somewhere."

"We'll see. Depends on how yur treatin' that child." Missouri closed the door and came in the living room to sit down. "I done washed my hands, give her to me. If ya'll want coffee and coconut cake, help yurself. Coffee's fresh, and the cake was made by the neighbor day before yesterdey. It's in the refrigerator."

Ben's eyes lit up as he hastily laid Sarah in Missouri's lap. The baby stirred a little, and he stuck a pacifier in her mouth before straightening up. "That'll keep her happy for a little while." he said. "Mint, you want cake?"

"Yes. And milk. You got milk, Missouri?"

"I thank thar's some in thar. Check and make sure it's still good, Ben." She looked down at Sarah's face and felt her eyes get watery. "She's a beautiful child, Mint."

"Thanks, Missouri. Who do you think she looks like?"

"Nobody but Sarah. Babies don't generally look like fam'ly to me until they git bigger. Now, I seen a few that was the spittin' image of somebody, but not many."

"That's what I think. But Mama swears she looks just like me, and Ben's mama says she looks like him."

Missouri laughed a little. "What did you expect 'em to say? The funny thang about babies is one month they'll look like mama and the next month they'll look like daddy. And sometimes they don't look like neither. You never know. However; I do remember when Beryl Dayle was borned, she looked so much like thur next door neighbor they upped and moved."

"Missouri! Is that a tall tale?" Ben asked as he came back in the room to hand Mint her cake and milk.

"Truth. I was newly married and was scandalized near to death. Preacher told me some people got caught sinnin' quicker than others, and that was a prime example. Never heared from the Dayle's agin in this town; far as I know, anyway."

Ben shook his head. "Sad story, for sure. Do you want some cake, Missouri?"

"No thank ye, Ben. I ain't hungry just yet."

Ben wondered back in the kitchen to get his own plate. Missouri looked at Mint. "How you doin', honey?"

"I'm all right. Sore as all get out, but recovering normal, I guess. I can tell we ain't gonna get much sleep for a while. That seems more bothersome than anything."

"That is so. Sleep's never the same after you have a young'un."

"When does it get back to regular?"

"I'll let you know, ifen it ever does."

Mint giggled, imagining Missouri still losing sleep over her 'child', Mint's grandmother. She reached and stroked Sarah's head, the blonde hair so fine it stood up like chick fuzz. "Weren't you a redhead, Missouri?"

"That's a fact. Always hated it till Preacher fell in love with it. He was pure-t mesmerized by my hair. Made up fer a lot of years envyin' Kizzie's blonde tresses."

"It's a wonder Grandma didn't have red hair, too. Ain't it supposed to be a dominant gene?"

Missouri stirred uncomfortably. "Don't reckon I know about that kind of stuff."

"What color was Preacher's hair?"

"It was a dark brown, nur black."

"The pictures of Grandma look like her hair wasn't that dark."

"No, it was nurly blonde, but more a light brown."

"Wonder who she took after. She don't look like you or Preacher."

Missouri felt herself become clammy and her heart beat rapidly. "I don't reckon I know who she took after."

Mint yawned, losing interest. "Oh, well. Like you said, some babies are spitting images and some aren't." She smiled down at the baby. "It would have been nice if she'd had your red hair, though."

Missouri grunted. "Blessin' she don't."

"Man, this is good cake." Ben came back into the living room, cheeks bulging. "We've still got a little bit of food that church sent over, and some from what Georgia cooked the other day. Wylene says she'll fix us a good supper tonight, but then I reckon she's going back home and we're on our own. Probably won't have a meal that good again until Easter. And that's two weeks away."

"That's only right. Ya'll need to start bein' yur own fam'ly, all by yur lonesomes." Missouri could see by

Out on a Limb of the Family Tree

Mint's expression, she was nervous about it. "Now, Mint, honey, you are gonner do just fine. It's an amazin' thang, what God's done. He somehow put how to take care of a baby right inside most of us."

"What if He left me out?" Mint asked. "Mama just takes over every time I start to do something except nurse, and I do believe she'd do that too, if she could!" Ben blushed, but before he could say anything, Mint rushed on. "I love Mama, you know I do Missouri, but she's made me feel like I ain't gonna be able to do none of this without her. I'm not sure I can either!"

"Oh, shaw! That is yur baby, Samintha Sanders! Yur mama didn't have her, God didn't mean fer nobody to be her mama but you! Now stop snivelin' and show me some backbone."

Ben patted Mint on the shoulder. "I've seen how sweet Mint is with Sarah, when she has the chance. And that baby already knows who her mama is. I do believe if Sarah had been give the opportunity, she'd have chosen Mint to be her mama."

Missouri felt her eyes start to water up. "That's exactly right, honey. Ben is exactly right."

****

Ben, Mint and Sarah had hardly driven out of the driveway when Kizzie called, ranting. "That boy ain't worth killin'!"

"Who in thunder you talkin' about?"

"Sumter, who else?"

Sumter Elkhorn Johnson was the youngest of Kizzie's brood. He had been given such an outlandish name because

Kizzie's first husband's granddaddy, at the tender age of fifteen, had been at Fort Sumter when the first shot of the 'Northern Invasion' had taken place. Elkhorn was for the Native American part of Homer's questionable and interesting heritage he had passed along to his son.

"Now, I know Sumter has always been a mite quar in the head, Kizzie, but ain't you bein' a tad harsh on him?" Missouri sighed heavily. "What's he done now?" Missouri longingly eyed the biscuit and gravy on her plate she'd popped into the microwave as soon as her company had driven off. She'd jus started to sop up the gravy with said biscuit when the phone rang.

"Well, first and foe-most, I blessed him out good. He got hisself drunk as a lord and received a DUI fer his efforts." Her voice trembled. "Old man Trouble surely visited me the day he was borned."

"Well, he ain't the first to git a DUI, Kizzie."

"Oh, that's just the beginnin'. The fool wadn't in his truck. No sir. He went next door and stole the neighbor's ridin' lawnmower. He was drivin' it down Main Street, right in the middle of Whistle, Georgia. That way nobody could miss him. Lord knows we don't want to keep no secrets from nobody."

"Have mercy! That boy does need a good killin', you was right! What did the little wife do this time?"

"Mrs. Bama Southern Johnson has done gone to the courthouse and filed fer her a dee-vorce, that's what. And I don't blame her one little bit."

"You gonner bail him outta jail?"

"Mayhaps I will, mayhaps I won't." Then resolution entered her voice. "Nope. I ain't gonner do it, Missouri. Let him sit thar till the cows come home."

"Good fer you, Sister. I know you love him. I do too, fer that matter. But he's just about done enough."

"I am so embarrassed, Missouri. I cain't show my face here in Sweetapple or in Whistle again."

"Oh, shaw, Kizzie. Remember when we wuz little and old man Deacon Brookshire got so drunk on moonshine Saturday night he was still drunk Sunday? And him tryin' to lead sangin' in the Lord's house!"

Kizzie giggled in spite of herself. "Yeah. And what give him away was the mule he had standin' in the choir loft, tryin' to git it to sang 'O, Susannah'."

They both roared with laughter then. "And don't fergit Pockets Satterfield nearly burnin' his own barn down thanks to drank. His wife come close to beatin' him to death with a mop handle, as I recall."

Kizzie took a moment to compose herself. "I know thar's been drunks since thar's been the devil's brew to drank. Don't make it no easier when it's yur own young'un doin' the drankin'."

"I spec not. You want Sam or Herb to do anythang?"

"I reckon not. Just make sure the fam'ly knows. I don't want to tell 'em."

"All right. I'll call Georgia as soon as I finish eatin'."

"I might want to come over after while. Reckon one of them will come git me?"

"You know they will if they can. I'll ast that too."

They hung up and Missouri found herself heating up the gravy in the microwave again, hurriedly eating, and making the phone calls Kizzie had asked of her.

In mid-chew, Missouri suddenly wondered how in the

Sam Hill she'd got herself in the middle of all this. "Old fools is the worst." She muttered before she laid down for her nap.

Before sleep overtook her, she remembered what she felt like was a close call with Mint talking about hair color, and Georgia not looking like anyone in the family. She knew Mint didn't mean a thing by it. She knew when you lived with a lie it haunted you, that's all. And she had been haunted this afternoon. She reckoned it was a small price to pay for her daughter.

CHAPTER FIFTEEN:

Come to Dinner!

The first Sunday family dinner that Mint was able to attend after Sarah's birth was an exciting event. Missouri had insisted on it being held at her house, because she wanted Sarah to always be told that her first Sunday dinner was held at her great-great-grandmother's. Georgia and Wylene brought enough food for an army, Kizzie brought two kinds of dessert, and Ben had managed to pick up potato salad at a deli. Nobody embarrassed him by saying that store bought food was under par for their Sunday dinners.

As plates were filled and then emptied, Kizzie and Missouri began to reminisce about their childhood dinners and regaled the rest of the family with stories.

"Remember when it would be ar turn to have Obadiah Frost over fer Sunday dinner?" Kizzie asked. "Lord, I was skeered of that man when I's little. He had that eye that was blind and poured tears all the time. But I finally got used to him, I reckon."

Missouri picked up. "He lived up in the Shake Rag settlement, as I recall. Everbody said Obadiah was brilliant when he was a child, especially about Bible thangs. When he was seventeen he got kicked in the head by a mule and they thought he was gonner die, but he didn't. After that he was tetched in the head purty bad. His mama passed away shortly after the accident. She'd always been a sickly woman, my mama said. When Obadiah was twenty years old or so, his papa died too. His papa had a will and had left some sort of trust fund set up so that Obadiah was to git so much a month to see to food, care of the place, and whatnot. I reckon Obadiah's papa was purty well off, even though they lived in a very modest home."

"Didn't take long fer that little house to come to near ruins, did it, Sister?" Kizzie tsked her tongue in disgust.

"No. Fer back as I could remember it weren't much more'n a shack. Anyway, he got to whar he wore this big, wool overcoat ever day, summer and winter. Said if it kept the cold out it orter keep the heat out too. Only time he took that coat off was when the town boys would talk him into jumpin' off the Clur River Bridge."

Mint sat up straight in an outrage. "Why didn't someone stop them? What a cruel thing to do to a poor boy who didn't know better!"

"They was some that did try to stop him from doin' it. Everbody knowed who was temptin' him, but they couldn't prove it, so they went and talked to Obadiah. He just laughed and said he had a secret them boys didn't know about. Obadiah always trusted Alba Slaughter a lot, even let him take him to the doctor one time when he got bad sick. So, Alba ast him what that secret might be. Obadiah leaned in real close and said to Alba, 'Right before I hit the water, I slow down.'"

"That'd be hard to argue with," said Herb. He shook his head. "I'm sure the poor feller believed it."

Missouri nodded her head in agreement. "He wore stove pipes around the bottom of his laigs above his boots. Fine-lee, Pin Butterworth got up the nerve to ast him why he was a'warin' stove pipes 'round his lower laigs. 'Well, madam,' Obadiah says, 'Don't you know it's for the rattle heads and the copper snakes.'" Missouri paused while the family laughed. "He stopped changin' clothes and takin' a bath 'cept on Saturday night, and thank the good Lord that he did then! Fer he was faithful at church. The coat by itself stunk so bad it was hard to sit close to him."

"But Missouri," Mint interrupted. "People didn't bathe much in olden times, anyway, did they?"

Missouri raised an eyebrow. "Well, I don't rightly know about *olden times*, but I do know about my childhood. It is true in the cold of winter we didn't git in the tub 'cept on Saturday night. But we had a wash basin we bathed in ever mornin' and especially ever night. Washed ar hair on Wednesday and Saturdays, too. It was hard, dragging that old wash tub in the kitchen and heatin' enough water fer a bath, which was why we didn't do it but onct a week when it was cold. But in the summer, why it was near ever day. We had that wash tub on the back porch yonder, and Mama would run a curtain of sheets around it. Papa had it set right up under the pump handle on the back porch, so it was easy to fill. And Papa had put a stopper like thang on the bottom to drain out the water. Mama used that bath water to water plants when we was through. Weren't never no reason to go dirty." She glared at Mint. "Any more questions afore I continue?"

"No'm." Mint said in a small voice.

Missouri cleared her throat and continued. " Anyway, the first Sunday rolled around that it was ar turn to feed Obadiah after church. By now, Mama had larned how to be one of the best cooks around. And she'd gone all out fer poor old Obadiah."

"And no wonder," Kizzie said. "No tellin' what he

was likely to say. Poor Mizriz Hedgerow's first prize winnin' meatloaf was served to him the Sunday before. They said he took one look at it and said real poe-lite like, 'I don't eat dog food, madam.'" Kizzie cackled at her own remembrance.

Missouri nodded. "That's truth. He was rail thin, that's why the church decided people had to start feedin' him some to start with, but not so's he'd thank it was charity. So Sunday dinner after church was perfect, as folks visited and ate together a lot anyway. Mr. Harper said all he bought at the grocery store was sardines, co'cola, and so-dee crackers."

"'Cept he called them Saltines." Kizzie interjected.

"That's right." Missouri agreed. "Anyway, Obadiah ast if he could say grace, much to my papa's surprise! O'course, Papa said yes. Why, you woulda thought we had us a great orator in ar midst! Obadiah always spoke like a perfesser anyway, but that prayer was suhum else! Well, when the rafters stopped shakin' from the last amen, we commenced to pass the food around. And what a feast it was! Fried chicken, pot roast, beans, taters, corn, fresh onions and tamaters, cukes, biscuits, cornbread; you name it, Mama had it on the table, all served on her very best dishes."

Missouri paused a moment, thinking back. "Now, let me say me and Kizzie may have been raised country, but we had been taught table manners." Kizzie nodded her head vigorously. "But Obadiah ate like a animal. He shoveled food in so fast his cheeks stuck way out as he hunkered down over his plate. Mama sat in shock. Kizzie and me didn't even know ar mouths was hangin' open till Papa give us a stern look. Finally, Mama braved a comment to Obadiah. She says 'Is the food to yur likin', Mr. Frost?' Obadiah looked up, startled like. It was as though he'd fergot we was even thar. He straightened up in his chair, finished chewin' the food in his mouth, and swallered. He wiped his face with his napkin, all careful like, and clured his throat. Cockin' his head to one side, considerin' Mama's question, he said in that boomin' voice of his, 'Beats eating a snowball'. And then he hunkered down again and set to on that food like nobody's business."

The table shook with everyone's laughter.

Kizzie said, "I remember goin' to Mr. Harper's grocery store one day when I was growed and married. Suddenly them double doors in the front of the store opened up and thar stood Obadiah. 'MIS-ter Harper! MIS-ter Harper!' he called in that voice of his'in. Mr. Harper come round and spoke and ast him what he could do fer him. Obadiah told him two or three thangs he needed, and Mr. Harper went and fetched it. Rung it up on the cash register, told Obadiah what he owed, handed him the food, and got the money. Obadiah thanked him and left, never settin' foot in the store. Mr. Harper said that's the way Obadiah always done business."

Missouri said, "I remember when Obadiah passed on, the deacons went to his home and waded through the filth. Found a big old sack of money chewed up by rats. But they was still plenty in the trust fund to bury Obadiah Frost proper. And he did have a fine fune'rul. The tombstone still stands today. Somebody puts flowers on it ever birthday he has. Don't know who tis, do you Kizzie?"

"Cain't say as I do, Sister."

"They say the preacher that did the fune'rul talked about what Obadiah had taught him. How we all want to be accepted by others, no matter how different we might be. He looked everbody right in the eye and said he hoped each and everone had showed some kindness to Obadiah Frost."

They ate on in silence for a few minutes, not only digesting the food in front of them, but the food for thought too.

CHAPTER SIXTEEN:

In Your Easter Bonnet

April 10, 1998

Mint was excited and scared too. It was the first time she was out of the house without the baby since Sarah had been born. Day after tomorrow was Easter, and Sarah would be three weeks old tomorrow. She and Ben both thought it a good time for her to get out. The church women were dying eggs this afternoon, and a hairdresser friend of Mint's family owned a grocery store and were willing to donate eight dozen eggs! Mint was picking them up, taking them to the church, and going back home. But it was freedom!

She pulled into the Sweetapple Grocery's parking lot and stopped to smell the spring fragrances in the air. It had come a good shower this morning and every plant in sight looked about to bust with blooms.

She walked into the store and was greeted by at least a dozen people before she could get to the back. Everyone wanted to ask about Sarah and make a comment. It was wonderful!

"Hey Mint! Need an egg or two?' She looked up to see Bobby Colowell stocking canned goods. He stood, tall and lanky, the grocer's apron wrapped around him nearly twice. He shook his curly black hair out of his eyes and grinned. "I don't know why, but you look in need of eggs."

Mint laughed. "I need more than one or two, Bobby. You gonna load them up for me?"

"Sure thing. How's that baby?"

"The most beautiful one ever born. How is your baby doing?" Bobby and his wife Pricilla had a six month old boy.

"Well, he's the most handsome, of course. Looks just like me." They laughed again and Mint followed him to the storage room where the eggs were waiting. "Pull on around the back and I'll put them in your car."

She walked out the back door and around the building to her car. Mint parked and opened the trunk. "Oh, no!" There was all of Ben's camping gear, and not an inch of room for eggs.

Slamming the lid shut, she unlocked the passenger side and pushed the seat as far back as it would go.

"We'll have to put them in the front floorboard and the seat, I guess. If we need more room, it's the back by the car seat."

"You're just going to the church, right? So, you outta be fine." Bobby carefully loaded the eight dozen eggs, softly closed the door, and told Mint to drive slowly. He wished her a Happy Easter and went back in as Mint drove away.

Mint stopped at the four-way and said a quick prayer about which way to go – straight or left? The church was just across the stop, and she decided straight would be best. She pulled out and the next thing she knew she was hit! The car lurched heavily to the left as she saw a car ramming into the passenger side. Her first thought was *'It was my turn!'* and the next thought was *'The eggs!'*

She closed her eyes and turned her head to the right and opened them just a little bit. Then moaned. "Oh, no, oh, no!" She threw her head against the headrest and started wailing. A part of her knew she was overreacting, she knew the hormones were kicking in. But she couldn't stop crying.

She heard someone banging on her window and turned to see a distraught man's face peering at her. When he saw her move, he opened her door. "Are you all right?"

Mint continued to sob. "Broken, all broken; what about dying? Oh, what will the children do?"

His eyes widened. "Don't move." He looked back over his shoulder. "Edna! Call 9-1-1! Quick!" Then he turned back to Mint. "I'm going to check on the other driver. Don't move!"

She squeezed her eyes shut. How could this have happened?

The man walked over to the other driver. "Are you hurt?"

"No, I'm okay." He was getting out of his car. "The sun was so bright I didn't see the stop sign until I was right on it! Then the pavement was wet and I just kept on sliding. Didn't even see the other car till I hit it." Trying to peer into Mint's car, he asked. "Are they hurt?"

The other man lowered his voice. "It's just one girl. I think she's hurt pretty bad. She's moaning about something being broken and dying. I told her not to move."

The driver paled. "Oh no. I won't be able to live with myself if she dies."

Mint heard sirens and cried even harder. This was the second wreck she'd had in less than a year. What would this do to her insurance? Ben was gonna kill her!

Her sobbing was interrupted again. "Ma'am! Ma'am! Are you all right?" She turned her head to see a uniformed man squatted down next to her. "Don't move. We are going to check you out. What do you think is broken?"

"Everything! All broken. What about dying now…"

"Ma'am! There will be no dying now!" Mint cried even louder. He turned to his partner. "She's delirious. We have to be very careful. Could be a head injury." He stood up to get the stretcher and when he turned back around, Mint was hopping out of the car. "No! Lady, don't move!"

"Why not? I can't stand to sit in that mess any longer! Just look! All eight dozen broke when that idiot hit me and it's all over me and the car. I'll never get it cleaned up. Where is he, anyway, I wanna give him a piece of my mind!"

She turned and showed the EMT her dripping, sticky right side, from her hair down to her knees. "What the heck is that?" He asked, taking a step back.

"Eggs. Eight dozen eggs, all broken. I'm supposed to have them to the church right now for dying. What are the kids gonna do now?"

"You're not hurt." He said it flatly.

"No, but somebody's gonna be. Where's the fool that hit me?" She squinted her eyes and looked around. It was obvious who the guilty person was, as he looked sheepish and more than a little scared. "You! Look at this mess!" She walked up to him and poked her finger in his chest. "As soon as we get out of jail for all this, you are going to go straight to the store and buy eight dozen eggs, and take them immediately to Sweetapple Baptist. Got it?"

"Uh, sure. I'm sorry about everything. But I don't think we're gonna go to jail." He turned to the EMT. "Are we?"

"I can't believe she's not hurt." The EMT shook his head.

"Well, I could have been! I had a baby three weeks ago. It's a wonder I'm not half killed."

The EMT perked up. "In that case, I need to at least check your vital signs, make sure you really are all right." He grabbed his blood pressure cuff and started putting it around Mint's arm.

Traffic was backing up and Mint saw Inez Parish get out of her car, see her, eyes grow wide, and get back in. Mint groaned. The grapevine would commence any minute now. "Miz Inez!" She hollered. "Don't you tell nobody about this unless you start out with *'Mint ain't hurt at all!'*"

Inez stuck her head out the window as she backed her car up to turn around. "That's what I'll do, honey. Don't worry!" and she zoomed out of sight.

Then Mint gave one last dirty look to the other driver, saw the damaged side of her car and started wailing again.

****

Missouri sat on her front porch, Bible in lap. Dawn was just a few minutes away, and she shivered a little, even though she was dressed warmly. The phone rang and she knew it was either very bad news or Kizzie. "Good Easter mornin'."

"So you wadn't asleep. I didn't know if I'd wake ye up or not."

"I'm on the porch with my Bible. It's a bit arish out, but I'm doin' what Papa did. Remember how he got up ever mornin' just before dawn and went to the porch? Said one of these days the Lord is gonner split the Eastern sky, and just in case it was that partic'lar mornin', he wanted to be one of the first to see Him."

"I can just see Papa now, Missouri. I miss him and Mama suhum fierce, and me a old woman."

"I reckon it won't be too awful long fer either one of us. It'll be good to see them again." Missouri watched the sky carefully. "It's gonner be a busy day. Church and Easter dinner. I aint' seen the baby fer five or six days now. I bet she's growed."

"Prob'ly. Lit'luns grow mighty fast."

"Here comes the sun."

They were both silent for a few minutes as the sun made its appearance in pinks, purples, and silver. The world seem to come alive with its rising.

"Purty sight indeed." Missouri closed her Bible and stood up. "I guess I best be inside cookin' me some breakfast. It'll be a long while before dinner's on the table. Got to git all gussied up, too."

"Be shore and put on that Easter bonnet. I'll see you thar. Is Wylene and Herb pickin' you up too?"

"Yep. Later, then, Sister."

They hung up and both went to prepare for the day.

****

Sweetapple Baptist Church was full on Easter Sunday. The singing was beautiful, the preaching poignant. Everyone gathered around them to see pictures of the baby in anticipation of the real thing when Sarah turned six weeks, and much concern was expressed (with some humor) regarding Mint's wreck.

In a flurry of decisions, Wylene and Herb stopped by

their house to pick up the sweet potato soufflé and dinner rolls, with Missouri and Kizzie in tow. Georgia and Sam left to grab the ham and creamed corn. Georgia was calling Mint, who was supposed to already be at Missouri's to turn on the oven so they could warm things. Missouri had a pot of beans cooked, and onions, tomatoes, radishes and deviled eggs were in the refrigerator. Mint and Ben were providing dessert, and Missouri had hinted at coconut cake. She'd hankered after some more ever since her neighbor had baked one for her when she hurt her knee.

Both Georgia and Wylene had tried to convince Missouri to have it at one of their houses, but Missouri was adamant it be at the home place. "As long as I'm able, we'll have it here. Fer one day I may be too feeble." And that settled that.

Missouri asked Ben to bless the food. He stood, cleared his throat, and thanked the Lord for this day above all days, he thanked God for family and country, for the church they attended, and finally, after some time, he thanked God for the food, and asked Him to bless it to their bodies.

When he sat down, everyone was staring at him. He blushed. "I guess I got carried away." He looked at bit tearful. "I'm just so overcome since the baby. And I can't blame it on hormones like Mint does."

Missouri patted his arm. "It's all right, child. We all feel purty thankful. But you did remind me of a few preachers I've knowed." Grinning, she turned to Kizzie and told her how it reminded her of the story of the preacher saying the short benediction because the preachers had preached too long.

Kizzie cackled. "That was Preacher Clemmons! He also opened that service with prayer. He said 'Lord, I don't know this man. You do. Use him if you can.' Poor man was half crazy and his wife was the other half." Kizzie shook her head, grinning. "Do you remember when the Reverend James Folsom got called up to the Clemmons' household? Old man Clemmons sent word and told him to git thar quick, so the reverend got in his old truck and flew up thar to see what the matter was. Old man Clemmons met him thar on the front porch and told Preacher Folsom that Mizriz Clemmons' dog had died two days ago, and she had him laid out in the parlor on the couch, waitin' fer the Lord to raise him up."

"Land sakes! I don't recall hearin' about this, Kizzie. What in the world did Preacher Folsom do?" Missouri sounded shocked.

"Well sir, he took hisself a deep breath and entered thur house. Thar laid that old dog with a blanket and a sheet up to his nose, just like he's in a hospital or suhum. Preacher Folsom says, 'Mizriz Clemmons, I understand yur dog died.' And she says, 'No, God told me He was gonner raise him up, and I'm a'waitin'." Kizzie shook her head. "Preacher Folsom ast her would it be all right with her if he called somebody to check the dog to see if he was dead, and she said that would be perfectly all right with her.

"So, Preacher Folsom, he gits on his two way radio and calls the EMT's and tells old Roam Patterson to git thar quick with a shovel and a stethy-scope. Roam says 'I beg yur pardon?' and the preacher says 'You heard me and make it snappy!' Here comes Roam in the fire truck with the lights a'flashin' and the si-reen a'blarin', screamin' up the hill, and comin' to a screechin' halt in front of the house. He gits outta that truck in a hurry, and Preacher Folsom meets him at the door, explainin' the situation quick like. Roam approaches the couch, and pulls the covers back, gentle like, looks in the dog's eyes, and puts the stethy-scope on the dog's chest and listens. Then he slowly shakes his head and says to Mizriz Clemmons 'I shore am sorry to tell you this, ma'am, but that dog is dead.'"

"Oh, lord, what did she do then?" Missouri asked.

"She said okay, they'd have to bury him. So, she sends all the men folk out in the yard to find a decent burial place. They pick a spot under a bloomin' lilac bush. Preacher Folsom told Roam to git the shovel and start diggin'. Just as they had a hole big enough, Mizriz Clemmons made 'em stop and she run back in the house and got this beautiful quilt to wrap up the dog. Preacher Folsom says 'But that's a good quilt!' and Mizriz Clemmons, she says, 'And that was a good dog.'

"They bury that dog in the three hundurd dollar quilt, and then Mizriz Clemmons turns to the preacher, and ast him to say a few words over the grave. He did." Kizzie finished with a satisfied look on her face.

"Reckon what Mizriz Clemmons did after that?" Missouri wondered.

"Well, she went out and got herself another dog, what else?"

What else, indeed.

The family pondered this for a while and ate in silence.

Then dishes were washed, the baby held by all, a

declaration that there wasn't anything worth watching on the TV, and families got ready to go back to their own abodes.

It had been a good Easter.

CHAPTER SEVENTEEN:

Escape from the Hen House

    Missouri awakened early the Wednesday morning after Easter and felt right spry. For one thing, this morning felt like mid-March instead of mid-April, as there was a thin layer of snow on the ground, and it was still snowing furiously. "Happens ever onct in a while," she mumbled to herself. "Won't stay long though, April 'uns never do." She sat with her second cup of coffee and her seed catalogue, scribbling furiously. She knew she couldn't have a big garden, but she would still have a garden. "Let's see now, I want me some pole beans and cabbage, a few cucumbers and maters…" Suddenly she had an overwhelming need to call Ben and Mint's house. "What in the world?" she said aloud. "Lord, is suhum wrong?"

    Missouri got up from her chair. It took five minutes to find the cordless. She'd given up on it and reached for the kitchen wall phone, where she found the cordless lying on the counter. Under the wall phone. "These time savers sure ain't," she grumbled as she punched the number that would call Mint.

    It rang about eight times. She was just about to hang up when Ben answered the phone. Urgency colored her voice as she said, "How's Mint and the baby?"

    There was a bit of hesitancy in his voice as he said, "Sarah is just fine, Missouri. And Mint is, well…"

    "Tell her I'm fine too!" Missouri heard Mint screech in the background.

    "Oh my, Ben. Sounds rough this mornin'."

"Yes'um."

"Would you like to come visit me fer a little while so's you can git a few minutes to catch yur breath?"

Ben's voice lowered to a mere whisper. "Don't know if I can." Ben replied. "Escaping from here is like breaking out of the county jail. It can be done, but it ain't as easy as it looks."

Missouri chuckled. "What if I needed you fer suhum?"

"Missouri, are your chickens loose?" Ben asked excitedly, aware his every word was being eavesdropped upon.

"Well, I reckon they could be, I ain't looked out in the last little while," Missouri said in amusement.

"Don't you worry. I'm sure Mint can handle things long enough for me to come help you out."

"When can I expect yur presence, then?"

"I'll be there in half an hour, tops."

Missouri hung up, having herself a good laugh. That poor boy! Knowing Mint, he was suffering needlessly. She shook her head. She'd do what she could, for all of them. She went to the kitchen and decided she'd cook 'em up something that Ben could take back.

Maybe that'd help things out on the home front.

In less than ten minutes, she heard Ben come pulling up like his tail feathers was on fire.

She met him at the back door. He grabbed her in a bear hug, and Missouri thought she might smother he was so big and all. But at the last minute, he set her free. She looked in his face and them big blue eyes was full of tears.

"Here now, calm down. Set at the table. You want some coffee?"

Out on a Limb of the Family Tree

"No thanks. Water. A glass of water would be good."

She opened the refrigerator and hastily poured him a cold glass full. She set it down in front of him. "Mint floggin' you this mornin'?"

"Well, she's got something stuck in her craw. Things have been rough ever since we came home with the baby – hormones, lack of sleep – whatever. But this morning, boy, I'm surprise she ain't hit me. She threatened to."

"Well, that's a fine howdy do!" Missouri exclaimed. "What'd she do that fer?"

"It had something to do with the way I folded her T-shirts when I got them out of the dryer."

Missouri was silent for a moment. "Did anythang happen last night to git her stirred up?"

Ben shrugged. "We went over to some friends' house. There was us and another couple, plus the couple we visited. One of the women is about four months pregnant, and I thought she and Mint had a good time, talking about that, and all. We got home early, slept as good as any night we've had since Sarah was born." He thought a moment, guzzling water. "Since the wreck Friday, she's been worse. She's fretting about not having a car when I go back to school next week, if the insurance doesn't come up with a loaner."

"You know good and well Wylene and Herb would let ya'll borry one of thur vehicles. They got three."

Ben sighed the sigh of the doomed. "That was the first thing I thought of, and mentioned it right off to Mint."

"Well, what'd she say to that?"

"It was like tryin' to pet one of the roosters in a cock fight."

"Huh." Missouri never felt so sorry for anyone in her whole days. "Let me ponder on this a bit." She got up and walked to the door. "I'll be right back. Don't you go no whar."

"I won't." Ben sounded morose.

Missouri walked on out in the yard a bit, right to where her garden spot would be. She stood with her hands clasped behind her back, looking out at what used to be a great field for all sorts of work. "Now Lord," she began. "You put me up to callin' them childern. So Ben come to me on account of You. That means thar's work to be done, and I don't have any idey what to do." She shook her head. "Nary a one, Lord. Now I'm gonner go back in thar, and I will be trustin' in You and not a'leanin upon my own understandin', just like the Good Book says I ort. Amen." She took a deep breath, and thinking of Mint, muttered, "Little idjit." And headed back to the house.

Ben looked up when she opened the door. His eyes held pure misery. "I'm sorry to dump all this on you, Missouri. I know Mint is the apple of your eye. But I can't talk to my mama, she'd just lecture me how we got married too soon, had a baby too soon, blah, blah, blah. She means well, but that ain't the problem." Warming to the subject, he got a little brighter. "Why, I knew within an hour Mint was the one for me. And Sarah is nothing but a blessing from God." He slumped. "I just don't know what to do."

"Well, that apple of my eye, as you call her, is actin' a little too rotten fer my taste right now. I'll tell you what to do."

"Tell me and I'll do it!"

"Go home and demand Miss Mint git fixed up. Then

tell her I need her, I'm a cookin' dinner fer ya'll. Make sure the baby stays with you, she can nurse her right afore she leaves. I won't keep her more'n two ars. I'll git to the bottom of this, me and the Lord."

Relieved, Ben stood. "I'll do the best I can, Missouri."

"Stand up to yur full height, beam them baby blues down on her, and use a stern voice. She may cry a little, but she'll do what you say."

Ben's eyes widened. "Really?"

"And don't go abusin' that power either, mister."

"I won't." He took a deep breath. "Okay, here I go. And thanks Missouri. I knew I could depend on you to come up with something."

She waved him off with her hand, and as soon as he was outta sight, she heaved a breath. "I'm glad somebody knows it."

CHAPTER EIGHTEEN:

Hemmin' and Hawin'

About an hour later, Missouri got the call from Ben saying, "She's on her way", so Missouri laid slices of a roast she'd cooked in the oven to start warming. Mint drove up and came slamming in the back door. Missouri turned and looked at her, one eye brow raised.

"The door closes real easy like. You don't have to put so much effort into it."

Mint almost rolled her eyes. "Sorry."

"What's the matter with you?" Missouri laid her knife down and started rinsing her hands.

"I am mad as a wet hornet and I'm standing on my last straw!" Mint exclaimed. "I'm tired, I'm hormonal, and I can't get anyone to cooperate with me!"

"Well, now, what exactly does that mean?" Missouri poured water over the potatoes and set them on the stove to start cooking. "I thought everbody was bein' right nice to ya'll. You seemed purty happy Sunday at Easter dinner."

"I was. At least for the moment." The wind seemed to go out of Mint's sails. She sat down at the table. "I'm up one minute and down the next, and I understand that. We aren't getting enough sleep, I understand that. Ben is prob'ly stir crazy having to do so much at home, and he sure doesn't know how to do most of it right!" She looked down at the table as her chin began to quiver. "But that's not really what's bothering me."

"Why, child, what is it?" Missouri turned down the potatoes and came to Mint's side. Laying a hand on Mint's arm, she patted her gently.

She looked up at Missouri with tear streaked cheeks. "Sometimes being dumb hurts."

Missouri felt pain encircle her own heart. "Come here, honey-lamb." She pulled Mint to her and held her against her bosom. "You ain't dumb. You git mixed up sometimes, but that ain't dumb."

"Last night was awful." She sat up, wiping her eyes on a napkin she took from the holder. "We went out to supper with some friends. I sorta knew the other couple that was coming, and she's pregnant, so I thought it would be fun to talk to her and I knew they all wanted to see Sarah. We were at Devin and Suzanne James house."

Missouri nodded. "Wadn't she that cute little freckle faced gal that spent the night with you here onct, and she lost a tooth that night? Her mama was a Sanford, I believe. They's all raised up on Chigger Ridge, right past Hard Scrabble Holler."

Mint tried not to look impatient. "That's right. She married Devin James a few years back. Anyway, things were going along fine until Suzanne started to tell us about the robbery she witnessed."

"Land's sake! A robb'ry? Whar was she?"

"She was at Andrew Jewelry Store in Marietta. She was shopping for her mama a birthday ring. You know, where there are birthstones for the month of each of your children's birth? Suzanne has three siblings, so they thought four would make a nice looking ring. It's a pretty big store, and there was some rich lady going into the vault when six men came in with big guns. They had those boggin thingies over their faces and were screaming bad words and told everyone to hit the floor and stay face down. The store clerk musta hit the panic button because Suzanne said sirens started heading their way in just a minute. It made the robber guys mad, and one of them shot the clerk right in the head. Suzanne said it was awful, people screaming and begging and moaning. The cops got there and those masked guys started shooting through the windows. They killed a person on the sidewalk and wounded more. Suzanne was close to the window, and glass fell on her. She said she could hear outside and inside and it was terrifying. The robbers started hollering more, and shot one of the customers that was just laying there on the floor, she said she just knew she was next. Then she said her heart froze when she heard one of the policemen say: 'Fire at will!'" Mint started sobbing.

Missouri kept on patting her. "Well, that's all awful stuff. Musta been hard to hear, too."

"It was pretty awful. We were all listening, fascinated. And I shoulda kept my trap shut. But I couldn't figure it out, no matter how hard I consecrated, and I just had to ask. I looked at Ben and said, 'How did they know one was named Will? Did they recognize him?"

Missouri felt her heart sink to her knees as Mint continued. "For a moment there was, there was, *stunned* silence. Then everyone started laughing. I mean really, really, laughing at me. Even B-Ben. I tried to laugh a little and maybe some of them thought I was joking, but the other guy there called me 'Blondie' the rest of the night. Ben said he was sorry on the way home, he said it just surprised him so, in the middle of the story and all."

"I'm a- guessin' you never heared that sayin' before."

"No. Ben explained it to me. But I still felt I'd been bush hogged by my own husband!"

"You mean bush whacked?"

"See? I can't get anything right!"

"Well, you just have a, uh, way with words."

"And this morning I started thinking about how I'm always saying dumb things. Don't think I didn't see the look that passed between ya'll on Easter when I asked Ben if genetics were hereditary when I was saying I wanted Sarah to be like me. I know ya'll laugh behind my back a lot."

"We do not! You make us smile, but we ain't makin' fun of you, Mint."

"I'm so dumb!" Mint cried. "Oh, Missouri, what if Sarah does get my genes?"

Missouri felt her mouth twitch. "Now listen here. You ain't exactly dumb. Yur just...far fetched in yur thankin' sometimes."

"And am I really inbred?" She asked in a small voice.

"Aw, no. Preacher was second cousins to yur daddy's granddaddy. The kin is purty far off. Besides, if you live in these mountains long enough, everbody winds up kin." Suddenly it come to Missouri! She knew what to say.

"I growed up with a family who had a boy named Cleveland Grover."

"Wasn't that a president?"

"That was Grover Cleveland. Anyway, it's a wonder they didn't name him Grover Grover after the president, none of that fam'ly was over bright." Mint giggled, which was Missouri's intention. "Cleveland was made fun of in school because he had trouble catchin' on, and it made me and Kizzie so mad we'd threaten to tell on the boys if they was mean to him." She patted Mint again, absent mindedly. "You need to understand Cleveland didn't just have times when he was funny oops like you, he really struggled to git by. Take yur worst moment and try to live in it all the time."

"Oh, lord." Mint sighed.

"Plus, bein' a boy, it don't come across cute like it does on you. Fellers have always thought you was just sweet and innocent. They thought Cleveland was just plain stupid. But one day, the teacher invited a special guest to the classroom. Mr. Richardson, ar teacher, was always doin' things like that. He said he wanted us to hear about a lot of things from diff'rent people, so we would be as edgicated as he could make us. This here partic'lar guest was a artist. He was passin' thru on his way to Atlanna to do some kinda art show. He had gone to school with Mr. Richardson and they'd been buddies, was why he come to ar town. Well, sir, he stood up and was talkin' about art, and showed us some of his paintins' and explainin' how he went about such, and how he'd knowed since he was a boy he'd wanted to be a artist. Then he looked out over the class and ast if any of us had ever wanted to paint. And lo and behold, Cleveland's arm raised up, slow like. A'course, the boys hooted and said thangs like 'he don't mean paintin' the barn', and 'you'd just stick that brush in yur ear', foolishness. Mr. Richardson quieted the class down. When his friend ast Cleveland if he'd like to come up and try suhum on the canvas he had thar, even Mr. Richardson looked strained. I reckon he was afraid Cleveland would be made the fool, as usual. But Cleveland went up and dipped that brush, and in front of my very eyes, ar teacher's own likeness appeared! In just a few strokes, too!" Missouri cupped Mint's face in her hands and looked her right in the eye. "What I'm sayin' is, everbody has weak spots and everbody has strong spots. You got plenty of strong spots."

"What happened to Cleveland?" Mint asked, appearing to have missed the point.

"He was accepted after that. Nobody made fun of him anymore. Mr. Richardson's friend tried to talk Cleveland's fam'ly into lettin' him journey down to Atlanna and take some courses, but they needed him on the farm. So he farmed. But he drawed a lot, and all the town went to him fer fam'ly portraits and such. When the new church was built, he did the picture of the Lord that hangs in the vestibule. He married a girl that wouldn't a give him the time of day before. They had six childern, I believe. And one of them went on to school to become purty famous, though I cain't recall her name."

Mint smiled. "Thanks, Missouri. You always make me feel better. I know I'm not all dumb. It's just things take me by surprise so much, and it makes others laugh. It gets old being the brunt of the joke all the time."

"I reckon that's true, honey. But in the end, be glad you can make 'em laugh, and laugh with 'em."

CHAPTER NINETEEN:

Family Reunion

When Georgia had called Missouri two weeks prior and informed her there was going to be a huge family reunion during the Fourth of July holiday weekend, Missouri thought about flatly refusing to go. But Georgia was all excited about showing off her first great-grandbaby and having all the family there together. So Missouri had swallowed her ill temper and said nothing, except, "What do you want me to brang?"

Georgia asked her to make a cobbler (peach or blackberry, either one would be fine). "I'm frying up chicken, Wylene is making potato salad. Ben said he'd make slaw for him and Mint to bring, and will you ask Kizzie to bring some of her pickled beets and some chow-chow?"

"Don't you thank it's high time Ben has a little talk with Mint about takin' back the chores of her own home? The baby is three months old."

"Mama, you know Mint. She'll milk this for all it's worth. I figure Ben will get fed up soon enough and we'll hear the big bang when it happens."

"That child is spoilt rotten, Georgia. Nobody's fault but Wylene and Herb's, especially her daddy. But I reckon yur right."

That had been two weeks she'd had to dread this family reunion. When it was all said and done, except for her immediate family, Missouri thought the lot of them was worth stayin' away from. "It'll prob'ly be the last one I have to fool with anyway." She muttered to herself. It usually took them five years to get over one, and Missouri figured if she was lucky, she'd done be passed over and Home before the next one got off the ground.

Mint was beyond excited, knowing Sarah would probably be the youngest there and preened over non-stop. And, of course, she'd want to show off Ben too. "Two feathers in her cap." As Kizzie put it.

And then, worser happened. Ben found out his family reunion was the same weekend and some fool decided to do 'em together! Missouri took her blood pressure reading faithfully, thinking maybe it'd be up a little bit and she'd have to stay home…but no.

They'd rented a giant camp ground and set up funeral home tents for people to sit under, as well as being situated next to the creek with lots of grills, and a pavilion with a refrigerator. The pavilion also sported picnic tables with ceiling fans overhead. Missouri told Georgia if she didn't get to sit at one of them, she'd make Sam take her home.

The big day arrived. Missouri tried to find the coolest dress possible and grumbled the whole time she was making the cobblers. She couldn't decide which, so she'd made one peach and one blackberry. She might not want to go, but she'd be durned if she'd be out done by some fool on Ben's side of the family!

Georgia said every single person was to bring enough food to feed at least four people, that way it was assured no one would go hungry. Kizzie had about split a gut when Missouri had repeated that little tidbit of information.

She went on the back porch to see if there was a breeze of any sort when she heard the phone ringing. It was Sam.

Their car had overheated about half way to Missouri's house. Sam had walked to Kizzie's to use the phone, and now he was overheated. Wylene and Herb were going to come get everybody, it would just take a while. "Now how in tarnation is all of us gonner fit in Wylene's car? That's six people!"

Well, Sam wasn't sure; she might have to have Mint and Ben come get her. Since he and Georgia were already at Kizzie's house, they'd make sure she got there with them. He'd call her back in a minute and let her know.

Missouri slammed the phone down and went back to sit on the porch. "Cars ain't worth a toot." She muttered. "Give me a good mule any day."

With that thought, a smile flickered across Missouri's face. There'd never been a mule before or since like Roddie.

The family had taken the horse drawn carriage to church that Sunday because it had been so cold, for the carriage was enclosed, unlike the wagon. When they'd stepped out of church there was snow everywhere, underneath a layer of ice. The way home had been treacherous and taken a long time. Half frozen by the time they got there, Papa had let them out at the back yard next to the porch and lower field.

When they had gotten out of the carriage the first they thing saw was their mule, Roddie, completely encased in ice. He was somehow trapped by a tether tangled into the old barbed wire fence. Unable to move around, he'd been helpless to do anything but stand there and take whatever the weather doled out.

He looked like a giant snowman in the shape of a mule,

but it was one of the most horrifying things Missouri had ever seen. And the most horrifying of it all, was that she knew she had been the one to leave the tether on him the night before, in too big a hurry to go back and eat supper.

Papa had turned to the squalling Missouri and Kizzie and told them to run as fast as they could and get Pozie Bottoms, he would be the only one what might be able to save Roddie.

As odd as Pozie's name was, no one had ever made fun of him. Standing several inches over six feet with skin blacker than night, he was respected. Not only for his size but his way with animals, which was better than any veterinarian Missouri had seen as of yet.

When Pozie gets there, he is out of breath from running. He takes one look at Roddie and big tears start streaming down his face, "Lawd have mercy," he whispers, then turns to Papa. "I done sent Lit'lun after Sir. The Lawd showed me I'z goan need hep here."

Kizzie and Missouri are right behind Pozie, riding on his horse, Lucy Belle. Pozie wouldn't have it any other way, so they'd ridden while the grown man had run.

Pozie Bottoms and Sir Elfe, who was also bigger than any other man Missouri had ever seen (then or since, because he was even taller and broader than Pozie) had come from slave stock owned by George Bottoms.

The reason Pozie and Sir's family were still neighbors after all these years, was when George had become elderly and near feeble, his only son, Lucious, had taken up with 'town trash' and sired an illegitimate baby. George had become enraged, not just because of this, but because his son would not take care of the child once she was born.

George had financially provided for them instead, setting up a small house and allowance for the mother.

Then he had called his lawyer, and writing Lucious out of the will entirely, left everything he had (which was substantial) to Pozie and Sir's family, splitting the rich farm land down the middle. George said the Nigra community had been more of a family to him than his own son.

The two men, Posie and Sir, had worked for him as hired help since adolescence. George's family had treated the two slave families, from which Pozie and Sir had descended, good enough that the sons had worked on after their freedom had been declared. Pozie's family had long ago taken on Mr. Bottom's last name, and Sir's family had taken on George's wife, Hilda's, maiden name.

Sir's mother had died shortly after his birth, leaving him an orphan. Just before her death, she had named her baby boy Sir, saying everyone would have to call her boy Sir now, whether they liked it or not.

Hilda Elfe Bottoms had not thought it quite so amusing, because there was no other female, black or white, to help raise Sir. So she'd done a substantial amount of that herself. Pozie's mama helped too, and was officially the one, as far as the community understood, raising the baby. But she was pretty busy raising her own seven children, and working hard for the Bottom's family as maid and cook and gardener and whatever else was needed. And since the black women had pretty much raised George and Hilda's son, Hilda figured fair enough, but would have never said that to her friends. The Bottoms may have been good to their workers, but the workers were Nigras, none

Out on a Limb of the Family Tree

the less.

No one but George knew how much his wife did take care of Sir, (or for that matter how much she loved him) and she would have been unable to face people if they had known.

Papa always told the naming of Sir Elfe story with amusement. He said when his Pa heard Sir's name for the first time he laughed until he couldn't catch his breath, then he'd laughed again. Said that woman was one smart Nigra, naming her boy that.

No one in Missouri's family had been allowed to say nigger, and had been taught to call them by their proper name. Missouri thought Nigra was correct until recent years, when they'd started calling themselves Black. She had never used 'colored' even though most folks had started doing that years before Black came into vogue, because she always wanted to do what was right.

Pozie said they needed to get the frozen mule warm, but he was afraid to do it too quickly, thinking it might thicken the blood too quick and 'muck up his innards'. He and Papa were attempting to move Roddie around, hoping to work off some of the ice, when Sir appeared. The three of them got the ice off Roddie, and wrapped Mama's good quilts around him, then half carried, half walked him to the house. With much cooing and persuasion, Roddie was walked up to the back porch, then the men pushed him into the kitchen. When Mama had protested at this, Papa had said, "Hush, Mama. This mule's been with me all my life. He's like a brother, almost."

Pozie and Sir had both nodded their heads in vigorous agreement, saying, "Yes'um, me too, yes'um, me too," and stroking that mule's back like he was their child.

Mama had the wood stove fairly hot, a back log in place so that dinner stayed warm until they got home. She'd put kindling in and got a blaze going. Missouri and Kizzie had gone around the front and lugged in a log through the parlor (as they couldn't get in the back on account of Roddie filling up most of that area with his giant hind parts), and Mama had stoked the fire.

Missouri and Kizzie had been instructed to get to the barn and find everything they could in the way of burlap sacks and whatever else to start drying off Roddie, as the ice was melting fast. Papa had looked at Mama and warned her with words and a look that her fine towels might have to be put to use. She'd put a fist to her mouth, eyes tearing up, but nodded mutely, and went to get what she could find.

Roddie had even got to eat most of the vegetable soup Mama had prepared for their evening meal, which had been kept hot in the stove's warming oven.

Mama's fine quilts, Mama's kitchen, Mama's best towels, and even Mama's vegetable soup, saved Roddie with the help of good neighbors and prayers all around.

But ever after Roddie had little to do with Missouri, throwing dirty looks at her whenever she got near.

That mule malingered as long as he could, knowing a good deal when he saw it. Every time he walked past the back porch, he attempted to turn in to it instead of continuing to the barn, harnessed up, or no. And every time Mama made her vegetable soup, you could hear Roddie hee-hawing out in the pasture, begging for some 'just like a dog under the table' Papa always said – and Papa always *snuck him a little bit of soup after supper, just like he would of a dog.*

****

"Thar must be two hundurd people here, at least." Kizzie said when Missouri finally arrived with Ben, Mint, and the baby. The pavilion was off limits for sitting, as that's where all the food was being placed, but the family had secured three tents, with big floor fans blowing into them from the pavilion. Georgia, Sam, Wylene, and Herb were to Missouri's right; Missouri shared her tent with Kizzie, Ben, Mint, and baby Sarah, who had a portable playpen in which to sleep. Ben's Mother, Cora, as well as Cora's mother, Gertie Carroll, sat to Missouri's left.

Missouri knew that Cora had Ben late in life, but was surprised that Gertie looked close to her age, instead of Georgia's. She leaned sideways and said in a loud voice, "It's nice to meet you, Mizriz Carroll."

"Eh, don't bother with the Mizriz. Just call me plain old Gertie."

"And it's Missouri to you, that's what I allow everbody to call me. And this here," she pointed, "Is my sister, Kizzie."

"Ain't we got us a fine baby?" Gertie asked, nodding toward Sarah.

"Law, yes. I prayed I'd stay around till I got to see me a great-great-grandbaby, and here she is."

Gertie laughed. "Now, Missouri, you better be a-prayin' fer suhum else to keep you here."

Missouri looked thoughtful. "I reckon we don't never say we's ready to go on Home unless we're a-painin' bad.

But I'm near ninety, so I guess I ort to 'spect to go on any time now."

"I'm near eighty myself. But I expect no such thang. I like it here just fine. Why, I wouldn't mind stickin' around and watchin' Say-rey here grow up and have her own young'un."

Missouri's eyebrows went up. "Well, that'd take some doin'. Folks live that long sometimes, but they's scarce as hen's teeth."

Gertie nodded in agreement. Then she looked up and frowned. "Lord help. Look who's a'comin' this way. It's a pure-t lie and it's dressed up like Fannie Renee Butler."

"She must be on yur side since I ain't never heared of her." Kizzie said.

"That's a true and unfortunate statement. And we are about to hear from the considerable depth of her ignorance. That woman wouldn't know the truth if it snuck up and took her by the throat. I cain't never recall a time she's been able to tell anythang without messin' it up with exaggeratin' and right out lyin'."

"That's a shame, that is." Kizzie warmed to the subject. "I don't know what makes some folks that way, but I seen a lot of them in my lifetime. Why, I remember old Shade Oakley. He would tell a yarn about his own mama, and her a'standin' right thar listenin' with her mouth hung open from the shock. On top of that, he was so lazy you couldn't blow him off the porch with a stick of diney-mite! And he was a ornery cuss too! He wadn't worth killin'."

"Don't sound like it." Gertie shook her head in sorrow. As she looked up, Fannie Renee came straight toward her. "Here goes it." She muttered and plastered a smile on her face.

"Hello, Cousin Gertie!" Fannie Renee shouted.

Gertie pursed her lips. "I ain't deaf, Fannie Renee."

"Of course you aren't." Fannie Renee yelled, patting Gertie on the shoulder. Her speech was slow, with an air of condescending superiority, and her voice was that of a nasal, rust worn hinge. "And who are these lovely young ladies with whom you are conversing?"

"I'm Kizzie Martin and this here is my sister, Missouri Pickett."

"It's so nice to meet you both. Are you twins, Mrs. Pickett?"

"No." Missouri didn't offer the usual 'you can call me Missouri'.

"I almost missed this reunion!" Fannie Renee continued on, fanning herself with her hand. "I've been on a business trip in Europe and just flew in yesterday. I'm exhausted! I must look a fright."

No one disagreed, and for a moment there was dead silence. Then Fannie Renee saw Sarah in the playpen. "Oh! What a beautiful baby! Is she your grandchild, Mrs. Martin?"

"No. She is Missouri's great-great-grandchild."

"How wonderful for you, Mrs. Pickett! You must be so proud. Why, I do believe she looks like you!"

"That's what everbody sez." Missouri deadpanned. Kizzie snorted.

"Well, girls, I must be moving on. You know how everyone expects me to speak to them individually."

"Yur Aint Ivy is a'settin' over thar by herself. You ort to go speak to her." Gertie said.

Fannie Renee's face fell a little. "I suppose you're right. But I sure dread it. You know how she whines."

"I reckon that's why she's a'settin' by herself."

"Well, here I go! Tata!"

"Tata." All three mimicked in tandem.

They watched Fannie Renee totter off in her spike heels. Every step she took, she sunk in the ground. "Reckon she'll break her neck afore the day's over?" Kizzie asked curiously.

"Nah. She won't stay much longer. She's exhausted, you know." Gertie said solemnly.

Then all three snickered as they waited on the next visitor.

They didn't have to wait long. Ben's cousin, Mike Teague, wandered over. He started talking once the introductions were over and all eyes in four tents were completely glazed over by the time he started bragging about who all his sister was acquainted with. "Let's see." Mike bent his head in concentration. They all admired the blooming bald spot on top of his head. "I think she was one of the Gibson girls."

"Like the hair!" Mint said brightly. Everyone turned and looked at her questioningly. "Um, that's a little hairdresser humor. It's an old style. We use it sometimes for girls...who, uh, go to the prom, or something." She finished in a mutter.

Mike was quiet for a moment longer, then giving Mint a scathing look, he continued. "Anyway, her name is Debra and she married either an Eves or an Adams, I can't remember which. What I'm trying to get at, is, she works at the CDC in Atlanta!" He puffed his chest up a little.

"What does them letters stand fer?" Kizzie asked.

Mike's eyes got big and he looked irritated. "I can't believe you don't know!"

Wylene leaned forward and said, "It stands for the Center for Disease Control, Kizzie."

"That's right," Mike said, nodding his head. "It's where they work on new germs, new strains of stuff, like the flu epidemic and such." He actually winked.

"Is that so?" Missouri asked.

"Yep. And she's very important there. And she's my sister's best friend."

"Is yur sister a'comin' to the dinner today?" Missouri looked at him suspiciously, as though his sister might be hiding behind his back.

"I don't know if she can make it. She says there was something real important at work in Atlanta today."

"I hope nobody ever invites yur sister to any dinner I'm at." Missouri said flatly.

Georgia looked shocked. "Mama! Why ever not?"

"Ain't no tellin' what she might pick up! Goin' around with that friend, why lord, Armageddon could fall right into her pocket book!" Missouri leaned toward Georgia. "If that girl shows up, let's us make shore we sit sommers else."

Ben was doing everything in his power to stop it, but finally he could control himself no longer, and he laughed until the tears came. That made everyone else twitch. At last, all the family was laughing, even Mike a little bit. Since he had no idea what he was laughing about, he moved on quickly to visit elsewhere.

When the time to eat finally came round, Missouri was

as ill as a sore tailed cat. She was hot, she was hungry, and fed up with some of the strangest people she'd meet until the next one of these reunions rolled around, if she was still alive to put up with this foolishness.

And to beat all, right when Herb had put her plate down in front of her some fool cousin twice removed decided that was the time to put her toy poodle right in Missouri's face. "Git that blame thang outta my face!" she had exclaimed, whopping the dog a good one. The dog yipped, the cousin was furious, and Herb had to start all over with Missouri's food.

The other highlight during dinner was when one of Kizzie's children, (Sumter, who'd gotten himself bailed out of jail) was holding Sarah and decided to hold her way up over his head and jiggle her. Kizzie had hollered at him, "Lord help, don't pitch that baby in the ar! You'll turn her gizzard plum over!" Sumter's feelings were hurt, Ben was half mad Sumter had dared treat his baby that way, and it took fifteen minutes to calm everybody down from that.

People mingled a good bit after the eating, and Missouri had to admit it was nice to sit with a full belly and watch the goings on. She squinted just a bit as she saw a tall woman headed their way. "Yonder comes yur cousin, Betty Jo."

Mint frowned. "I don't remember her."

"You know, she's that real sweet gal who become a teacher."

Mint's eyes widened. "The math teacher?" she asked in horror.

"Oh, fer land's sake, Mint, she ain't gonner ask ye to cipher. She cain't be all that bad, she married a preacher."

Out on a Limb of the Family Tree

Mint watched the tall woman as she smiled and spoke her way across the yard. But the sun kept glinting off her glasses so her eyes couldn't be seen. "Oh, lord," Mint breathed, as Betty Jo headed straight for her. Mint closed her eyes. "Please let me remember my multiplication tables."

Missouri and Georgia looked at Mint with a mixture of awe and disbelief. "Mint, honey, I know you was scarred by that awful Mr. Thompson, but all math teachers ain't pure devil. This here woman is nice. Trust me."

"Okay." Mint said in a small voice. Straightening herself up, she put on a smile and embraced Betty Jo's hand with her own.

Betty Jo cooed at the baby and had Mint eating out of her hand. Not once did she ask Mint any math questions, and soon was on her way to find her husband so they could leave.

Just as the musicians started tuning up, Kizzie poked Missouri in the ribs. "Look who's headed ar way."

"Who is it? I don't recall that face."

"It's Amaryllis Patterson, that's who. Remember her daddy, Ira Peevy?"

"I shore do. Little bitty feller. Sold liniment and such door to door. He was knockin' at the door of Fancy Whitecap —what *her* mama was thankin' I'll never know, namin' a child such as that, maybe that's what made her so all fired ill all the time — and the door flew open. He got caught in all that calamity. She was slangin' a belt toward all her childern at onct, knocked the clock right off the fireboard, and busted it all to pieces. Then she clobbered him!" Missouri cackled right along with Kizzie.

"Said he told later it was the worst whippin' he ever got, even from his pa."

They both wiped the tears from their eyes and composed themselves just as Amaryllis closed in and had a fit over the baby.

The guitars, banjos, and keyboard were brought out, and singing began as dusk settled. Gossip stopped, visiting stopped. The day was finished with a prayer from one of the many preachers attending. It was a very long prayer. Missouri firmly believed that what finally stopped the man was Sarah's whimper turned into outright screaming to be fed.

Missouri teased Mint on the way home about pinching the baby. Mint grinned. "I was about ready to. I thought that man would never shut up. Seemed to me he was giving a speech to be heard instead of praying to the Lord."

Instead of being scolded like Mint anticipated, Missouri laughed. "Reminds me of a revival years ago when all them long winded preachers stood up, one right after another. All of them had preached but one, and he was somewhat tetched in the head, so no one ever ast him to preach outside of his own church. But it was a bit glarin' to just plain old ignore him, so the last preacher of the day ast him to do the benediction. He stood up slow like, as he was old and stiff, and lifted his face to the ceiling. Word fer word he prayed: 'Lord, we know, and You know, we been here far too long. Amen.'"

Ben and Mint whooped. "What happened then?" Ben asked.

"They filed out quiet like, but thar was a lot of grinnin' bein' hid behind hands."

Out on a Limb of the Family Tree

Ben and Mint saw that Missouri got in the house. Mint told her she'd see her mid-morning about getting her old jeans let out so she could wear them now.

Everyone was exhausted and Missouri couldn't wait for them to leave. She was in her bed within the half-hour, and asleep before her head hit the pillow.

She slept with a smile on her face, amazed at all the goings on she had witnessed that day.

People was a wonder, wadn't they?

CHAPTER TWENTY:

A Day in the Life

Missouri heard a knocking on the front door. She'd nodded off in the chair and it startled her, so she had to sit a minute to get her bearings. She finally opened the door to Wylene. "Ain't you early?" she asked, yawning.

"No. Were you asleep?"

"Guilty as charged. Dozed off, I reckon." She turned back around and really looked at Wylene. "Why, you got on specs!"

Wylene sighed. "I know. Glasses make me look worse."

"That's not so. They look right nice on you."

"I don't mean they hurt my looks, I mean now I can see, and I look worse than I thought."

Missouri hooted. "Child, you don't look a day over thirty-five. How old are you gittin' to be, anyhow?"

"Grandma age." Wylene sighed again. "I think Sarah being born has made me feel old. And then I had to get glasses because my arms are suddenly too short. I'm forty-one, Missouri. And I don't much like it."

"Wait till yur nearly ninety-one and come talk to me about it." She patted Wylene on the back. "So it's gonner be us girls this afternoon, is that right?"

"Correct. The men folk are going to the football game in Atlanta. Big deal to them, foolishness to me."

"Let them boys have thar fun. They don't hardly git to be anywhar we women folk ain't. I reckon if I was a man, I'd git awful tired of me."

Out on a Limb of the Family Tree

"Nobody gets tired of you, Missouri. In fact I wish I could be with you more."

"Yur my onliest grandbaby. 'Course you do." She glanced at the clock. "And speakin' of grandbabies, whar's yurs?"

"You know Mint, forever late. Mama said she would be late, she's baking a cake, and said it'd have to cool some before she could wrap it."

"That's an excuse I can live with. I got green beans and cornbread cooked, and I have taters and okry cut up to fry. Fried pork chops early this mornin'. Got a big fat juicy Vidalia onion, too. Mint said she'd brang tea, she shore does make good sweet tea."

Wylene laughed. "That's because she puts so much sugar in it." She cocked her head. "Is that thunder?"

Missouri went to the door. "Shore is. Looks like a storm's a'brewin'. Hope they git here before it starts too fierce."

About that time Mint arrived. She pulled up close to the back steps and handed her Mama the jug of tea. She went back to the car to get the baby as thunder rolled around them.

She barely stepped onto the porch when the thunderstorm moved in like a two year old's temper tantrum. Suddenly the branches on the trees were furiously whipping back and forth, and as they hurried into the kitchen, the loud squalling of the rain was overpowering.

"Hope we don't lose the lights." Missouri hollered over the racket. They sat huddled in the living room, Sarah sleeping soundly through it all. In about ten minutes the storm stopped as suddenly as it started, the clouds moved out, and there was nothing but clear skies and sunshine.

"Sweet baby Sarah will give you a fit one of these days like that storm just throwed." Missouri commented. "I remember the fits yur grandmama could throw. Laws have mercy! The best thing I larned to do was ignore that child till she was done. Anythang else and she'd just git worser. I was beginnin' to thank she was tetched in the head or suhum."

"Speak of the devil, there's Mama now." Wylene said.

They all got up and went to the back porch, Sarah beginning to stir. "Looky thar!" Missouri pointed to a big toad frog on the walk. "When I was little I liked to put the top of a empty acorn shell on thur heads fer them a little hat. They just set thar blinkin' up at me and let it set on thur heads. My Papa told me one time it looked like it had on a yarmulke. I ast what in the world was that and he explained it was what Jewish boys wore on thur heads. After that I always thought toads was boy Jews. Then a Jewish fam'ly moved in to Sweetapple and me and thur little girl got to be fast friends. When I told her all toads was Jewish boys she laughed till she couldn't stand up. Embarrassed me to death. She was real kind to me after, though. We wrote to each other after she moved. She was kilt in a plane crash in nineteen-hunderd and sixty. Miss her still."

Georgia handed the cake to Wylene, picked up an acorn shell, and put the top on the toad's head. He did exactly what Missouri said he would, blinking up at them in his little beanie. Shaking her head, she climbed the steps and they all went in to cook dinner. "Whar's Kizzie?" Missouri turned to ask her daughter.

"Said she had a headache and asked if I'd wait till

dinner was ready and come back and get her. It's just two minutes away, figured I could do it when we put the bread in the oven."

"I ain't talked to her since this mornin'. She didn't say nuthin' about the headache then." Missouri frowned.

"Now, Missouri, you know as well as we do that headaches come on you quick like sometimes." Wylene shot Georgia a look.

"She told me she was taking some ibuprofen and laying down till I got there. She didn't sound bad off or anything, Mama."

"True enough, I reckon." She turned to Mint. "I thought you was gonner git here early so I could may-zure that new dress of yurs that needs hemmin'."

"I *knew* I was forgettin' something!" Mint huffed. "Sarah was crying, and Ben was trying to leave, and the dryer cut off, and I plumb forgot. Can we do it day after tomorrow? Sarah has a pediatric appointment tomorrow and that will probably be all I can take in one day."

"I'll check my dance card and let you know."

Mint giggled and hugged Missouri. "Thanks, Missouri, you're the best."

"I'll just hafta find my pankin' shears so's I can trim it good. Don't want no ravelin' when I try to hem that kind of material."

They bustled about and Missouri called Kizzie to tell her the bread was in the oven and Georgia was on her way. "You all right?"

"I reckon. Just the dad burn headache. Cain't stand them thangs. But the ibuprofen's made me perk up a right smart, so I'm ready to journey on over thar."

"Maybe that'll put the quietus on it."

"Lord, I hope so. Here she is, honkin' the horn. That'll make my head better." She groused as she hung up.

Missouri grinned. Kizzie sounded all right to her. And she looked fine when she got there.

"Boy, you sure smell good, Kizzie." Mint told her as she hugged her great-great-aunt tight as she entered Missouri's kitchen a few minutes later.

"Thank ye. I didn't have time fer no bath, so I washed up as fer as possible, then I washed down as fer as possible," With a twinkle in her eye, she finished. "And then I washed possible!" She cackled and slapped her knee.

"Lord, Kizzie, that's plumb awful!" Missouri exclaimed.

"Aw, hush, Sister, you have said worser yurself."

"That's truth." Missouri agreed, and everyone laughed.

As soon as they got dinner on the table, and blessed it, they began talking a mile a minute.

"Sakes Alive! I near fergot to tell you, Missouri. Mizriz Mentor Patterson passed away. Cain't say as I remember her first name."

"Elvira or suhum like that. Mr. Patterson was a ferner from up north sommers. I bet she was a pill to live with."

"When my young'uns was purty small," Kizzie said. "Mizriz Patterson had me over fer tea or some such foolishness. I had to excuse myself, and while I was in her bathroom, I looked in her drawers, uh, searchin' fer a aspren. It was like openin' one of them canned tricks full of snakes that jump out at you."

"Ort not to a'been snoopin'." Missouri said. "Remember that daughter of hers? She was older than you,

Georgia, by a year or two, I guess. She was sorrier than the bottom of a greasy paper bag. Her whole house was like the wreck of the Hespers, and her childern was heatherns, carryin' on all the time like they'd had all ten toes stepped on at onct. She died drunk as a skunk, she did, and owin' her own child a thousund dollars."

"I didn't know she had children, Mama." Georgia said.

"Two of 'em, as I recall. I reckon they's still livin', but I don't know thur given names."

"Wadn't she at the lady's social at the church that time Kendall Brown made a spectacle of hisself?" Kizzie asked.

"I thank so. Lord, what a calamity! They was havin' one of them lady's socials at the First Baptist Church in Whistle, and Kendall Brown showed up, come to eat. He was crazy as a bess bug and everone just sorta tolerated him. His mama died, and his wife left 'cause she couldn't put up with him no more. The sheriff had already put him in jail twice fer peepin' tom business, but he was fairly harmless. Just somewhat alarmin' to be mindin' yur own, and turn around, and old Kendall peerin' into yur winder. Anyway, he eat at ever fune'ral and fam'ly gather'un he could catch, so it weren't no surprise when he showed up at church at the end of the social fer the goodies. Why, he was prob'ly standin' and peerin' in the winder thar to see when it was time to eat! Well, sir, he had cake and ice cream and a cup of tea. Mizriz Applegate insisted on the tea so's she could use all her best china that had come straight from Angland. Then he excused hisself and went to the men's room. In about five minutes, lo and behold, he come out as nekkid as the day he was borned! He strolled in thar like it was nothin' unusual to appear at the lady's social circle buck nekkid. All across the room, at least five of Mizriz Applegate's fine china salad plates crashed to the floor at the same time. She was so mad about the dishes she tried to have poor old Kendall arrested on destruction of private property!"

"What did they do with the man?" Mint asked, eyes big around as saucers.

"The preacher heared the ruckus, and come down and escorted him back to the men's room, and had him put on his clothes. Then he took him home. Mizriz Applegate called the sheriff and he just laughed at her fer wantin' him arrested."

Sarah began to stir and Mint got up to tend to her, which broke up the hen party. The others started clearing the table when the phone rang. Georgia answered it and told them it was Ben on the phone. The game had been rained out. They'd stopped to get a bite to eat and were almost home.

"Soon as we finish up the dishes I guess I better scoot on home. Kizzie, do you want me to take you?" Wylene asked.

"I'm ready when you are. I'm tard and needin' my nap."

"Don't fergit yur pocketbook like you did last time." Missouri warned.

"I got it settin' here by the door. Can I take a piece of that cake home fer later?" She asked Georgia.

"Of course. Mama, you keep a piece for yourself, too."

"I's plannin' on it, child. Wylene, you ready to ride?" Missouri asked Wylene as she watched her load up her arms with clean dishes and her purse.

"I am. Going home to let Herb regale me with tales of woe about missing out on a ballgame." She kissed Missouri, Mint, the baby, and her mother and sailed out the door with Kizzie in tow.

"Mint, don't fergit day after tomorrow fer us to hem that dress." Missouri said.

"I won't." She pecked Missouri on the cheek. "See you then."

"Is there anything else I need to do before I go, Mama?" Georgia asked Missouri.

"I reckon not. Ya'll left the kitchen in better shape than it was afore ye got here." She walked Georgia to the door. "You drive careful on them wet roads."

"I will. I'll talk to you tomorrow. Call if you need anything before."

"I will, Sugar. Tell Sam hello."

Missouri closed the door behind them, glanced at the clock and decided she'd feed the chickens and call it a day. She was tard out too.

CHAPTER TWENTY-ONE:

Rain, Rain Go Away

Missouri woke up as the grey dawn pushed through the rain clouds. She snuggled down under the quilt, stroking the outside of it with a smile. This was the quilt her mama had made her when Missouri was a girl, and she'd been sleeping under it ever since. She listened to the storm. The thunder was now a distant rumble, lazy and slow. The rain beat steadily on her tin roof, a serious melody if she'd ever heard one. She reckoned she'd get up d'rectly and fix breakfast, as she had a hankerin' for blackberry pancakes, but for now, as long as her bladder would allow, she decided she'd lay right here.

The phone rang about five minutes later, jerking her mind back into her bed. She'd been dreaming about a boy who'd been raised out on Wolf Pen Gap…what was his name… "Hello?" she answered.

It was Kizzie. "Mornin' to you, Sister. A good rain, ain't it?"

Missouri stretched, thankful for the cordless phone the kids had given her for Christmas. "It's so good I have laid right here in this bed listenin' to it."

"Well, what I called fer is to ask you if you know whar I can borry one of them zee-rocks machines."

"What in the world would you want a machine fer?" Missouri rolled her eyes. "I swan, Kizzie, you can come up with the most confounded thangs."

"I need me copies of papers about Sumter, that's all. And I don't want nobody's nose in the middle of it, copyin' and sneakin' looks the whole time they's doin' it."

"I don't know, but I'll ask Georgia if you want me to. I'm sure her or Wylene will know."

"Thank ye kindly. I knowed some of yur young'uns would figger it out fer me."

"Yur welcome. Now, I's dreamin' about a boy we used to know. Raised out on Wolf Pen Gap. A real looker, too. Know who I'm talkin' about?"

Kizzie was silent for a minute. "Well, now, I thank I do. Hmmm…was it Cot somebody…"

"Aiken! Cot Aiken! Lord, remember that purty strawberry blond hair and them green as grass eyes? And he could sang better'n anybody I ever heared, then or since."

"Truth. Reckon why you was dreamin' about him? I ain't thought of him in about a hundurd years."

"Me neither. I'll have to ponder on the why." Missouri rolled over and sat up. "I'm gonner have to hang up. Bladder's callin'."

"You let me know about that zee-rocks machine, here?"

"I will. Don't fret." Missouri hung up and rubbed her forehead. "Lord, my head's just a-thobbin', as my Papa used to say. I need me some breakfast right quick."

After breakfast, Missouri took her a cup of coffee and sat down on the back porch in her rocker. The rain was gently dripping off the eaves, and a light mist still fell from the skies, giving the morning a cool break from the late summer heat.

Closing her eyes and thanking the Good Lord for all her blessings and this day ahead, Missouri let herself drift back to girlhood...

She and Kizzie went to ever dance they could talk Papa into attendin', because the only ones they could go to was the ones Mama and Papa went to.

*Cot Aiken was a tall, lanky fella and he was at ever dance. He sang like an angel, played the fiddle nearly as good as Papa, and that was sayin' a lot. He and Papa would spell each other on the fiddle, which gave them each a turn at dancin'. And Cot could dance anything that was called. All the girls loved him, but none of them was **in** love with him, not until Kate Hillsong moved to town, and then it was all she wrote.*

Cot led the singing most times at church, especially during revival time. That giant mop of hair would swing back and forth as he led the singers, and them green eyes twinkled so much you could see them all the way to the back pew.

After him and Kate got married, he'd laugh and say it's 'Cot n Kate' anytime they'd come calling. Kate got pregnant ever time Missouri did, but she had the babies, and Missouri lost them. So, when Kate came to call after they come home with Georgia, Kate was plumb tickled. Told her they'd been 'a'prayin' up a storm' fer her and the baby and 'it was a blessin' to see the baby so healthy.'

Missouri had cried, both tears of sorrow and joy, and of course, Kate took them all for the joyous kind.

After a while, Cot and Kate and their three (or was it four?) children had moved to one of the Carolina's where someone had offered up a job to Cot where he could teach and lead a choir in a big fancy high falutin' church, and teach fiddle too!

Her and Kate wrote to each other four or five times, Missouri guessed it was.

It was some years later she learned they'd had another child who had been severely disabled in some way, but they had all rallied around, and that young 'un was took everwhar they went. Named him Cleaborn, Missouri thought.

Missouri reminded herself to chew this over with Kizzie when they talked again this evenin'. But of course, by then, she'd forgotten all about Cot and Kate Aiken.

Mint had called mid-morning saying Sarah was sick with a high fever and they were on their way to the pediatrician with her. Missouri fretted for an hour, then called Wylene.

"I haven't heard yet, Missouri. But I think Sarah has an ear infection. She was fussy yesterday, pulling at her ear some. You know how that happens to babies."

"Papa used to blow tobaccy smoke in ar ears if they hurt. Helped, too."

"I guess the heat, don't you?"

"I reckon. You promise me you will call the minute you hear."

"I promise."

Three hours later, Mint called. It had been an ear infection, they'd given Sarah meds for pain and fever and she was already feeling better. "The only reason I called you in the first place, Missouri, was to pray."

"Well, I did plenty of that. You just let me know when thar's a conclusion to suhum."

"I always will. I won't leave you hanging."

Then Missouri had gone out to the chicken house and

one of her hens lay dead. Body was still warm. In spite of herself, Missouri felt tears prick her eyes. She reckoned everything had to die eventually. But this hen didn't look sick nor had it been attacked. Strange, she thought. Made her skin crawl.

Two hours into the afternoon her electricity went off. She called and they didn't know what was wrong, so she sat two more hours in the cloudy darkness waiting on somebody to do something. Too dark to read, no TV and she knew Kizzie was down for her afternoon nap while she watched them soap operas.

By the time the power came back on, she was in a foul mood, for sure.

Fixin' her supper she realized in all the to-do she'd fergot all about askin' anybody about a durn zee-rocks machine for Kizzie! Turning off the stove, she called Georgia and told her what Kizzie was wantin'. Georgia said she'd call her right back.

Just as Missouri put the first forkful of food to her mouth, the phone rang. It was Wylene, saying Herb could take the papers with him to work and copy them. It would cost Kizzie ten cents a page.

"I ain't got no inklin' how many pages she's got, Herb, but I'll talk fer her and say she'll pay it."

Missouri ate her supper, cleared the dishes, fed the chickens, put food out for the wild cats, watched a moment from the door as they came running to eat, then called Kizzie.

They talked about the zee-rocks business, and Kizzie like to had a hissy fit, but said she reckoned she'd have to pay, even if it was 'highway robbery'. Then, after a brief argument over that, they discussed Sarah's ear infection and how the old way of soothing a ear infection was probably better, but they wadn't gonner stick their noses in the young'uns business.

Missouri hinted around, wantin' to know what kind of papers it was Kizzie wanted copyin', but Kizzie was shut mouth about the whole thang.

When she told Kizzie about the hen she found dead, Kizzie just preached she needed to get rid of the whole lot of 'em. No sympathy there!

Missouri grumbled to herself after she hung up that the whole day had been like tryin' to hug a porcupine.

Just before she went to bed, she called to see how the baby was and Ben answered. Baby was doing fine, he said. And when Missouri told him about the hen, he was upset and sympathetic.

Somewhat mollified, she got ready for bed, read her devotionals, turned out the light, and was nearly asleep when she remembered that she hadn't mentioned Cot and Kate Aiken to Kizzie. Well, maybe tomorrow would be more pleasant and it would be a nice conversation of reminiscence.

****

Kizzie died early the next morning.

Missouri had just got up and was cooking her breakfast when Ben drove up. Her heart lurched in her chest because he was crying, and she saw no signs of Mint nor baby.

"Dear God in Heaven," she whispered as she opened the door. "Tell it now. I cain't wait no longer."

"It's Kizzie, Missouri. She passed sometime this

morning, I reckon. Sumter found her a little while ago."

Missouri felt immediate relief and intense grief at the same time. "My baby sister," she said softly, and sat down at the kitchen table. Ben pulled up a chair and sat close to her.

"I'm real sorry, Missouri."

Missouri nodded. "T'was bound to happen to one of us sooner than later. I just figured it'd be me, somehow." Tears glistened in her eyes. "But Kizzie had a rougher life than me in many ways. And I thank she was scared of me dyin' afore her. She ain't got good fam'ly all around her like I do." Missouri patted Ben's hand. "My fam'ly keeps growin', too."

Ben smiled a little. "I sure am proud to be a part of it." He cleared his throat. "Do you want us to go to the funeral home in a little while? I think her body is still at the hospital right now."

"Who found her this early in the mornin'?" Missouri asked, glancing at the clock. She and Kizzie usually had their morning arguments an hour from now.

Ben's eyes held a flicker of concern as he'd told Missouri only a minute before. "Sumter," he repeated. "I don't know why he was there. I do know he had some kind of spell, and they rushed him on to the hospital too."

"Ain't no surprise thar. He's a weaklin'. I'd rather wait a bit afore we go. Have you eat?"

"Not yet. Georgia called and asked me to get here quick like before someone else called you or came by."

"Well, I got biscuits in the oven, and sausage in the pan, and aiggs ready to fry. Might as well make good use of the waitin' time." She stood and braced herself against the chair, but still staggered a little as she headed for the stove. "I reckon you'll have to help me some, Ben. This news has made me all feeble."

Ben helped her back to the chair. "You need some coffee while I finish cooking breakfast." He reached over to the pot, poured her a cup, checked on the biscuits and turned on the eye to start the sausage frying. "How do you take your coffee?"

A shadow of a smile crossed Missouri's face. "I take a little coffee with my cream and sugar, I reckon."

Ben took care of that, pouring in the half n half and scooting the sugar bowl close to her. Then he flipped the sausage over, and stepped over to the sink to wash his hands.

"You shore know yur way around a kitchen, fer a man."

"I was a bachelor for some years. And Mama, well, she's a fair cook, but she ain't never been all that excited about it. After Daddy died, she sorta gave it up and I took over what little cooking we did. Now she goes out to eat with some other ladies three or four times a week, and she lives outta cans and boxes the rest of the time."

"I remember after Preacher died I couldn't stop cookin'. It was a solace to me. Funny how we all handle grief diff'ernt." Ben saw a tear streak down Missouri's cheek. His own chin trembled in response. "I missed him so bad. Still do. And now, looks like I'm the last to leave. I cain't hardly thank about what I'll do come night time, and Kizzie not on the other end of the phone to tell me what to do about gittin' rid of chickens and such. I'm shore gonner miss that bossy old thang."

Silence followed as Ben cracked eggs, took up the biscuits and sausage, and started frying the eggs. In spite of the emotional upheaval, his stomach was rumbling with anticipation. He set their plates down and Missouri asked him to bless the food. "Lord, please nourish our bodies with this food. We are troubled this morning in a way only You can comfort. Please, Lord, give us Your strength and comfort today. We thank You that Kizzie has just stepped over and will be waiting for us all. Amen."

"Amen." And they commenced to eat.

****

Soon, a flurry of family began arriving, first Georgia and Sam, who had already been to the hospital and seen to the arrangements of getting Kizzie's body to the funeral home. Wylene and Herb came as soon as he finished off some business over the phone so he didn't have to go to the office, and lastly Mint and the baby, both bawling their heads off.

After everyone settled down, Missouri asked to be excused. "I just need to be by myself fer a little while. If ye can stay off the porch, I'll go set a spell in my rocker. I mean don't come out thar unless I holler, which I won't." As she started out the door, she turned. "And no snoopin' out the winders nor door, neither." She gave them her best glare and walked out.

As she sat there, an incredible sadness filled her, just as she knew it would. She bowed her head, letting tears fall onto her lap. She looked at her gnarled hands and wondered why she would be surprised that Kizzie passed. They both had far outlived God's promise of three score and ten. Plus, she knew Kizzie always was adamant about going first. Well, she'd got her way. "Lord, I know it ain't none of my business about Kizzie goin', or me either, as fer as that goes. But I don't know if I can do this. Seems like another lonesome tomorrow is more'n I can take."

She got no answer, no comforting word. Missouri sighed heavily. "It's true I miss Preacher ever day. But it's also true I don't want to leave yet. That baby puts another anchor here, that's fer shore. I'd like to live long enough fer her to remember me, at least a little bit." She shook her head. "O'course I don't want to suffer none while I'm here. Ain't that just like us? We want it all clean and neat. And Lord, I do thank Ye that Kizzie musta not suffered a'tall. Seems she went to sleep and left her body easy like. That's a blessin' I thank Ye fer."

She raised her head and looked out over the back yard, into the fields. She wondered idly who'd go first, her or that poor old barn. The cats had seen her and were sitting watching her. She could hear the chickens once in a while, clucking, and a cackle as one of the girls laid an egg. It was already warm, but wouldn't get blistering hot any more. September had arrived and the worst of the hot days were over.

"Seems like it will be good weather fer the fune'ral, Kizzie. I remember part of what you want, but I hope you got it wrote down sommers. Them young'uns of yurs will be a'fightin' before yur in the ground if ye don't. Probably will be anyhow. Hear me now, I ain't gonner have no part of it. They'n kill each other fer all I kere. I know you got Mama's table and chairs and a few other doo dads, but I'll faint dead away if they offer to let me have 'em fer my remainin' years. That's fact. I reckon you are doin' more happy thangs right now, anyway. I bet Mama and Papa shore was glad to see yur face! And Homer and Preacher, too." Her voice became a whisper. "And my three babies. William, the one nobody knows about here – though I've made sure my obituary says three babies, and told old Vernon at the fune'ral home not to let nobody change it-" She choked up. "And Georgia's mother that birthed her. Let her know what a fine woman ar Georgia has been."

She studied a few more minutes, searching her heart. She believed she could make it now. She heaved herself out of the rocker and stood for a moment. Then, squaring her shoulders, went back in to be with her family.

CHAPTER TWENTY-TWO:

Happy Birthday, Little One!

March, 1999

Missouri awoke to the sound of banging on her back door. She glanced at the clock as she tried to sit up straighter in her arm chair. "I done it agin!" She exclaimed. "I'm a'comin'! Stop bangin' on the door!" she hollered.

She stood for a moment, to be sure she wasn't going to have one of her 'spells', then hobbled on into the kitchen.

"Missouri, are you all right?" Wylene had a frightened look on her face.

"I'm fine. Just went to sleep in my chair accidental like. I'll hurry so's we won't be late."

"No, no, I'm a little early anyway. You look fine. There isn't going to be anyone there but family and Ben and Mint's friends, the Thompsons, with their baby."

"I heared they was in thur-pee."

"What kind of therapy?"

"Marriage. One of my friends from church called me and said they was in trouble with money and him drankin', so she said git help or I'm gittin' out with the baby. Said she weren't raisin' no baby with a drunk."

"Oh, my! I hope it helps. I don't think she works outside the home."

"I heared she dudn't do nuthin' if she kin hep it."

Wylene shook her head. "We are standing her gossiping about people we hardly know. Shame on us! Go get ready so we can celebrate little Sarah's turning a year old."

Missouri shook her head. "I cain't believe that child is a year old. My, my."

She washed her face, tidied her hair, changed shoes, and stuck a stick of gum in her mouth.

"I'm ready. Such as it is."

"Make sure you've got your door key."

"Right here." She held it up. They locked the door and Wylene helped her down the porch steps. She opened the door and Missouri got in the back, saying howdy to Herb who was waiting patiently in the car. It pained her heart to get in that empty back seat, when Kizzie had always been there waiting on her before. Missouri reckoned she'd miss Kizzie for the rest of her days. The missing didn't seem to get any better as time went by. Of course, her family made sure she was checked on. Somebody called her every morning and every afternoon if they didn't come by. There were very few days she was alone all day, but it happened. The pastor came by once a week, and his wife called twice a week, like clockwork. Missouri figured they had a schedule they went by. She still had a few friends (all younger) that checked on her some. Still had her chickens and feral cats, but everybody was trying to talk her out of getting any more chickens. She only had four hens left, and although she wouldn't tell anybody for the world, she, too, was thinking seriously of not having any more chickens after these were gone. She was just getting too feeble to get out much on her own. And the cats, well, they came up on the porch now to be fed, as long as she went back in the house after she put the food down. She sighed heavily.

"You all right back there?" Herb asked.

"Just fine. Are they gonner let Sarah have at the cake like some of them pitchers I been seein' of babies, with it all over 'em?"

"Beats me. I don't care as long as I don't have to clean up the mess."

Wylene laughed. "That's always been Herb's motto."

"Sounds like a good 'un."

They pulled into the driveway of Ben and Mint's tiny house. Georgia and Sam were already there, and there was a strange car that Missouri supposed was the Thompson's.

Sarah squealed when she saw Wylene and reached for her. She gave her a big sloppy baby kiss on the cheek, reached for Herb, did the same, reached for Missouri, and did the same. Then she took Missouri's face in her chubby little hands and said "Wuv!"

Georgia laughed and told Mint she had some competition for Missouri's attention. "Hers and everybody else's!" Mint said, laughing too.

Mint came over and hugged Missouri herself, extra long and hard. "I miss coming over there every day, Missouri. Sarah keeps me so busy I don't have the chance sometimes."

In reality, Mint did well to get to Missouri's a few minutes a couple of times a week. But Missouri understood, truly she did. She remembered how Georgia had kept her in circles the first two years. "It's fine, honey. Just glad to see you when you kin git over. And what a day today is fer blessins' galore!"

Mint smiled. "Let's get settled. I want you to meet the Thompsons, too."

The Thompsons were sitting on opposite ends of the

living room, and Mrs. Thompson looked fit to kill over something, and would dart a look at Mr. Thompson occasionally like she was going to snatch him bald headed. Missouri glanced at Wylene and raised her eyebrows. Wylene shook her head a little.

Introductions were made, presents were doled out, (Missouri had given Ben and Mint a gift certificate that Georgia had picked up for her), and then the cake was brought out. One fat candle was in the middle and Sarah had help blowing the candle out. The Thompson baby and Sarah were each given a cupcake to make a mess of while the adults ate from the real cake and added ice cream to it.

There were many photographs made, and when Missouri was told she'd get a framed picture of herself with Sarah, she was satisfied. When the five generation picture appeared in the Sweetapple Weekly, she was thrilled. For once, Missouri kept the phone lines hot, calling everyone she had a speaking relationship with. She got out the church directory to make sure she didn't miss anyone. She even called Kizzie's children, painful as that was. (Although there was some satisfaction in hearing envy in their voices).

She had that picture and article framed too. It was the first thing she checked on in the mornings, and the last thing she checked on at night.

By the late afternoon, the non-speaking to each other Thompsons left, and Sarah had gone to sleep in Missouri's arms in the rocking chair.

It was more than Missouri could ask for of any day.

CHAPTER TWENTY-THREE:

Well, I'll Be Dogged!

Georgia opened Missouri's back door. "Mama?"

"In here!" Missouri hollered back. "I'll be out shortly."

Georgia heard the flush, and Missouri appeared. "I cain't believe I left that back door unlocked agin. I'm gittin' older by the minute."

"You didn't. I knocked and you didn't answer so I used my key." Georgia held up the key, showing Missouri. She was smiling, big.

"What's so blasted funny?" Missouri asked, giving Georgia a stern look.

"We have a surprise. I haven't been this excited since Sarah was born."

Missouri's eyebrows rose. "You and Sam got suhum to tell me?"

"Ha, very funny, Mama. But that's close." She stepped back to the door and nodded to Sam, who was still in the car. "He's coming."

As Sam stepped up on the porch, Georgia opened the door for him. In his arms was a wiggling puppy. "Meet Winston."

Missouri shook her head. "Ya'll shore are brave." She stepped toward the puppy who wiggled even harder, his black mask split by a big old doggie grin. "Now, what kinda bulldog is this 'un?"

"He's a full blooded Boxer, Missouri. Ain't he purty?" Sam beamed.

"That he is." She stroked his fawn colored fur, making

Winston whine in ecstasy. "I reckon if you put him down he'll pee ever whar."

"Probably. But I'll clean it up if he does." Georgia said.

Sam put the dog down and he immediately peed in the floor, then tore around the room as fast as he could.

"Acts like you put a stick of dinny-mite under his tail."

Sam laughed. "They tell me he'll be that way for about three years."

"Then does he drop dead of a heart attack?"

"No, I reckon he just calms down." Sam stooped a little and whistled. "Come here, boy." Winston immediately turned and zoomed toward Sam, banging into him and licking his hand furiously. "We are gonna sign him up to obedience school."

Missouri snorted. "Wish they'd a'had that fer you, Georgia."

"From what you tell me, Mama, it wouldn't have done much good."

They watched as the puppy began to wind down, then fall dramatically in the middle of the floor, instantly asleep.

"Come on and take advantage of that nap and drank some coffee." Missouri headed for the coffee pot and Georgia put down three cups as Sam cleaned up puppy pee.

As soon as they got settled, Missouri, nodding toward the sleeping pup, began story telling: "Thar was a man named Trudy Wilson some years ago. He was one of the meanest men I ever knowed of. He was mean to his wife, she was as cowed down as you can git. And I reckon he was just as mean to his daughters, fer they was as bad off as thur mama. Had one boy, name of Thomas. And he was the sweetest boy you'd ever want to meet. He tried to be good to his mama and sisters, mostly havin' to stand up fer 'em and make up fer what his pa weren't.

"Old Trudy had bulldogs, like yurs here, but rougher. The males was big old thangs, I'd say weighin' up toward a hundurd and fifty, if not more." Missouri laughed. "Tale is old Trudy hired a feller to do some work up under his wagon, so he was on the ground, half under and half out, fixin' suhum, and one of Trudy's old bulldogs come and laid down across the feller and went to sleep. Poor man couldn't git him off, and he laid thar nur two ars afore the dog got up on his own, and ambled away. Said that man cussed old Trudy and swore he'd never come back fer nuthin'.

"Anyway, Trudy bred them bulldogs to brang down wild hogs when he was a'huntin', and they brung down bulls some, too. But he weren't no better with the dogs. He kept one bitch at a time. When she had pups, he'd pick out the finest male, and sell the others. If he didn't sell all the females, he kilt them poor little thangs. Said he didn't need but one bitch at a time, so he'd get shed of the rest, one way or the tuther. They was folks that come at the last minute to git a female pup, just to keep 'em from bein' kilt." Missouri shook her head, in memory and disgust.

"Anyhow, what goes around comes around, they say. I don't know whar his fine male dog was, but Trudy was by hisself in the pasture, and a bull got agitated. Gored him and stomped him near to death. Thomas heared the commotion, and set the bitch they had on the bull. I reckon she saved old Trudy's life, what thar was left of it. The doc come, of course. Said thar weren't nothin' he could do fer

Trudy other than sew up the gashes. Give him some sort of medicine fer the pain and left him. Trudy suffered suhum awful, and it didn't git much better as time went by. Mizriz Wilson had to nurse him. Only help she had was one of her daughters. The other one refused. Said she hoped he died and suffered a lot afore he did. Other ladies tried to talk to her, tell her she was just makin' it hard on her poor old ma, but the one time she went to the sick room, they said she just stood thar, grinnin' at him, and then spit right in his face afore she walked out."

The puppy whined in its sleep. "Story's so bad it's upsettin' the baby's nap."

"It is awful, Mama. I just can't imagine treating your daddy that way, even if he was mean."

"That's because yur daddy loved you good'ern anythang. Of course you cain't imagine it."

"My papa was pretty stern," Sam said. "But he was fair and I never doubted his love for us."

"I guess the Wilson's never doubted the lack of it." Missouri shook her head. "Anyway, months went by. Thomas got married and brought the wife to live thar on the farm. She was a sweet little thang, and she did help Mizriz Wilson. I guess she didn't have no hist'ry with Trudy, so she was able to put up with his foul mouth, and blame it on his pain, not his nature.

"It was comin' up on Christmas, and they had a tree in the front winder fer the first time. Trudy never let 'em celebrate what he called 'foolishness of the most expensive kind'. Mizriz Wilson and her daughter-in-law cooked a fine Christmas Eve dinner, and the daughter that was willin' to help her ma, fed her pa afterwards. He was wastin' away purty bad, but they said he eat good that meal.

"Thomas went out after that, and a while later come back with one of the finest bull dog pups anybody had ever seen. Seems he'd heared about a man who'd kept one of Trudy's bitch puppies, then bought a male from another state and bred 'em. First litter resulted in one giant pup, so Thomas scraped up money and purchased it. He took it in the sick room and told his pa 'Merry Christmas'. His pa took that pup's looks in. Thomas was a'holdin' it so its paws hung over Thomas's forearms. Old Trudy told Thomas to brang that pup closer. Said it had the biggest feet he ever seen on a pup. Fine head, perfect mask. Pronounced they was to name it Brute. Thomas said, 'Well, all right, Pa, that's what we'll call her.' Old Trudy actually sat up half way. Said 'What you mean brangin' a bitch puppy in here to me?' Thomas always spoke real soft like, but he told his pa it were a female that brought him into the world, and he knowed she was a mean 'un. But that his pa was just like her, and hadn't bothered to look around at all the fine women in his life. Told him it were a female that saved him from the bull, and it was females what was savin' him right then. Trudy snarled at Thomas, and swatted so as to knock that pup off the bed. But as Thomas reached to catch it, that puppy got her balance. She turned on old Trudy, hackles raised and teeth bared, growlin' fer all she was worth." Missouri laughed out loud. "That was one female that weren't gonner take no mistreatment from Trudy Wilson! Said old Trudy sat back, shocked, and then commenced to laugh. 'Might be we ort to name her after yur sister yonder. But Brute she is!' he declared. As soon as Brute calmed down, he held out his hand, and that dog never left his side much after that.

"Well, sir, the day after Christmas the preacher come to visit. He happened in about the time Trudy was speakin' worser'en harsh to Mizriz Wilson. That preacher marched in the sick room without so much as a fare thee well, and give Trudy the what fer. Rained hellfar and damnation on that man, I reckon. Quoted scripture about how the good Lord Hisself treated women. When the preacher finally run outta breath, Trudy said he shore was glad he had come because he'd been thankin' on it and knew he needed the Lord. Said that sweet little Brute had showed him how wrong he was, but that he hisself didn't know how to stop bein' what he'd always been." Missouri sighed. "Ain't the good Lord wonderful? Took a lowly creature like a bulldog, and got a man saved."

"Mama, how in the world do you know that story?" Georgia asked.

"That would be because my best friend was married to Thomas."

"Miz Rheba! She always called him 'her Tommy', didn't she?"

"That's truth. But everbody else called him Thomas. They was married sixteen years when Thomas up and had a massive heart attack at thirty-six years of age. Left her with a twelve year old daughter. Rheba just kept on livin' with Thomas's ma and sister. And when his other sister was widdered some years later, she moved back home, too. So Trudy's house was filled with women fer years. Fact is, Rheba died last year and I reckon her daughter lives on thar."

"That's terrible that Thomas died so young!"

Missouri nodded. "And that dog died the very next night. She was nigh on to fifteen or so, I reckon. Buried 'em together, too. And if you don't thank that caused a ruckus at the church house! Nobody much wanted the dog buried in the graveyard."

"How'd they get it changed so they got their way?" Sam asked.

"Well, sir, the preacher stood up and said unless somebody could show him in the Bible whar it said not to do such, and if they couldn't find nothin', and still didn't allow it, why, they could be findin' thurselves another preacher, cause he wadn't gonner stay with a bunch of self-servin', superstitious, religious hypocrites."

"Wow! I don't think our church would allow it today."

Missouri sighed. "Prob'ly not, child."

"What I'd like to know is what the tombstone says." Sam shook his head. "That's one I'd like to see."

Missouri thought a moment. "I know Rheba spent money she didn't have fer a tombstone big enough fer all the engravin'." Missouri cleared her throat and recited: 'Thomas Albright Wilson and Brute: Both used by God to do good works.' And the dates, of course."

"Was Rheba buried alongside them?" Georgia asked.

"She is. Hers said: 'Rheba Hollister Wilson: Loved by both."

Georgia sniffed. "That's the sweetest thing I've ever heard."

"Sweet maybe, but I don't want Winston buried with me." Sam said.

Georgia glanced at her watch. "Sam, we have to go. I've got a Bridge game with the girls in an hour."

"Free time fer Sam!" Missouri grinned at him.

"Well, fact is, Missouri, it makes me kinda nervous when she goes to play with them. They are all widows but Georgia. Sorta creepy." He shuddered.

Georgia rolled her eyes. "Good grief Sam." She leaned in and gave Missouri a cheek kiss. "Bye Mama. We'll see you Sunday if not before."

"Sam, don't you thank fer a minute I don't know that pup is really fer Sarah." Missouri said, patting the puppy on the head.

His eyes lit up. "Won't she fall in love with this puppy? She'll be beside herself!"

"That's truth. Ya'll take care." As she started to close the door she hollered, "Especially you, Sam!" He laughed and waved.

Missouri watched them as they drove away, shaking her head. That puppy was gonner be a world of trouble. But she reckoned she knew by now: you'd do anything for a grandchild. Even put up with a puppy.

Missouri and Kizzie were sitting in the middle of a revival meeting when Thomas Wilson purely ran up the middle aisle, sobbing like a much smaller child than he was. Missouri remembered looking wide eyed at Kizzie, wondering what could be causing Thomas such sorrow. The preacher stopped preaching and got on his knees at the altar with Thomas, soothing him in soft words no one else could hear. In a moment, Missouri's Papa was on the other side of Thomas, and slowly Thomas calmed down. Nodding his head, he stood to his feet. The preacher put his arm around Thomas's shoulder and Papa sat down on the front pew.

Out on a Limb of the Family Tree

"This child is in trouble, folks. He has just accepted ar Lord Jesus Christ as his Savior."

The amens and praise the Lords rang out, but the preacher held up his hand to stop it.

"It is right we should rejoice, as the angels in Heaven are rejoicin' as we speak. But this boy will be harmed when he goes home to share this wonderful news with his family. His ma is with him. If his pa finds out they's here, he will consider it his business to do what he wishes with them both."

There were mutterings in the congregation. Some men were outraged, some uncomfortable because of 'their business way' of mistreating their own children and wives.

About that time the doors flung open and Trudy Wilson marched in. He glared at Thomas and yanked his wife up from the pew. With a jerk of his head, he motioned Thomas to follow as he half drug, half carried his wife out of the church house. A few men stood to stop him, but Thomas pleaded. "Please don't. It'll be worser if you do." And then he followed his parents out.

Ten days later, Missouri's Papa was one of the three folks who witnessed Thomas's baptism in the creek. Not exactly secretly, but oh so very discreetly.

Missouri shook her head, hands cupped around a cooling cup of coffee. Thomas Wilson had grown up to be a fine man. And she thanked God right then and there that Trudy lived the last few months of his life learning how to be a man from his son.

CHAPTER TWENTY-FOUR:

True Tall Tales

"Pure foolishness," Missouri muttered as she stood at her closet in her slip. She had three good Sunday dresses for this type weather, and now she'd have to put on the grey one she had planned on wearing Sunday. All because Georgia insisted she go to the surprise birthday party at the church for the preacher's wife. Missouri had declined at first, but Georgia had chided Missouri, reminding her how much the preacher and his wife had done for her. "That's truth." She muttered again. Georgia had also fussed on her because she said Missouri just wasn't getting out enough lately. "Hmmph! That's my business." Seemed to Missouri, the older and less inclined she was to go anywhere, the more determined her family was to make sure she was somewhere besides home!

Didn't they know she was just plain tired a lot? She never missed church (yet), and her home was always open to any of them that wanted to visit. She knew they was all just afraid she'd give up if they didn't push. "And that's my business too."

Georgia arrived and helped Missouri with her hair. Finally finding her hand bag, Missouri said, "Let's git this show on the road. I ain't wantin' to stay a long time, neither."

"Oh, Mama, you'll enjoy it once you get there and start talking to everyone."

And she did. There were about twenty-five women there, ranging from their twenties to Missouri, and the food was good to boot.

Someone asked why the walls in the fellowship hall matched, save one. "That's because we had a far one time." Missouri told her.

"A fire! When was that?" The preacher's wife asked.

With the older members putting their heads together, they came up with sometime around the mid-nineteen sixties. "And it's a wonder the whole thang didn't burn to the ground." Some of the women smiled and nodded, already remembering what Missouri was going to tell. "You all got to remember Sweetapple was even littler then than it is now. Ar po-leece chief was also the far chief. And he weren't no genius, neither. His name was Rail Duncan."

"Surely that wasn't his proper name, Missouri." The preacher's wife chimed in again.

"Oh, no. I thank his proper name was Jack. But he was so skinny he had to run around in a rain storm to git wet. Somebody musta seen smoke comin' from the church house and found Rail. So he gits in his fartruck, turns on all the lights and si-reens and heads out to the preacher's house."

Everyone started to laugh, and the preacher's wife looked confused.

"Rail, he banged on the house till the preacher come to the door wantin' to know what in the world was wrong. 'Preacher', he sez, 'The church is on far!' The preacher is dumbfounded. 'What! Then why are you here?' By now old Rail was bugged eyed. 'I ain't goin' in no church house in the middle of the night! It's too dark and skeery.' So the preacher hopped on the truck and they went and put out the far before it got too big."

"Why was this man scared of the dark so badly?" The preacher's wife asked with curiosity.

"Always was a common thang. People thought they was haints in church houses. Especially old 'uns like this."

The younger ones were shocked to hear this, and the chattering got louder until Missouri spoke up again. "Rail was tetched a little, anyhow. When he was a young'un they had a hard time with him larnin'. Plus he stuttered suhum awful."

Georgia looked alarmed, knowing where this was headed. "Mama, I'm not sure you should tell that story here."

But pleas from the audience drowned her out. Missouri grinned and continued. "Rail's mama was tryin' to bake a pie and realized she didn't have enough sugar. So she told Rail to go over to her sister Martha's house and borry some. Now, Rail was only four years old, and Martha lived across two yards and two good sized gardens, but he didn't have no roads to cross, and besides, it was safer back then. Folks didn't thank nuthin' of young'uns bein' off by thurselves.

"Rail gits to his Aint Martha's and try as she might, she cain't understand what it is he wants. She holds up shortnin'. He shakes his head no. She holds up flar. He shakes his head no. Finally, despurte, she holds up clothespins. That child exploded in a fit. 'Hellfar, Aint Marfie,' sez he, stompin' his foot. 'You cain't wheaten no pie wif dam cwosepins!"

The younger ladies looked shocked that Missouri would use that language in the church, but the older ones guffawed. When the preacher's wife tittered then laughed outright, the rest did too.

Wiping her eyes, the preacher's wife sighed. "I've heard that the preachers here years ago always had an interesting time." Her eyes twinkled. "Do you have any more stories, Missouri?"

"Well, you know my own husband was a preacher here." She nodded. "Onct the sheriff come to Preacher (my husband), and said a travelin' salesman by the name of 'Juice' Mahoney had been throwed by his horse and kilt. He was with another man, and the sheriff was told by him the dead man had no fam'ly, and had ast if a preacher in this town would do a burial service. Preacher felt like he had to do it, but he ast the sheriff to leave his gun at home. Fer at the last fune'ral Preacher had preached, the sheriff had accident'ly fared his gun, and a bullet had went through the people's parlor floor. It was plumb embarassin'. With that agreement, two of the deacons went to build a coffin, and Preacher took off to talk to the feller that was with Juice when he was kilt. He couldn't even tell Preacher the man's proper name, just 'Juice'. All he could tell Preacher was he was a smart salesman and liked to have a good time. Well sir, when Preacher got back to the church house, the deacons was all wild eyed and couldn't wait fer him to git in thar. When Preacher looked at the body they had placed in the coffin, he liked ta choked. The deacons told him after they placed the body in the coffin, his friend come and ast to be alone with him fer a few moments. A'course, they said yes. When they come back, thar in the corpse's arms was a fishin' pole and jar of corn liquor!"

The ladies "Oh my!" and "Good grief!" and "What!"

rang out.

Georgia noticed Missouri wasn't in any big hurry to go home.

****

On the way home, (finally) Georgia asked Missouri about a woman she didn't recognize. "She was sitting over there with Illa Mae Cochran. An older woman. Looked about your age, actually."

Missouri snorted. "Georgia, *you* are a older woman. Why don't you come out and say it: people are amazed we're still langerin', and wonder how much longer before they have to drag out thur fune'ral attar."

"Mama!" Georgia sounded really shocked. "You know exactly what I mean. Don't say that about yourself." She shivered.

"Oh, don't git so upset. And, yes, I know who you are talkin' about. When we was little we got caught dippin' snuff one time at school. Each got a whack with the paddle to the backside. It'd been worser too, if we both hadn't been so sick we was green. Patricia Monroe's her name. Cain't remember her married name. She's been widdered fer many years. I had heared her family moved back here and she come with them. Always liked Patricia. Her Mama called her Trixie. We wuz playin' house one day out in thur yard. My Papa had taught me how to whistle and I was tryin' to larn her how to. Her mama heared us and come a'flyin' out the door. She told Trixie she never wanted to hear her whistle agin, fer a whistlin' woman and a crowin' hen, both will come to no good end."

Georgia looked puzzled. "Whatever does that mean?"

Missouri shrugged. "Unlucky, I reckon. They was a superstitious lot. Ever time I went over thar to play, I was admonished about some sort of foolishness to watch out fer. I never told my Mama, fer I was afraid she wouldn't let me go play to a heathern's house."

Georgia laughed. "As I recall, you taught me and every boy I ever dated how to whistle loud enough to make dogs howl."

"Kin ye still?"

"Yes ma'am, I can."

Missouri reached over and patted Georgia's lap. "Good fer you, child. Good fer you."

****

As Missouri did more and more often, she dreamed of the past that night:

She and Patricia were about eight years old. Kizzie had stayed home with Mama that day because she wasn't feeling well. Missouri believed it was because Kizzie didn't like Patricia much, for she was jealous. The two girls had gone behind the spring house and up the creek a ways to play. It had come a real gully-washer earlier that day, and the friendly little creek had turned into an angry, churning roar. Nevertheless, they had brought the dipper and were determined to get a cold drink from there instead of out of the spring house. Missouri tried to hold onto Patricia's skirts, but it was no use, and before she knew what was happening, Patricia fell into the fierce water. They both started screaming, and Missouri remembered lying on her belly, trying to grab at Patricia as she swirled by. To this day, Missouri had no memory of how Patricia was saved.

For years, she would wake up in a cold sweat, dreaming that Patricia had drowned.

As she did now.

Waking up, her heart was flying, and she was having a hard time breathing. Trying to shake the nightmare from herself, she slowly calmed down. Turning over on her side, she wondered why in the world she hadn't asked Patricia today what had happened then. Maybe that would have stopped the dreams. "I'll ast her if I ever see her agin, that's fer shore." Missouri declared out loud before she turned over and went back to sleep.

CHAPTER TWENTY-FIVE:

Dot or Feather?

Watch the Weather!

Missouri was washing her dinner dishes (she'd fried herself some chicken and mashed some potatoes to go with her last jar of home canned green beans from last winter), when she heard a car coming from around the front of the house. She took a moment to thank the good Lord that she still had good hearing at her age, and grinned for a moment remembering her birthday bash a few days ago when she turned ninety. She'd missed Kizzie, real bad. But other than that, it had been nice, with the baby and all. She determined the car was Mint and Ben's, then waited a second for the car to come around the corner of the house and stop at the back door.

Mint hopped out of the car and bounded up the steps. Missouri opened the door for her and she came in, giving a big hug to Missouri.

"And whar's my baby?" Missouri demanded.

"At home with her daddy. I can't stay too long, we are going out to the movies tonight. Mama said she'd babysit for us so we can get out alone."

"Looks ta me like you done accomplished that."

Mint giggled. "Shhhh. Don't tell Mama!" Mint sniffed the air. "Have you fried chicken?"

"That's truth. I always cook a little extry in case the likes of you show up. Got beans and biscuits, too. Ate up all the taters, though."

"A piece of chicken and a biscuit sound wonderful, Missouri. I ate a sandwich a little while ago, but I'm still hungry." She sighed. "I've been trying to cut down and get rid of some of the left over baby fat." She looked down at her figure.

"Yurs or the baby you had?"

"Ha, ha. Do I look fat?"

"No. You ain't even headed towards plump. All you need to do to look like you did before Sarah was borned is walk in the afternoon. You'll shape up. Don't need to lose no weight."

Mint brightened. "That is one great idea. I could do that for fifteen minutes right after Ben gets home. He could play with Sarah and then we could finish getting supper ready."

Missouri poured Mint iced tea, and Mint closed her eyes in ecstasy with her first bite of chicken. "Nobody can do this to a chicken but you."

"Thank ye. I ain't seen you in nur a week. Ya'll are findin' out what busy means now."

"You'd think I'd have plenty of time since I'm not working. But, lord! Sarah takes up so much time, she's into everything! I have to watch her like a hawk. It seems like I barely get one mess cleaned up before she's creating another one. I try to do laundry and empty the dishwasher when she naps."

"Umm hmmm. Reckon how hard it was afore washin' machines and dishwashers?"

Mint shook her head. "Don't go there." She finished her biscuit. "I came here to tell you something!" She giggled again. "Missouri, you are gonna love this! Finally someone made a bigger goof at a table than me!"

Missouri raised an eyebrow. "Well, now, that's a rare bird." She said dryly. "I know that made you proud."

"It did! Of course, they didn't do it dumb like I do, they did it snooty, but that made it all the more funny."

Mint told as how they had been out to supper with a few friends and Ben's cousin. She had recently married a guy, who from the moment he was introduced, clearly looked down his nose at the Southern folks gathered around. He made a snide remark or two about the way words were pronounced, correcting his new bride more than once. "I could see Ben getting mad. He loves his cousin, she is the sweetest thing! And she was acting all cowed down and embarrassed. Then, one of Ben's co-workers, who has a Master's Degree in English, by the way, was talking about his Cherokee heritage. Except he said something to the effect that his great-grandmother was full blooded Indian. And Mr. Better-than-everybody-else stopped his chewing, put down his fork, and waited for our attention. Then he looked at Ben's friend and asked, 'Dot or feather?'"

"What in tarnation did he mean by that?" But Missouri had a feeling she knew.

"It confused everybody at the table too. This blank look took over everybody's face. Then Charlene – that's Ben's cousin – you could see this look of 'getting it' dawn on her face. And she started shaking a little. By this time we were staring at both of them. Charlene finally lost it and nearly brayed like a mule she laughed so hard. You know how it is, Missouri, when somebody starts laughing that hard, everybody else does too. Well, except for her nasty old husband, who just got red in the face mad. When Charlene could stop laughing long enough, she explained he was asking was the person from India or a Native American. *Dot or feather?!* Come on! This made us laugh even harder. Ben finally said that around here if we say Indian we usually mean Cherokee Indian." Mint rolled her eyes. "Missouri, he was trying to be so haughty and smart. All he did was make a fool of himself."

"How did ya'll pick up after that?"

"I think he was furious, and embarrassed too. He finished the meal, but he didn't say much more. He kept cutting his eyes at Charlene, who wouldn't look back. When they left, he made some snotty remark about how he had so enjoyed the evening with the natives. Can you believe he said that?"

Missouri shook her head. "Takes all kinds, I reckon. Sounds like Charlene's got her work cut out fer herself, if she's gonner stay married to that 'un."

"I'll say."

After Mint left, Missouri thought she'd take a rest in the rocker on the back porch. It was a pretty day, and Mint had given her something to think about. It always aggravated her how people treated Southerner's as though they weren't very smart. Missouri knew many highly intelligent people who had thick accents and were proud of it. She hoped Charlene's husband ran into a few of them and got educated himself before it was too late for his marriage. Or, she feared, it went a whole lot deeper than that, and the man was just plain mean.

There were plenty of them in the world too, she thought, as she began to remember a day in the early

Out on a Limb of the Family Tree

seventies:

Missouri, Georgia, and Wylene had excitedly decided to visit the new mall near Atlanta. Missouri still felt young at age sixty-eight, and with money to burn and a tank full of gas, they set off early on Friday morning. And what a trip! As Missouri said later, they spent money they didn't know they had. Lunch had been good, and a tired trio had started out of the mall.

Missouri thinks what caught her eye was the beauty of the woman sitting with her husband, about to have their portrait taken by a young professional photographer. He had his set-up right in front of the big plate glass window, she supposed to help bring more customers in. At first, Missouri thought they were in costume (more her own ignorance than anything), but looking at the woman's large eyes, dark skin and 'dot' in the middle of her forehead, she realized these were 'foreigners' for sure. The three of them slowed to watch the process. Missouri didn't know what was going on, all she saw was the man suddenly drawing back and slapping the woman in the face. The three of them stood stunned for a moment, then the fury of a redhead set in and the next thing anyone knew, Missouri was inside the studio.

'What in blazes is goin' on?' she asked the photographer. He looked scared to death. 'I don't know. All I asked was for her to hold her head a certain way, and said it again, like I always do…' she turned to the man from India. 'You ort to be ashamed!' the woman answered Missouri first: 'It is all right. I did not pay attention.' Missouri's eyebrows almost disappeared under her hairline. How she wished Preacher was with them! The

man literally snarled at her. 'This is none of your concern, woman.' Missouri whirled on the photographer. 'What are you gonner do? Nuthin'? Yur as big a coward as this 'un.' She turned back to the husband. 'I'm findin' a po-leece! And you will someday have to answer to the Lord Jesus Christ, and I fer one, cain't wait!'

She had found a security guard and demanded he intervene. Whether he did, she never knew, as they had left as quickly as possible and headed home.

Preacher had comforted her and prayed with her and told her she could not change the world altogether.

Missouri had prayed for that woman for years.

As she sat on the porch, she wondered why that had bothered her so much when she knew abuse went on all the time between married folks. She supposed it was the man's lack of anger when he slapped his wife, and their exotic beauty she had been so taken with until he had slapped her. A fairy tale had been instantly and violently shattered.

Poor Charlene, too. She was apt to be heading down that very trail if someone, especially Charlene herself, didn't put a stop to it.

Didn't matter what kind of heritage folks came from.

Dot or feather.

****

Missouri ate a bite of supper long after Mint left, and glancing at the clock decided she'd better go feed her few remaining hens before it started into late evening. As she stepped outside she realized clouds had gathered and that's why it had seemed dark so suddenly. The first few sprinkles hit her head as she started toward the chicken yard and she quickened her pace. Feeding them hurriedly in the ever heavier rain, she rushed out of the gate.

She and Kizzie were with Papa at Crane's Corn Mill. Both of them were half in awe, half in terror of the two story building towering above them, the great iron wheel turning, spraying water so far that they often felt the mist even as they got out of the wagon. The flume was made of high wooden scaffolding, and the wood dam across the creek that backed the water up made a deep pool. The two water gates, one in the dam wall, and the other one at the end of the water flume, were closed, as Mr. Crane had backed up the water to make the wheel grind the corn.

Lance Crane was old Harold Crane's grandson, and his grandpa had given him permission to open the water gate at the flume end to start the water flowing over the wheel that day. Lance had waved proudly to the girls as he found his footing on the small ledge at the base of the window. Then showcasing a bit, he climbed into the open window and pulled the latch open. Trying to keep an eye on his audience and watching the water flow, he misjudged the timing, and with a mighty roar, the water hit him with a force so strong it knocked him over.

Kizzie and Missouri had screamed for all they were worth, both thinking Lance had plummeted to his death under the great wheel. Screaming turned to laughter as they saw his blond head pop out of the water like a cork, spluttering and gagging, but swimming toward them.

Missouri awoke with a gasp, water pouring into her face. She looked about, confused. Suddenly she realized she was lying on the ground in the pouring rain. "No wonder I was a'dreamin' about that water wheel." she muttered. She moved slowly to see if anything was broken, but apparently not. Trying to figure out if she had one of her 'spells' or if she'd slipped and fallen in the wet grass, she felt of her head. There was a knot, and she guessed she'd knocked herself out. She didn't remember. Trouble was, she couldn't get up, try as she might, her old body wasn't having it. Then a thrill of fear went through her as she realized if she caught pneumonia at her age, it could very well kill her as easily as the dreaded broken hip that haunted the elderly.

Not having any idea how long she'd lain there, she tried to figure out if someone might come check on her. Mint wouldn't call, as they had spent time this afternoon together. If Wylene knew that, she probably wouldn't call either. Maybe Georgia would call. Missouri sighed. Where was Kizzie when she needed her? "Lord, I know Yur Word says the saints are a'prayin' fer us up thar too, and I need You or them to start nudgin' some of my fam'ly right quick. Amen."

She was pretty sure she dozed, although she wondered how on earth anyone could doze in the pouring down rain on wet ground. But what got her attention was the droning of a car engine and a door slamming. "I'm down here!" she tried to holler. But much to her surprise, only a croak came out.

She heard Herb hollering her name, coming back out of the house. Missouri almost got tickled, wishing she had a red flag to wave over her head so he could see her. But even with no red flag, see her he did.

"Good Lord, woman! What happened?"

"I reckon I slipped on the wet ground. Don't rightly

remember. I don't thank nuthin' is broke, but if I don't git offa this here ground, I'm gonner git nu-moanie fer shore, then I'll be as useless as a back pocket on a shirt."

She could see the indecision in Herb's eyes – fear of moving her versus fear of not – and the fear of not won out. He squatted down. "Put your arms around my neck. If I can't get you standing, I'll have to call someone." After moments of struggle, she was sitting, then in a few more, standing. She held on to him for dear life until he got her seated in the living room.

He sprinted for towels, and she could hear him crank up the heat. He went in the kitchen and put on the tea kettle. The phone started ringing and Missouri picked it up as it was right beside her.

"I'm fine. Just got a little wet. Herb is tryin' to bake me like a turkey. He's got the heat turned up to a hundurd."

He promptly took the phone away from her and barked orders to Wylene to get a doctor over, and for her to get there RIGHT NOW, and help Missouri into dry clothes.

As soon as he hung up, Missouri said, "You know they is gonner start fussin' about me gittin' rid of my hens."

"Sam and I have already talked about that. We're both fools for not already taking care of it – "

"I ain't gittin' rid of my chickens."

"That's right. You ain't. Sam is gonna come every evening and go with you to feed them durn foul fowls."

"Ain't no point–"

"Grand Mother-in-law, for once, and just once, you are going to listen and mind me." Herb sat down by her. She was surprised to see tears in his eyes. "We love you. This isn't going to happen again. If you want a kitchen garden next spring, we're coming to help plant. If you don't, we don't care. If you want to keep the chickens, we'll be here. Got it?"

Missouri huffed. "This gittin' older ain't worth a flip. Who knew I'd outlive my own usefulness?"

"You think you're useless? You are the glue that holds us together. Everyone comes to you for advice, and you know it. But if you keep knockin' your noggin, your advise ain't gonna be worth squat."

Missouri couldn't help but grin, until she heard tires squealing. "I hope yur ready fer this. I ain't."

"Neither am I. But here comes the Calvary, so hold on."

CHAPTER TWENTY-SIX:

To Serve and Be Served

Six Months Later:

Sam and Herb held good to their word, and suddenly Missouri no longer had to wonder if anyone would visit her on any given day. The 'girls' took turns, and every day someone spent a good chunk of time with her. When she demanded to know why Wylene wasn't at work anymore, Wylene said she'd gone part time and was only working three days a week. Missouri was suspicious this was an outright lie, but nobody was talking.

And after a family dinner where Missouri had called Sam Preacher - twice - and hadn't noticed, they had a family meeting for the first time without their matriarch. What in the world should they do? But what cinched another move forward was when Georgia received a phone call at three a.m. from Missouri asking her why was it dark in the middle of the day. Georgia and Sam had got there as quickly as possible, only to discover Missouri sound asleep in her bed and mad as an old wet hen that they'd awakened her. When confronted about the phone call, she'd snorted and said it was thur own durn fault. The digital clock they'd given her hadn't been set right for a.m./p.m. When she'd gone to sleep on the couch watching television and awakened at three a.m., she thought by looking at the clock, it was p. m. "Thought a durn eclipse had happened."

Missouri's house wasn't as clean as it should have been. She lost weight (which she told them was because she was nurly a hundurd), but they could see she wasn't cooking much at all. So they ramped up the family duties to include bringing her food almost every day and made the announcement (with fear and trembling) that a woman was coming to clean for her once a week.

As predicted, she'd been 'maddern far', but nevertheless acquiesced.

And Missouri was glad she had. The woman had been a young thing of twenty-nine who cleaned like a tornado and then spent time chatting with Missouri over coffee.

A few weeks after their routine had been set, Stevi practically waxed poetic about how much Missouri's family loved her and how much they depended on her.

"They're scared to death something is going to happen to you. They think they'll all fall apart beyond repair."

Missouri shook her head. "That tells you what a poor job I done, then. I have recently turned ninety years old. My baby is seventy and you tell me she cain't take care of herself nor her own. Her baby is over forty. If they cain't do it now, they ort to fall apart."

Stevi laughed, but Missouri thought she saw tears, too.

"Child, what's the matter?"

Stevi wiped her eyes. "Oh, Missouri I can't seem to stop getting all weepy sometimes." She bowed her head for a moment. "Saying your baby made me think of my own. He died six months ago."

Missouri patted the woman's hand. "That's a turrible thang."

"Yes. He was an early baby and always had health problems, but he'd pull through every time. I guess I had convinced myself he would grow out of it. And maybe he would have, too, if he hadn't got a really bad respiratory infection. He just couldn't fight it off." She sniffed. "Sometimes I don't think I'll ever get over this."

"That's truth. You won't. That's just the way of it. But you'll git stronger and time will heal some of it. I lost three babies and it's hurtful."

Stevi put her hand to her mouth. "Three? How did you stand it?"

"It was a hard thang. Ever time a baby boy was born not breathin', I wanted to stop breathin' myself. The first time, the baby was early, like yurs, I guess. I'd had a fall and went into labor early. That was heart breakin'. But I thought it was because of my accident. But when the second one happened, and I had been extry careful, I didn't thank I could stand it. I had a fine husband who loved me through it. You got a good man?" Stevi nodded. "That's helpful. Then the third time I carried that boy nur full term. He was still born dead. I was shore it was me, that I kilt my own babies."

"What a relief you must of felt when Georgia was born."

Missouri's eyes flickered for a moment. "She's the most wonderful blessin' the Lord ever give me."

"And you didn't try to have any more?"

Missouri cackled. "Honey, back then you either stopped all together or did or didn't git with child agin. I didn't."

Stevi blushed. "What helped you, finally?"

"First off, I remembered suhum my Papa told me after Mama lost a little one. I believe she was a change of life baby, and the poor little thang was deformed. Mama was in turrible shape after that, and I remember Papa sayin' they was all diff'ert sizes of graves out thar in the graveyard. Ar days is numbered afore we's born, and that's fact. You have to believe the Good Lord knows what He's a'doin', I reckon.

"But more'n that, it was a woman who had worser tragedy than me. She was some older'n me, and I didn't know her much, they lived out on Stone Pile Gap across the county line. They started comin' to ar church after thur preacher died. Warn't but a few members, and they couldn't find another preacher, so they all just picked out sommers else to go. Lenora and Glenn picked ar church. I remember the first thang I noticed was she had the cutest little girl, who was about the same age as my Georgia. And she had two more young'uns, one a year or so younger and a baby. They was all friendly like, but thar was suhum else too. Lenora never really looked at her childern. They was took care of, and they clung to her suhum awful. The daddy hovered around them all, enough to make me plumb nervous. I had invited them to Sunday dinner, and she had politely declined, sayin' she might later on, when the baby got a little older. Then she ast me the oddest thang. She ast me did we have water on ar property. I said, you mean a sprang fer water? And she said, no, she meant like a pond or such. I reckoned as we did, but it was some distance from the house, not in sight. She nodded her head, kinda thoughtful like, and said she'd see about it, later. Then she thanked me fer the invite." Missouri shook her head. "I groused to Preacher – that was my husband – about it, and he told me thar was a story behind the whole thang and he'd explain it to me when Georgia was outside playin'.

We got home and had ar dinner, and bein' as it was Sunday we had a day of rest. Georgia did go outside to play, and I inquired right off the bat about Lenora. Seems two years before, she'd took her young'uns to fish in the river. Times was hard fer them, and her husband was out of work, except fer helpin' saw mill. They'd married awful young, and already she had a ten year old, a seven year old, and a five year old. The little girl I seen at church was just toddlin', and the younger one at the breast. The three older boys got in the boat to fish, and somehow or 'nuther the boat capsized. She stood right thar on the bank and watched them young'uns drownd. She couldn't leave the toddler and the baby alone, nor could she swim anyhow."

Stevi gasped. "That's one of the saddest things I've ever heard."

"I don't know how the woman kept any sanity. But I watched her over the next year or so git better. She begin to pay attention to the childern she had, not just take care of 'em, but smile at 'em and look 'em in the eye. And after some months, she come to dinner at ar house, like I'd ast her to. She never shared her tragedy with me, even though I knowed her fer years. But I thought right then and thar, that what had happened to her was far worser than anythang that had ever happened to me, and I had a child God blessed me with, and I intended to be the best mama I could be."

"We're hoping to try again in a few months. But I'm scared half to death. The doctors tell me there's no reason to be, that I should have a normal pregnancy next time." She sighed. "We have no guarantees in this world, do we?"

"Nary a one, save ar Lord Jesus Christ."

"You are a marvel, Missouri. No wonder your family thinks they can't go on without you."

Missouri snorted. "Well, they better start practicin'. If they'd take notice of my advanced age, they'd wonder like I do about how much longer I got here."

"Advanced age or no, you have blessed me today. You have no idea how much you have helped me."

Stevi got up to finish what little laundry there was, and Missouri sat with her hand on the TV remote, but sat in silence.

Stevi had no idea how much she'd helped her, either.

CHAPTER TWENTY-SEVEN:

As Time Goes By

March, 2000

Georgia and Sam stepped up on the porch and waited as Wylene and Herb brought up the rear, Herb helping Missouri navigate the three steps. They all entered Mint and Ben's house together, with Sarah squealing at the sight of them.

"It's my birfday! It's my birfday!" she said, over and over, twirling in her new pink tutu.

"My, my!" Missouri said, clapping her hands together. "What a handsome outfit you got on, baby."

"Fank you! Mama!" Sarah hollered to Mint. "My toot is hansome!"

Everyone laughed as Mint corrected her daughter. "It's tutu, honey." She looked up at her family. "Ya'll come on in to the dining room. She's about to drive us crazy about the cake, so we thought we'd do that first, then presents, then we'll talk and eat supper. I know it's backwards, but you can have dessert again, if you want it."

They all dutifully sat around the table and Sarah clambered up in a chair to watch the lighting of her candles. Her eyes danced with anticipation. "I'm gonna blow 'em out!" she shouted.

"Make a wish first." Ben said.

"Okay, Daddy-o." she squeezed her eyes shut, lips moving. "Okay. Now?"

"Now!" everyone shouted and she blew for all she was

worth. The candles went out, she applauded herself, looked expectantly toward her assembled adults, and on cue, they too clapped.

Presents were ripped in to; Sarah's favorite immediately became a fluffy yellow stuffed animal in the shape of a baby chicken that cheeped when she squeezed its wings.

She scrambled up onto Missouri's lap, squeezing the chicken for all it was worth. "What's that little chickie's name, honey?" Missouri asked her.

"Fevver!" Sarah exclaimed, ruffling the yellow downy feathers on its back. Jabbering on, Missouri only caught every third word or so, but it didn't seem to make any difference to Sarah.

Missouri grinned. "She's gonner be a little clatter-trap, ain't she?"

Mint rolled her eyes. "She talks like a plugged in radio all day long."

Sarah pulled down her tutu, proudly displaying her underwear to Missouri. "Big girl pannies!"

"Well, now, ain't that fine? I didn't know you was so growed up."

"Just during the day," Mint said. "At night we are still using pull-ups. But she's been doing real good for the last week or so."

Sarah nodded her head. "Real good!"

"Come here, squirt!" Ben said, grabbing her and making her squeal. "Let's see if you need to do real good right now. It's been a while."

****

Out on a Limb of the Family Tree

Missouri had thought long and hard about the garden space. She told Sam and Herb she'd come to a decision that all she could handle was 'tamaters, cucumbers and green onions'. They agreed. When they told the wives, they were suddenly confronted with the fact that none of them could live without the regular garden. Georgia told Sam since they were retired; they'd be the official caretakers, with everyone else helping out. Sam meekly agreed.

Missouri, when alone, chuckled. She had just knowed she was gonner git her garden!

When bean pickin' time came, duties were shifted a little. Missouri informed them she could 'still strang' and 'look 'em' but the rest was up to the other three women, who did a fair job, in Missouri's opinion.

That fall, two of the feral cats disappeared. Grapevine had it that there were coyotes on the prowl, killing and eating cats and small dogs. Missouri went into action and had Ben buy a small doghouse and put it on the porch with the opening facing the wall of the house, with just enough space for the cats to get in. She had their food and water dishes pushed up close to the doghouse, so they could get in quickly if needed. What the family didn't know was Missouri searched down an old flannel blanket and cut it up in sections. She kept parts washed and dried, and on cold nights she'd heat up the clean parts of it and put in the house, so the cats would be real warm. She wasn't sure if it was safe to put flannel in the microwave, but if it caused a fire, well, it was her durn house.

All the hens had died, but Herb couldn't stand to tell Missouri, so he and Sam smuggled four new ones into the lot.

Missouri pretended she didn't know. Them aiggs was too good to pass up.

Thanksgiving had Missouri doing more sitting and ordering around than doing. She gave detailed instructions on how to make her dressing: 'a dab of that, a peench of this here, don't choke us to death on sage!' This continued until the meal was on the table.

Much of this was done with Sarah in her lap, or playing at her feet. Missouri prayed every night that she would live long enough for Sarah to remember her, even if just a little bit.

CHAPTER TWENTY-EIGHT:

When the Mornin' Comes

June, 2001

Missouri had insisted that three year old Sarah spend the night with her, even though Missouri had not been strong for some days. She could see the apprehension on Ben and Mint's faces, so she rustled up all the sternness she could come up with and let them know she and baby Sarah would fare just fine without any adult supervision, and they could come by and pick Sarah up late morning. Missouri assured them if she tired out or felt bad, she'd call them right away. Reluctantly, they had left Sarah alone with Missouri for the night.

It was a time Sarah carried with her all her life:

Age three: Missouri washing off Sarah's face, hands, and feet, and Missouri letting her cover herself with expensive lotion. Missouri had laughed and said somebody better git some use out of it, she shore wadn't gonner use it much longer. Missouri and Sarah snuggling up in the bed, Sarah nestled in the crook of Missouri's shoulder, and Missouri telling her to 'scrooch up real close like', and Missouri reading a little story book that she always told Sarah (before she started the story) her Mama had read to her when she was three. She told Sarah that book now belonged to her and she could take it home with her in the morning. Sarah clapped her hands in excitement. She'd never been allowed to take it home until now. Just before prayers, Missouri told Sarah she was going away pretty soon and would miss her, but was real excited about leaving. Sarah listened intently as Missouri explained she was going home to see Jesus and be with her mama and papa and Preacher and her babies that were waiting on her. She told Sarah not to dare be too sad because she and Missouri would see each other again.

Sarah had been lying on her belly, her face propped up in her hands. She had frowned at what Missouri was telling her, she didn't like it one bit. "That bodders me a wot." She told Missouri.

"Now, lamb, don't let it be a'botherin' you. It's a wonderful thang fer this old woman. And we won't be separated any longer'n that!" she snapped her fingers, "till we are back together agin ferever."

Sarah thought on that for a moment. "You pwomise?"

"If you love Jesus, I promise that will be true."

Sarah sighed and sat up. "I wove Him, aw right. We tawk aw the time." She put her arms around Missouri's neck. "I'll miss ya wil bad."

"I'll miss you too, Lamb." Missouri had sighed. "I'll miss you too."

The next morning Sarah awoke to an empty bed. She padded into the kitchen to find Missouri cookin' coffee. She sat at the table, and Missouri gave her a bowl of oatmeal with lots of cream and honey. Missouri sat down with coffee, and when she saw Sarah eyeing it, she poured a little into the saucer; added more milk and sugar, and let her slurp from the saucer. Grinning, Missouri told her not to tell her mama and daddy about the coffee. Sarah never did till she was grown.

Till Sarah's dying day, she could see herself, curls a

tousled mess, bare feet and sleepy eyes, slurping coffee from Missouri's saucer.

July 2001

It was the worst news Mint ever had in her life, and would be until Ben died nearly fifty years later.

When she answered the phone, she heard her mother's choked voice say, "It's Missouri, honey." Not Missouri fell, or Missouri's sick, or we've headed to the hospital with Missouri. Just, 'it's Missouri'.

Her mother said other things Mint didn't hear as she slid to the floor, phone cradled in her bosom.

Sarah came and squatted by her, placing her chubby hand on Mint's arm. She looked at her mama with a solemn face and intense blue eyes. She asked softly, "Has Miz-ur-ee gone on to Heaven now?"

Kathi Harper Hill

Mrs. Missouri McGuire Pickett

Died Tuesday, July 3, 2001 at age 92.
She was born to Esther Eliza McFarland McGuire and
Jacob Tobias McGuire, on February 7, 1909.
She is preceded in death by husband,
Benjamin "Preacher" Pickett, and three children,
Who passed at their birth, and
One sister, Kizzie Mae McGuire Johnson Malone.
Survivors include daughter and son-in-law,
Georgia and Sam Hillside,
Granddaughter and grandson-in-law,
Wylene and Herb Sanders,
Great-granddaughter and great-grandson-in-law,
Samintha and Ben Sanders, and
Great-great-granddaughter,
Miss Sarah Esther Sanders,
Nieces and nephews.

Mrs. Pickett was an 85 year member of Sweetapple Baptist Church, where she taught Sunday School to little ones for many years.

A wonderful celebration of her life was held inside the church house on July 5, 2001 at two o'clock in the afternoon.

She was buried in the Sweetapple Baptist Cemetery next to her beloved Preacher and two of their children.

She will be missed by all who knew her.

Epilogue

Part 1

May, 2002

Mint sat on the back porch steps of Missouri's house – she still thought of it as Missouri's house - and watched her daughter play in the dirt with a shovel and pail. It was one of those hazy, warm days when summer was just beginning to make itself known. A cow lowed and Sarah raised her head and pointed excitedly "Moo-cow, Mama!"

Mint smiled. "That's right, honey, moo-cow." After Missouri's death, she and Ben had purchased the old home place from Georgia, and Ben had purchased a few head of cattle, as well as some more chickens to join the few hens Missouri had left behind. She teased him and said she felt just like Farmer Sanders and he'd told her she *was* Farmer Sanders.

Sarah came over and put a sweaty arm around Mint's neck and tried to sit in her lap, which proved to be difficult as there wasn't much lap left. Mint was eight months gone, and this time they were expecting a boy. She reckoned he'd make an appearance about the time it got really hot. She scooted over a little so Sarah could sit beside her on the step. "Zat Miz-ur-ee's moo-cow?" Sarah asked. It never failed to amaze Mint that Sarah could remember Missouri, even though Missouri had been gone nearly a year and Sarah was barely four now.

"Well, no, honey. That's Mama and Daddy's moo-cow. Missouri probably has her own in Heaven."

Sarah nodded her head, satisfied. "Good. She got chickies too?"

Mint hugged her. "Yes'm, I guess she does. And they are pink!"

Sarah giggled, covering her mouth with a grubby hand. "No dey are not!"

Mint feigned surprise. "How do you know? They might be."

"Jesus' chickies are all brown."

"Oh. Well, why didn't you tell me?"

"Oh, Mama," Sarah sighed, rolling her eyes dramatically. "Do I hafta tell ya everthing?"

"Come here, you little squirt. I'll get you for sassing your mama."

Sarah squealed with delight as Mint hugged her and shook her a little. "We better get in before Daddy gets home and wonders where supper is."

"You goan cook?"

"A little. Want to help me?"

"You bet!"

"Let's go wash up then, so we don't cook dirt too."

Sarah flew into the kitchen, but not before she stopped to pet their cat and say he was "cuteful, didn't you fink so?" Agreeing the cat was cute, Mint followed at a more leisurely pace.

She had put chicken in the oven to bake an hour before, and figured two vegetables with it was enough. She still wasn't a magnificent cook, but they weren't starving, either.

"Do you want to come by the sink and climb up to help?"

"I'll get my bee stoof." Sarah went to the corner where the little stool Missouri had passed down to her was stored. She stopped, and cocked her head. "Hmmmm." Then she nodded, and touched the arm of the rocker next to the stool, and started it rocking slowly. "I fink I'll just sit here and talk wif Miz-ur-ree."

Mint felt her eyes prick with tears. She missed Missouri so much! "Well, okay. What has Missouri got to say?" she tried to sound bright and happy.

Sarah looked as though she was listening intently, her little brow furrowed. "Well...she says she is one of the fousands of saints prayin' for you and baby Claire, my sistah."

Mint felt chills run up her back. Where had Sarah heard about the host of saints? "Sarah, remember, we aren't having a Claire, we're having an Adam Joshua. Remember seeing his picture inside mama's tummy?"

"Ummm hmmm."

"Well, maybe you better tell Missouri she's made a mistake!"

Sarah just looked at her mother. "I reckon she can hear you, Mama."

"Oh. I beg your pardon. So what does Missouri say to our baby being a boy?" She knew Sarah had badly wanted a sister, and had pouted for a few days when told it was a boy.

Sarah shrugged her shoulders, making her curls bounce. "She don't say nuffin'. She is just laffin'."

Then Sarah let out a shriek that made Mint jump a foot and nick her thumb with the paring knife she was using to peel potatoes.

"Daddy! Daddy's home!" and Sarah shot out of the kitchen like a rocket.

"Don't go off the porch!" Mint said, managing a feeble holler.

"I ain't!"

Mint glanced back at the door, then crept to the rocker, her bleeding thumb in her mouth. "Missouri? Are you really there?" Absolutely nothing. The rocker had even stopped. Mint felt foolish.

Later that night she told Ben about the whole thing, and he said Sarah probably heard the biblical quote about the host of saints praying from Wylene or Georgia. "And you know she's heard that whatever Missouri Pickett said went around here, so maybe she thinks if she tells you Missouri says the baby is a girl, it will be a girl."

Mint still felt a little spooked, and made sure the light was on the next morning before she walked all the way in the kitchen.

Three weeks later she went into labor. Everything went wrong, and she was pretty sure she was dying (the doctors were too). The last thing she remembered was Ben telling her the baby was fine.

She woke up two days later to the relief of her family. After Ben kissed her and covered her with his tears, she asked to see their son.

He placed Claire Julieann in her arms with care.

Mint never had a spiritual doubt again for as long as she lived.

Neither did Ben.

And Sarah? Well, she never had any to start with.

Epilogue

Part II

Spring, 2063

    Sixty-five year old Sarah Sanders Teague came through the door and threw her coat across the sofa. Then she threw herself onto the sofa. What a week!

    For six months she had consoled her sweet mother, who, in Sarah's opinion, grieved herself to death over the illness and death of Sarah's baby brother, Adam. He was five years younger than Sarah, and she had her own overwhelming grief to deal with, but it had pretty much been put on the back burner for her mother's sake.

    She tried to understand. After all, it seemed unnatural for a son to die before a mother, especially a mother who was already well into her eighty-fifth year. But die he did, and it had turned their lives upside down.

    And on top of everything else, she had to deal with her Mother's death now. Once she could catch her breath, that was.

    Sarah didn't know what she would have done without her sister Claire and her own sweet husband, David. He and Adam had been close friends, so he'd had his own grief too. And then, there was their daughter, Rachael, who had dearly loved her Uncle Adam, who had been a childless widower, and always treated her as his own. And sweet five year old Amanda, Rachael's daughter, cried inconsolably all through the funeral.

    Today had been the reading of the will, much to

Sarah's surprise. She hadn't thought that would be necessary. She knew everything would be divided between her sister and herself, unless Mama had lost her mind and left it to some charity or a bunch of cats. The thought made Sarah grin. Her mama sure had loved her cats. As if the thought conjured one up, Toby jumped on the couch and curled up next to her. He was a sweet cat and Sarah thought 'no wonder Mama loved him so.'

Rachael had called Samintha 'Mommy Mint', and they'd been thicker than thieves while Rachael was growing up. According to family legend, the women in this family were always that way, from generation to generation.

Sighing heavily, Sarah reached over to her coat and drew out the envelope given to her at the end of the reading of the will. Apparently this envelope had been left for many years with the law firm, with strict instructions as to when it would be shared.

On the front of the envelope, scrawled in firm, Victorian style handwriting, the instructions were clear: 'To be opened only after the death of Georgia Pickett Hillside, Wylene Hillside Sanders, Samintha Sanders Sanders (Sarah had smiled at that). It was signed Missouri Pickett and dated June 7, 1998. Almost fifty-five years ago! What on earth?

She turned the envelope over, and as she started to open it, she heard the key turn in the lock. It was David. She smiled as he opened the door. "Just in time. I'm about to unravel a mystery."

He raised a brow. "Really?" He pulled off his coat, threw it on top of hers, and sat beside her, making Toby scoot over. "I'm always up for one. What is this?"

She showed him the front of the envelope and he shook his head. "This ought to be good. Hurry and open it before the phone chimes or the door calls."

Sarah slowly slit the envelope with her fingernail and pulled out the stationary inside. She unfolded the paper and began to read:

This here is Missouri McGuire Pickett writing, and I dread every word of it. But I reckon it needs to be done. The Lord has placed it on my heart to let the truth be told. It still feels like I'm going out on a limb to do it, but here goes:

My daughter, Georgia Pickett Hillside, is not my biological child. My husband, Preacher (Benjamin Pickett), and I had gone out of town when I went into labor with our third child. This child, William, was stillborn, just like my other two previous children. A young girl was giving birth at the same time I was. She died shortly after childbirth, and having no family or friends, begged us to take her daughter as our own, which we did.

If anyone is still living to testify to the fact that she was my daughter in every sense of the word except birth, all would testify the truth in that statement.

Me and Preacher never told a living soul, and neither did the doctor who birthed the babies, as far as we ever knew.

Somehow, I cannot take this lie to the grave. But I am not brave enough to say it out loud. So, I'm writing it. It seems to be an injustice to Georgia in some way by denying her right to truth.

Since I am too much of a coward to do it while living; and felt I could not leave this information to others still living after my death to deal with shock and maybe anger, I thought the least I could do was tell people who might have a historical interest in this fact.

So, whoever is reading this, (I hope baby Sarah or one of her young'uns!) Here's the truth.

But more truthful is this: Georgia was loved as much as anyone could love a child, and her generations of children became mine.
No one could take that from me, or her.
Sincerely,
Missouri McGuire Pickett
May 14, 1998

"Well. Wow." David cleared his throat. "So Mint never knew her grandmother was adopted. Well, sort of."

"Guess not." She looked up at David. "It's strange, isn't it?"

"Georgia lived till you were an adult, right?"

"I was fourteen when she died. I remember her well. I loved her very much. Grandma Wylene, Georgia's daughter, is the one you remember. I was almost thirty when she was killed in that car wreck. You and I had been dating a short time."

He shook his head. "There are so many women in your background I can't keep up."

She got tears in her eyes. "Not anymore."

"Aw, honey, I'm sorry. I didn't mean to sound cold."

"I know, I know. It's just, well, there's always been all these women surrounding me. And it was that way for

Mama, for sure. I heard about Missouri all my life. She was as real to me as everyone walking around. I barely remember her, I was so little when she died. Just vague moments, you know?" Smiling, Sarah recalled, "The most vivid memory is Missouri and I sitting at the kitchen table, and her letting me slurp surgery coffee from a saucer, and making me promise not to tell."

David laughed. "I just remembered something. Your mother was so excited when Rachael was born with red hair. She kept saying Missouri finally showed up. She totally negated the fact that almost everybody in my family is red headed but me."

Sarah grinned and ruffled his still strawberry blond hair. "You didn't miss it by much." She sighed. "I think Missouri did the right thing. Maybe it would have made things change."

"Does it change your feelings because our Amanda is adopted?" Rachael and Ted, her husband, had tried for years to get pregnant. Then Amanda 'fell into their laps and hearts' and nobody cared anymore.

"You know it doesn't. Lord, I love our grandbaby! I don't care if she was hatched." She flapped the letter in front of his face. "So, what do we do with this?"

"We could burn it."

"No!"

"We can put it in the old family Bible after we share it with Rachael, so when Amanda is old enough to understand it all, she can hear it too."

"The Bible it is."

Sarah got up and took the big antique family Bible off the shelf and carefully placed the letter under the front cover. Turning to David, she said, "I guess by now it doesn't really matter. I'm sure they're all up there in Heaven and have the whole family tree mess figured out."

He smiled. "Can you imagine the joyful reunion those gals had when Mint showed up?"

The doorbell rang. Claire opened the door without waiting and came in. "I need to be with you, Sarah. I'm just so sad!"

She ran into her older sister's arms and they cried. After a few moments, Sarah parted enough to hold her sister at arm's length and smile a little. "You came by at just the right time. I've got something to show you. You know that letter I got at the reading of the will?" Claire nodded. "Well, it's gonna knock your socks off."

Going back to the shelf she pulled the Bible out and motioned her sister to sit on the couch.

They read together, and quickly made a decision to trace their beginnings as soon as possible.

It didn't matter if the tree's members were from roots or grafts.

Family was family.

THE END

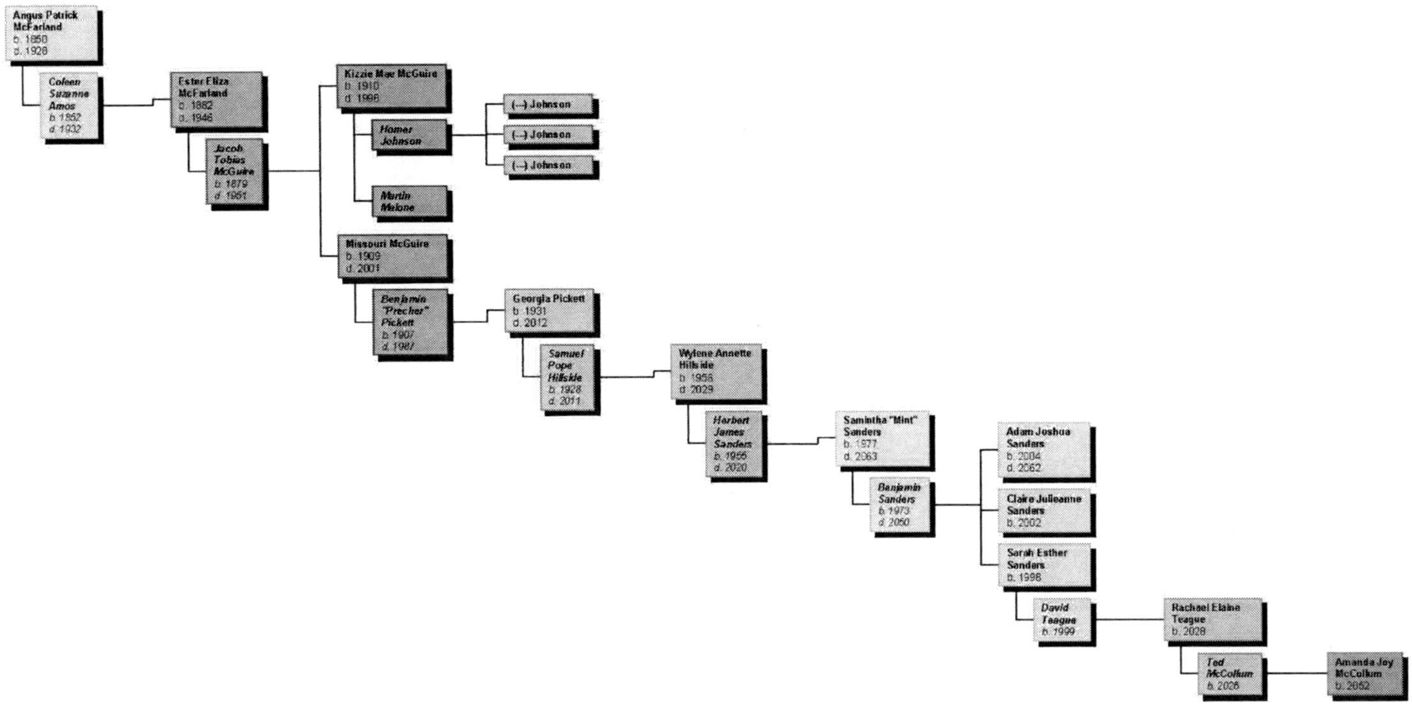
Angus Patrick McFarland b. 1850 d. 1928
Coleen Suzanne Amos b. 1852 d. 1932
Ester Eliza McFarland b. 1862 d. 1946
Jacob Tobias McGuire b. 1879 d. 1951
Kizzie Mae McGuire b. 1910 d. 1996
Homer Johnson
Martin Malone
(--) Johnson
(--) Johnson
(--) Johnson
Missouri McGuire b. 1909 d. 2001
Benjamin "Precher" Pickett b. 1907 d. 1987
Georgia Pickett b. 1931 d. 2012
Samuel Pope Hillside b. 1928 d. 2011
Wylene Annette Hillside b. 1956 d. 2029
Herbert James Sanders b. 1955 d. 2020
Samintha "Mint" Sanders b. 1977 d. 2063
Benjamin Sanders b. 1973 d. 2050
Adam Joshua Sanders b. 2004 d. 2062
Claire Julieanne Sanders b. 2002
Sarah Esther Sanders b. 1998
David Teague b. 1999
Rachael Elaine Teague b. 2028
Ted McCollum b. 2026
Amanda Joy McCollum b. 2062

About the Author

Kathi Harper Hill has lived in the North Georgia Mountains all her life. She has been writing since the age of ten. After taking early retirement as a professional in the mental health field, she began devoting more time to her craft. Her stories focus mainly on relationships between people, and how relationships force growth in the characters.

Besides loving to write (and read), her other interests include teaching Bible classes, interior design, and music. Kathi has been a soloist since the age of fourteen.

Hill is the author of five books. Her first, "Falling", was published in 2009. Her children's book, "The Crow and The Wind" a little book about a Big God, was first runner up in the mid child division at the 2011 Georgia Author of the Year Awards. Hill has been the recipient of numerous awards for her short stories over the years. One of these winning stories appears in "The Christmas Closet and Other Works".

She and her husband, David, (who illustrates all her books), live in a Victorian cottage with their daughter, Anna Kate, and current menagerie of pets: American Bulldog, Molly, The Great White Cats: Lily, Frost, and Eli. Anna Kate's cat, Mimi, joins the fray.

WHAT OTHERS ARE SAYING ABOUT KATHI'S BOOKS:

On Falling:

I really enjoyed Falling. It kept me interested in what was going to happen next and it had a lot of substance and meaning about morals and God. It had a happy ending but had a few turns here and there, like real life. I hope she writes more books like this, our society is lacking in morals and this book appeals to all ages. J. Rogers

The book was a well written respectful romance book that anyone would be proud to read. M. Pierce

The book "Falling" told an interesting, beautiful love story without using any vulgarity - what a refreshing concept! I enjoyed reading it from start to finish and have given this book as gifts to friends.
They gave it a thumbs up as well! Kathi Hill is a gifted writer who uses her talent to uplift others while telling stories that are relevant to today. Jeanne Addy

"This book should be read by every girl - and boy - for that matter - before they begin to date to find out how to have a Christian relationship. James Holt, Pastor

I thought: It must be a great book since James never reads anything unless it pertains to his sermon. He came to bed at one a.m. and said he'd read "Falling" in one sitting! So I thought I should read it too! (I did and enjoyed it!) Betty Jo Holt, pastor's wife and retired teacher.

"Falling" is an enticing book which asks and answers many questions that face young adults today. From the chance meeting of the famous and the wounded through the delicate plan of God, the author weaves a story that is fast paced and delightful for audiences of all ages. Marsha Benson

I couldn't wait for the book signing, so I ordered the book off Amazon. From knowing Kathi I wasn't surprised that it was a great book! A. W.

My wife purchased the book but I picked it up to read first. I cried in the middle of the story. What a book! I really enjoyed it. Morris M.

Falling is an excellent, well written book. With humor, Christian values, and a great story-line, it is a book that girls -and guys- will love. Would recommend it to all, especially young adults, for an all-around enjoyable story! David Lawrence

I just happened by the bookstore on the day of Mrs. Hill's book signing for "Falling". Since I work with young people, I purchased a copy and went home to begin reading it over lunch. I sat for one and a half hours without moving until I finished it! What a great book! I rushed back to the bookstore and purchased two more copies, and have been passing those around to "my kids" ever since. Bravo! P. Miller

A copy of "Falling" was donated to the high school library where I attend school. There has been a constant waiting list to read this book. When I finally got a turn, I could see why! I could picture the characters and scenes just like they were real. I hope she writes another book like this. Amanda W.

ON: The Crow and The Wind:

This book is a great book for little kids because of the simple story line and wonderful illustrations. But it has a deeper meaning that my 11 year old classroom really discussed, as we are studying symbolism. I recommend this to any parent or teacher who wants to get across the idea that there is someone bigger than us! Mary Sawyer

This book is a must read for both young and old! A beautiful creation and the author has a great idea of how to get through to people and share the beauty of God. The drawings alone are worth the purchase to see! Awesome book. Fos B.

The Crow and The Wind is a wonderful book for the child who hears it and the adult who reads it aloud! Both will be blessed by the content of the message and the detail of the illustrations. It's a book that belongs on every bedside table to be shared at bedtime. It will ease the troubles of the day by reminding readers that there is Someone bigger than us who is in charge! Jan B.

The Crow and the Wind is a children's book. Or is it? This book can be enjoyable and meaningful to Children of all ages. For anyone who still has an imagination and a belief in things not-seen. Actually it is love story about a crow and the wind. They find each other and ultimately God the Creator. The illustrations by David Hill only add to its charm. Nancy Vaught

The Crow and The Wind is a wonderful little children's book with a great big message! Kathi Harper Hill captures the reader and any little listener within earshot as she takes the crow on a journey of discovery. The beautiful illustrations provide the reader with colorful imagery as the story of God's presence, love and power are told. Hill's words are teaching and the lessons learned are indeed blessings of affirmation! Tony Smith

I enjoyed reading this story even though I don't have small ones. The story reminds us that we can stray from out creator. Then circumstances lead us back to the fold. Well written and beautifully illustrated. I loved the book. I recommend the book for middle schoolers. A great edition to a child's Christian library. Sue H.

This book takes a child back to an earlier and more rural time. It can be enjoyed by a child for its' visual appeal and its' very positive message. The group of children to whom I read were all attentive and were stimulated to ask many questions. David Lawrence

One Old Crow's Journey to the Truth: In an enchanting mix of old-time Appalachian religion, George MacDonald, and C. S. Lewis, Kathi and David Hill tell a smart and engaging tale of one old crow's journey to the Truth. You couldn't own a better bedtime story. Tina T.

This is a lovely book, with a gentle humor and beautiful illustrations. I was enchanted and have shared it with my friends. Lynnie O.

The Crow and The Wind is such a wonderful book. The story is great. I love the illustrations. I have already recommended this book to several people. This is a "must have" book! Connie G.

I bought this book for my grandson. We have thoroughly enjoyed reading it together. He loved the story and the illustrations. I'm sure that it will be one book that we will read over and over again. Would highly recommend this book. Cathy R.